UNDER THE SHADOW

Children of the First Star: Volume I

By

J.M. Kay

Books Endependent

Under the Shadow:
Children of the First Star

Volume I

Published by BooksEndependent, LLC

www.BooksEndependent.com
Copyright © 2014 by J.M. Kay

Cover Art by Amit Tayal

Cover and Book Design by J.D. Woods Consulting

ISBN: 978-0-9887687-6-5

Dedication

For Amy
… Without remorse,
Without any such consideration of choice,
Lifted you, your human form,
Sleepily through the in between to now,
To a point in space and time
Where, only by the happening of each
Single instance of history
Were you and I to meet,
To talk, to laugh, to become friends…

Table of Contents

Author's Note

I grew up reading a heavy dose of Fantasy and Science Fiction. With their potent talent, Margaret Weis and Tracy Hickman, Kristine Kathryn Rusch, David Eddings, Tad Williams, Orson Scott Card, and Robert Heinlein, opened my mind to incredible worlds and ways of looking at things that shaped my youth. But one thing that remained consistent in many of their stories, is a struggle between an unquestioned evil and an unquestioned good. This is truly a theme that seems to permeate much of not just fantasy/sci fi, but literature in general and especially popular Young Adult reading. There is good reason for this: it makes for very exciting stories! But I think sometimes, even the world of imagination is not that simple. The story I tried to tell is therefore not a traditional tale of good versus evil or of heroes and villains but hopefully I managed to capture a somewhat different yet equally intriguing and suspenseful spirit.

J.M. Kay

–◉↑ട–

"What are the roots that clutch, what branches grow
Out of this stony rubbish? Son of man,
You cannot say, or guess, for you know only
A heap of broken images, where the sun beats,
And the dead tree gives no shelter, the cricket no relief,
And the dry stone no sound of water. Only
There is shadow under this red rock,
Come in under the shadow of this red rock,
And I will show you something different from either
Your shadow at morning striding behind you
Or your shadow at evening rising to meet you;
I will show you fear in a handful of dust."

From "The Waste Land"
Thomas Stearns Eliot

–◉↑ട–

Chapter 1: A Disappointing Sun

Another morning crept into the sky as Jason Swann lay in bed examining the ceiling of his room. He focused on tiny cracks in the paint, and the dwindling final strands of an abandoned spider web. He could've slept for another half hour before his alarm sounded the evidence of what he was already sure of -- another day -- but he didn't see the point in trying to sleep. Jason hoped this morning would feel different, but he was still in Ashton. His friends, his real home, his real life, were in Chicago.

The shadows cast on the wall next to his bed, fighting the intruding light skimming through the blind slits, recalled a past morning: the day of his father's funeral. Jason remembered wearing a grey suit bunched at the seams, dead grass beneath his feet and the chiseled letters of his father's name, Michael, glowering back at him from the gravestone. He was just a kid then, only eleven years old. Now at thirteen, he stared at the ceiling of his new room and wondered if there wasn't some way to escape the inevitable progression of time.

When his alarm cried out, Jason pushed the unhelpful fantasies of returning to his old life back into the deep corners of his mind. Resigned, he got out of bed and made his way down the carpeted hallway to his bathroom. His feet were warmed by the carpet's spiral knots, but the softness lacked the comforting creak of the hardwood floor in Chicago. Jason still didn't understand why his mom insisted they move the few hundred miles away to the little city of Ashton, a place in every way the opposite of the life he left behind.

Jason brushed his teeth in lazy strokes, watching toothpaste and saliva congeal in his mouth and drip down the side

1

of his lip into a soupy mess in the sink. The sparkling mirrored cabinet revealed a familiar reflection of his hunched shoulders, stained undershirt and rumpled boxer shorts, but his face looked like a stranger's.

Jason waddled back to his bedroom, glaring at the portraits on the wall with suspicion. The smiling faces of his father and mother seemed like ghosts resurrected from a past long gone. He inspected the minute details, picking apart the pixels of light radiating from the corners of the wood frames, but to him they were fakes, a hoax, meant to recall events that never really happened.

He dressed in distrust; dark blue jeans threading at the hems, a faded red t-shirt and a grey windbreaker to sheer the brisk fall breeze. Then he grabbed his wallet and house keys from his dresser and lastly, begrudgingly, thrust his cell phone into his right front pocket. The phone was a gift from his mom and had a million different features he didn't need. In his mind, his mother found a way to interrupt him whenever and wherever he was, not exactly a 'gift.' His simple solution, of course, was to rarely charge it. He grabbed his backpack, heavy from the burden of a number of books, and headed downstairs for breakfast. As he descended, always one step at a time on school days, he thought he smelled pancakes and for a moment was distracted by hopeful anticipation. His delight transformed back to bland misery as he entered the kitchen and witnessed the sad reality of oatmeal and toast.

"Good morning sweetie!" his mom said from her seat at the kitchen table.

"Morning," he replied.

"How did you sleep?"

Jason rolled his eyes. Did he really have to answer this question every day? "I slept awesome. Everything was great. Comfy bed, good dream…I think."

"What was your dream about?" his mom asked.

"Don't remember. You should really start asking me, 'How did I wake?'"

Jason watched his mother's face, wondering how she

could be so put together. Wasn't she in pain? *Apparently not*, he thought as a cheerful smile crossed her face.

"Okay honey, how did you wake?" Anne Swann indulged her son.

"Thinking about dad," he said and spooned a glop of oatmeal into his mouth.

"I miss him too, Jason."

Not good enough, he thought, but that was all his mother said as she rose to put away dishes. Her movements through the kitchen appeared calculated and robotic, like she was clinging to a silly routine to hold herself together.

Jason had already been down this path many times. His questions about his dad, and the events leading to his death were always met with hesitation, like his mother didn't think he deserved to know the details. He wanted to scream at her, tell her he could handle the truth, could handle anything she had to say so long as she was honest, and not just move through the day with a phony smile on her face. But he was too tired.

"Did you finish all your homework?"

"Yes Mom," Jason replied dully. "Why don't you put up a piece of paper on the fridge and every morning I'll check off that I slept great and finished my homework, and we can skip this whole thing?"

His mother's smile faded, replaced by an expression of stone.

"Finish your breakfast, Jason; you need to leave for school."

Time for school already? he lamented in an oatmeal daze.

"I bet it's nice riding your bike to school, isn't it?" Anne asked. "Better than sitting on a smelly bus in traffic, right?"

Jason sighed. "You mean the bus that all my friends are on right now?"

"You'll meet new friends here Jason, I promise," his mother said. "We've only been here six months. I know you're having a hard time, but you aren't giving Ashton a fair chance."

There's nothing fair about any of this, Jason thought. He left his bowl of half-eaten breakfast and trudged out the front door.

Riding his bike through Ashton's downtown, Jason marveled at how small everything was. The biggest building in the city of thirty-five thousand was a ten-story pile of glass and steel, home to Barton Mineral Corp. Surrounding the building were smaller shops and stores that crisscrossed through a carefully planned network of streets around City Hall, which reminded Jason of a snow-globe-sized version of the capital building in Washington, D.C. The skyline he loved, the one with massive towers overlooking the coast of Lake Michigan, was replaced with this unobstructed view of a giant, intimidating sky.

Before long he passed downtown and found himself on yet more neatly tree-lined, suburban streets. As the bright brick of Jameson Middle School came into view, Jason gazed at the small, quiet houses, and imagined the no-doubt perfect and happy families living within. He wanted to open the door of a pretty red house and find his nightmare over, his father waiting for him on the other side. His mind drifted away, but was lurched back to reality when several kids zoomed by on bikes. Jason cringed, knowing nothing and no one better waited for him but the unfriendly building looming above.

Chapter 2: Saved by the Volcano

Jason came to view his science teacher, John Baker, as a large man, not fat but stocky: thick arms, thick legs and thick movements. His firm, angled face was framed by a pair of black-rimmed glasses. Baker was a bit of a klutz, which made his habitually desperate attempts to be careful as he walked, careful as he read, careful even as he called roll, all the more humorous. His boisterous voice carried quickly through the classroom.

"Who would like to present their project first?"

A shock of terror spread across Jason's face. He'd spent the last two weeks so focused on being angry at his mom and frustrated with having to live in Ashton that he'd forgotten all about the stupid science project! How had he not noticed all the other kids bringing in their projects?! *Please don't pick me, please don't pick me, please don't pick me...* was all he could think as he peeked at his classmates, praying for a volunteer.

Twenty-five blank faces were the only response. Jason slunk down inconspicuously, hoping Mr. Baker would some-how miss the guilt on his face. He felt the teacher's eyes scouring the class, taking time to seek out the perfect victim for embarrassment.

The slow-moving eyes didn't fool Jason for a second. He prided himself on being a good judge of character and he could tell that despite Mr. Baker's bumbling presence, inside the man was secure and watchful, even devious. At least as far as school projects were concerned.

"No one? How about you Jas--"

"I'll go Mr. Baker!" Ashlyn Bluent's annoying singsong

voice had never sounded sweeter to Jason's ears. He recalled his first day at school when she casually held out a small, firm hand and said, "Hi I'm Ashlyn from Ashton." His reply of "Good rhyme," was met with Ashlyn's confident words, "Actually, it's alliteration, not a rhyme." That was the last thing they'd said to each other.

"Ashlyn," Mr. Baker replied, "let's give Jason a chance to share."

Jason muttered under his breath as he began to rise, wondering how he was going to get out of this one. *Is Baker playing with me?* he thought. *He must have noticed I didn't bring a project... unless, well, he was bumbling about writing notes... Maybe he really didn't see?*

"Mr. Baker, I'd really like to present first... If that's okay with Jason."

Jason swung his head to regard Ashlyn with a puzzled expression. He might've been dreaming, but he could've sworn she gave him the slightest wink. He swiveled back to Mr. Baker, who seemed oblivious.

"I'm very pleased you're so eager to present your project Ashlyn, but Jason is new here and he hasn't had much of an opportunity to express himself in class so I'd like to..."

Jason cringed as he stood up completely. He gave Ashlyn a small nod of thanks, but there was no escape, he was—

"Mr. Baker, I'm sorry but I must protest your discriminatory practice. I don't doubt that you have the best intentions, but in the interest of fairness, I think that since you started out by asking for a volunteer, and I volunteered while Jason did not, it's only fair, as far as real fairness is concerned that..."

"Fine, Ashlyn... You've made your point," Mr. Baker conceded. "If it's all right with Jason, you may go first."

Mr. Baker shifted to Jason inquiringly, and an amenable grunt was all Jason could do to keep from erupting into joyous celebration, running over to Ashlyn and planting a big fat kiss on her cheek. As he sat back down, he flashed a small, thankful smile her way and... *Is she blushing?*

This unlikely observation crossed Jason's mind as he watched Ashlyn hop out of her seat in a flurry; her ponytail bouncing in delight as it brushed the hood of her purple, zip-up sweatshirt… He noted her vibrant green eyes as they stared confidently at Mr. Baker. He had to admit she was cute, definitely annoying, but…

Ashlyn half-skipped to the side of the classroom, where the science experiments sat on the ground. She located, and then carried, her science experiment to the front of the class. The excitement of the moment shined on her face, and Jason could tell she was proud of her volcano. *It certainly looked interesting,* he thought, although he wasn't sure if "volcano" was accurate. The entire structure drooped to the right like an old man leaning on a shopping cart, and the craggy sides of the papier-mâché contraption were covered in glittered designs. There were magenta swirls, sparkly gold stars, and a frolicking goat of a decidedly blue hue.

"That's a very… interesting design," Mr. Baker proposed. "What book did you use as a reference for the exterior of your volcano?"

Ashlyn ceded her teacher a puzzled look. "What do you mean?"

"I don't recall seeing blue goats and gold stars in the picture on page thirty-two of your textbook."

"Oh, I know that!" she exclaimed. "Just a bunch of boring brown rocks and stuff. This is much more energetic, don't you think? Conforming reality to our wills is what science is all about right?"

"I don't know if I agree with that-"

"And you also didn't specify that artists' interpretations weren't allowed."

Jason marveled at Ashlyn's perfect posture as she lightly berated their teacher.

The side of Mr. Baker's mouth twitched like he was reluctant to admit she was right. "I suppose I didn't," he finally relented. "Why don't you explain what a volcano is, and how it works?"

7

"Pretty self-explanatory, don't you think?" she asked genuinely.

A meaty hand clumsily pushed the spectacles back onto the bridge of John Baker's nose. As he glared at Ashlyn, Jason glanced around the class to find out if he was still in fact, at Jameson Middle School, planet Earth. Not once in his life had he heard a student speak to a teacher in such a condescending tone. Ashlyn's lively sureness was endearing. She was a say-it-like-you-mean-it kind of girl, and that was fine with Jason. But, if she didn't buckle down, Mr. Baker was going to get mad, make her sit down and then surely call on him.

Come on Ashlyn, stay focused, he thought, praying for a miracle.

"Well Ashlyn, maybe to you the inner workings of a volcano are second nature," Mr. Baker contended, "but I think there might be some kids in class who would like to know a little more about them."

"I suppose you're right Mr. Baker," Ashlyn said without rotating to face him. She'd been sneaking peaks at Jason. He was so cute, and so shy. But the shyness didn't seem like his real personality. Something was making him that way. Maybe nobody else could tell, but she was sure he'd lost something important; after all, so had she and Ashlyn recognized the signs. It must have been something really important to make him forget to do his science project. *Don't worry Jason, I'll-*

"Ashlyn, do I have to ask you again?" Mr. Baker questioned, bringing her back to the task at hand.

"So this is a volcano," erupted from her mouth, as she used her arms and hands delicately to display her project's greatness. "A volcano draws hot magma from underneath the earth, and when the pressure builds up enough the whole thing essentially goes Kabloom."

"Very descriptive Ashlyn, please continue," Mr. Baker nodded.

"When a volcano erupts, the built-up pressure can literally blow the mountain-top miles into the air. Now, a quick side note; when I was very young my brother told me this story, he's in college, Mr. Baker," she said, turning to face her teacher without drawing breath. "A long time ago, over in Italy, where spaghetti comes from, this volcano blew up, except nobody in the city below knew it was going to happen because it was a really long time ago and they didn't have seismic sensors like we have now. They tried to run away from the lava as it came crashing down the mountain-side, but they couldn't outrun it and they were all going to die so they sent their fastest runner, this guy named Hermes, I think --"

"Ashlyn, let's save the history lesson for another day and get back to the *science* of how volcanoes work."

"Mr. Baker," Ashlyn remarked, firmly placing her hands on her hips, "it's not a real story. I was just trying to illustrate a point."

Mr. Baker rolled his eyes in frustration.

"Why don't you just show the class how it works?" he pleaded.

"Very well," Ashlyn sighed.

Jason couldn't believe his good luck. *Was she stalling on purpose?* He hoped by the time she was done presenting, Mr. Baker would have forgotten all about his desire to let Jason "express" himself.

Jason wheeled to the student in the chair to his left, a small boy named Daniel, who had dark features and a brow that always appeared nervous. Nervous or intrigued, Jason wasn't sure, because he'd barely spoken to Daniel in the time they'd spent sitting next to each other. Up until now, there hadn't been much to say.

"Hey Daniel," Jason whispered.

Shocked, Daniel whirled to him.

"Yes, I can talk like other humans," Jason said. Daniel returned the sarcasm with a frown, which Jason chose to ignore.

"What's the deal with Ashlyn?"

Daniel shook his head in wonder. "What do you mean?"

"I mean, you guys grew up together, right?"

"I guess, why?"

"What do you think she's up to?"

"Keeping me from presenting my project," Daniel whispered, narrowing his eyes. "She loves attention, and she's kind of weird too. She used to hang out with this kid but-" Daniel suddenly stopped talking and his eyebrows descended into a defensive position. Jason peeped back at the front of the class in time to see Ashlyn shoot some very sharp eye-daggers at the small boy.

"This kid... what kid?" Jason whispered back.

Daniel was scared. "I don't know. Stop talking to me in class."

Jason responded with a bewildered expression. *What's his problem?*

"As I stated before," Ashlyn exclaimed like a veteran Master of Ceremony, "pressure builds up inside the volcano until everything goes Kabloom, scientifically speaking, of course. I will now attempt to replicate this feat, on a much smaller scale using my model. I already poured a bunch of baking soda in there, so now I'm popping the top on this bottle of vinegar..."

"Only a little bit of vinegar, Ashlyn!" Mr. Baker interjected. "Otherwise --"

"Yeah, I tried doing a little bit at home, but nothing spectacular happened, so I followed your advice about the scientific method and kept adding more and more. When I poured the *whole* bottle in, that's when the cool stuff happened!"

Mr. Baker's eyes widened to the size of bowling balls as he rushed to grab her hands with all his bumbling speed, but he was too late. For a moment, time stood still, all motion ceased and the empty space between atoms and electrons clenched tightly to nothing. Then, with building speed, the innards of the trembling miniature Mt. St. Helens burst forth from the prison of paper walls! Frothy waste careened from all sides of the multi-colored model onto the table, then all over the floor, spreading out like a flood in a great open plain.

Every science experiment lining the side of the classroom fell victim to the rush of the volcano's mighty flow: cut-up straws mimicking radio towers, masses of pipe-cleaners disguised as various arachnid species, and foam balls masquerading as the solar system, all drowned beneath the baking-soda-and-vinegar lava.

Jason stared at the damage in awe, overcome by his fantastic luck. He snuck a peek at Ashlyn, and this time there was no mistaking the wink. He couldn't help but blush; she really was pretty cute, and any girl who could make miracles was not nearly as annoying as he'd thought.

The room was in chaos, as Jason's classmates rushed to rescue what they could of their work. He noticed Daniel staring in abject horror at the destroyed remains of whichever of the projects had been his. Jason almost felt bad for him, but a little guilt was a small price to pay for his freedom. He relaxed, slid down into his chair, and thought about how he could thank Ashlyn for what she'd done.

Chapter 3: Treasures

Tote Street's small, handsome houses passed by without notice as Jason rode his bike home after school with a lackluster cadence. The solitary ride gave him time to think and Jason's good mood from class dimmed with each recollection of the past. Despite how hard he tried to focus on the wooden posts of a fence, or the types of trees lining the empty streets, these memories led to a mental image of his dad. Nobody really knew what Michael died from; at least, that's what his mom said. Jason didn't believe that; how could she *not* know? *She must,* he thought angrily, she must know and she assumed he was too young to understand! Jason remembered his dad changing almost overnight, becoming distant, like he was living in a far off place.

"That was a pretty crazy science class today, huh?" Daniel said, pulling up on a well-maintained bike with glistening chrome pegs. Jason's memory shattered under the startling sound of Daniel's voice. The sight of the boy's black-and-white, oversized windbreaker and cuffed, brown pants made Jason cringe, though he wasn't sure exactly what was so irritating. Jason cast his unwanted companion an angry glance, "Which part?"

Daniel glared back. "The part where Ashlyn's volcano erupted all over the floor!"

"Oh," Jason said, secretly amused. "Yeah, that was okay, I guess."

"Okay? My project was completely ruined!"

"Well I-"

"How annoying are girls, right? Ashlyn especially. She

thinks she's really cool, so take it from me and don't be offended if she makes you angry."

"She didn't-"

"She's just like all the other kids in our class," Daniel continued, oblivious to Jason's response. "I grew up with all of them and I can tell you that they're a pretty mean bunch. They make fun of me a lot because I don't like to do the same stupid things they do, and probably because I'm smarter than them... just as a matter of fact."

"Yeah, I guess--"

"Don't be surprised if they start to treat you the same way, especially Ashlyn."

"What did Ashlyn do-"

"Hey, you know what would be a good idea?" Daniel exclaimed. "Maybe you could come over to my house and we could work on our projects together. I spent forever getting the color schemes of Jupiter just right, but I guess I could do it again. Maybe you could help; are you a good painter?"

The desperation on Daniel's face wasn't lost to Jason. "You don't have to do it again; Mr. Baker said so in class."

Jason almost relished the confusion that overtook Daniel's face. "But Mr. Baker said we could, if we wanted extra credit. Don't you want extra credit?"

"Not really," Jason said with a grin, as he pedaled along. "I don't see what the big deal is anyway. So a bunch of foam balls got ruined, who cares?"

He cast a sidelong glance at Daniel and could sense the anger of a perfectionist brewing within his classmate's diminutive frame. However, Daniel's features cooled, and his face took on the expression of a person who wants something, but doesn't know how to ask for it.

"Yeah, I guess that's kind of silly, huh? All that extra work..." Daniel sighed, and an underlying sadness was clear to Jason. Daniel reminded him of a boy he used to know who'd say anything, to have a friend. Jason supposed he couldn't be too angry about that, everyone needed a friend.

"So then... what are you doing this afternoon?" Daniel

asked abruptly.

Jason cocked his head, "Probably nothing; Ashton is really boring."

Daniel's brow furrowed with annoyance, and his puckered mouth let out a resounding "Humph."

"You're from Chicago, right?" Daniel probed.

"Yeah."

"I've been to Chicago. Maybe Ashton isn't the same--"

"You're right there. Chicago is awesome. This place is tiny and-"

"That's what I like about it!" Daniel chimed. "I can hear myself think, and the air smells clean, and it's my home!"

"That doesn't mean it isn't boring," Jason retorted, but regretted the comment. He didn't used to be so angry and mean, what was happening to him?

"It's only boring because you're trying to be bored!" Daniel shot back.

Jason met Daniel's glower and relented. The smaller boy had a spark of courage Jason hadn't anticipated. He waved his hand invitingly. "Okay then, let's do something fun. What did you have in mind?"

Daniel's eyes lit up. "Well, I mean, there's lot's we could do like...uh, oh we could maybe go to the...no... or oh I know, we could... uh--"

Jason stared at Daniel coolly amidst his jabbering. "Why don't you let me know when you think of something?" he replied, regretting giving in to his compassion.

"No, wait, I'll think of something right now!"

Jason sighed and pedaled away without giving Daniel a chance. *Besides*, he thought, *if Ashlyn doesn't like this kid, maybe there really is something wrong with him.*

"Damnit," Daniel seethed, angry at himself as he watched Jason become smaller and smaller in the distance.

–◯⋔ဒ–

The refrigerator revealed itself to be as lacking as Jason anticipated, so he sluggishly climbed the stairs to his room. He regretted having been a jerk to Daniel, and was angry because he felt like he'd been left without an option. Why couldn't everyone leave him alone? He entered his room, tossed his backpack next to his desk and fell onto his bed.

Jason awoke at dusk, his favorite time of day. Old memories he'd thought lost could, by his observation of the simplest of things -- a chair or a book catching the amber glow of a fading sun -- return in vivid detail. The not-quite-light, not-quite-dark sky illuminated the hiding places of these misplaced possessions.

He narrowed his eyes to concentrate as he welcomed the waning rays peeking through his blinds. He formed the outline of his father in his mind, but filling in details was becoming ever more difficult, even at dusk. The just-right color of his father's eyes, the exact angle of the crook in his nose, and the other, near infinite features that made up his dad's face were torn from him by the unsavory smells of a waiting dinner wafting from the kitchen.

His mind lost the precious spark of memory. His father's imagined hair thinned, and fell away. His father's eyes peeled until the shining new layer of paint decayed, leaving a chipped iris and fading pupil. Dad's beard turned from brown to grey, shriveled, and receded back into skin. Skin melted away to bone, then bone melted away too, leaving the original outline, lifeless and emotionless as a sculptor's wooden model.

Even Mom's cooking is trying to destroy my memories, Jason thought furiously.

He sighed, and propped himself onto his elbows. The smell of overcooked, steamed vegetables was getting stronger. He didn't have much time before his mom called him to dinner, and he needed something stronger than dusk to help him remember. Jason snuck across his room, sliding on his socks to his closet. He cocked his head and listened, but there were no footsteps heading upstairs. He waited another moment, just to be sure, and then opened his closet door.

The interior of the closet was a mess. Despite his mother's

weekly demands that he clean it, he always found a way to leave the disarray. But what seemed like simple chaos was a carefully constructed ruse to hide the treasure within from prying eyes. He clawed away jackets, moved aside board games, parted boxes of old shoes, and reached into the deep trench of the closet bottom, relying on his sense of touch to feel for his treasure: a plain brown box left over from a birthday long since passed. Jason pulled the box to him, paused once more to listen for sounds from the hallway, and sat on the floor to investigate the contents.

"Happy Birthday Jason! Love Dad." He read the card first, running his fingers over the script. He put the card down and pulled out his favorite picture.

Jason was seven years old at Grant Park in Chicago, and sat smiling on top of his father's shoulders. His dad seemed like a giant at the time, a huge powerful force with hands that could break boulders and a voice that could frighten a roaring fire into cinder and ash. He knew back then his dad could take care of anything; like a god. And he knew, of course, that gods didn't die. Even at eleven years old, though he knew his father wasn't any god, Jason couldn't fathom the idea of never seeing him again. And he knew he was being silly, but part of Jason was sure they'd see each other again. His father would wake up from a deep sleep and find his way home.

The picture and the card were put carefully back in the shoebox. After the lid was secured, Jason recognized a familiar awareness of the lack of something wonderful.

As the dim, dusk light swirled about him, whispering of the coming night, he remembered the feeling of having, and now the feeling of not having. Though he couldn't name this feeling, he knew what his house was missing, what made it an empty cavity, a place to eat and read and rest his head.

Chapter 4: The Shadow of Home

A dull brick of salt-free fish and broccoli digested in Jason's stomach as he sat on his bed trying to ignore the gurgling of discontent. The clock read 9:44 pm. He had less than a minute until his mother came up to say goodnight, and she would, as on every night, be right on time. He counted down from ten and waved his hand towards the door as he heard her voice: "It's nine forty-five, can I come in?"

"Yes," was his bland reply.

She entered, and Jason watched her routine with practiced disdain. Her right hand lifted to the top of the dresser to set the alarm clock. She moved beyond the clock to switch on a little lamp. She turned off the overhead room light, took six careful steps to Jason's bed and sat down. His lips curled as she followed this nightly path.

"You didn't talk much at dinner Jay, did something happen in school?"

"I was saved from an 'F' by an exploding volcano."

"Very funny," his mother deadpanned.

He threw up his arms in protest, "No, seriously, a girl's papier-mâché volcano exploded all over the place and we had to end class early."

"Oh, well then…"

An expression bordering on despair crinkled his mother's face. What else could she say? So much, in his estimation, and yet all she asked was, "Did you make any new friends?"

"No," Jason stated.

"Give it a little more time," she pleaded in a tone both empty and strained. He found strange comfort in the fact that

17

she didn't seem to believe her own words.

"Mom, how old do I have to be before we can talk about what happened to Dad, I mean for real?" he asked, sensing a chink in her armor.

He saw her fighting back tears welling at the bottom of her lids, but she didn't give in to them. Instead, she pleaded, "Give me a little more time, okay?"

"What do you need more time for? Just tell me what happened! How come everyone gets to know what happened but me?!"

Jason's stone eyes watched as his mother stammered in surprise, "I... Jason, I..."

Her tears began to flow. The realization that he'd made his mother cry wilted the stout frame of Jason's fury. For the first time since they moved to Ashton, he let himself see his mother's pain. He felt terrible, but didn't know what to say. He didn't *want* to be angry with his mom all the time; he didn't want to be angry at all! He sighed and let his head sink into his pillow.

She always asked for time. From the day his father died her one plea to him had been to give her more time. Jason didn't understand what she meant. He and his best friends from Chicago became friends instantaneously in the moment of meeting. He'd said, "Hi, I'm Jason," and then they gave their names, and the bond was there. His love for his father and mother hadn't taken time to develop, nor had his grief at the finality of his father's death. So why should talking about something that mattered dearly demand so much unbearable time?

As Jason gazed into his mother's eyes, finally allowing pity to find his heart, he wondered if that's what getting older means: making friends, finding love, and everything else in life, would take much more time. But if she needed more time, he'd give it to her.

"I'm sorry, Mom. You can tell me when you're ready."

A tiny smile crept across his mother's lips, and while he'd hoped this would make him happier, the sight was more heartbreaking than anything else. Jason allowed her a salty kiss on his cheek before she turned off the light and left the room. He peered into the darkness, imagining a different life, before descending into dream.

Anne peeked through the crack in Jason's door and watched the rhythmic breathing of her only child... for how long, she didn't know. Her grief didn't make her cry, but anguish at seeing Jason's while knowing there was nothing she could say that he'd believe. He was so sure she was keeping a secret from him. But the truth was, the secret wasn't hers to tell. Anne didn't know why Michael died either, no one did.

–◎↑§–

Endless violet sky surrounded Jason as he soared above speckled granite canyons covered in ancient trees sparkling in many shades of green. He chuckled as he gleefully admired the great eagle wings extending from his body towards both horizons, carrying him effortlessly in a calm breeze.

The violet sky faded into deep turquoise on the horizon as he flew like a graceful blade towards the house. He knew he was getting close even though the ground far beneath him didn't change from a static shade of light grey rock. In the past, each time he'd approached the house, before the welcoming and handsome lines became more than a shadow hiding in a fog, the gold bands securing the wings to his arms unraveled into dust, leaving the wings to fade into the cloudless sky.

Each time in the past, he fell gently and without fear, as if being guided to a river in the canyon miles below by an invisible grip that held him like a mother sheltering an infant. When he reached the river, its calm current drifted him along, hollow and weightless, through the canyon that never changed, beyond the trees and the rock and the whole of the world. He moved back through time, which, like a heavy stone, sat quiet and unmoving as he stared up at the violet sky.

This time, Jason was prepared, and as the tips of the eagle feathers began to dissolve, he maneuvered his hand into his jacket pocket and pulled out a small vial of powder, a speckled mix of blue and white. Jason put the vial to his lips and thirstily drank. The golden bands strengthened, the wings reformed and carried him through the sky. An enormous grin crested Jason's mouth as the outline of the house came into view. He saw light reflecting off windows and small chips in the paint on the shutters. Red brick walls, thick oak door. He'd found his way home!

The canyon came to an end. Steep sides of the ancient stone shot up like angled spearheads rising miles from the river below, which cut into the converged cliff face and disappeared. The stone formed a ridge and on top of the ridge, parting gigantic pine trees huddled in masses on either side, was the simple house he loved.

Jason landed on freshly cut grass with barely a sound, weightless as a wisp of air. The wings folded into the gold bracelets around his arms. The bracelets melted and flowed like water over Jason's body until he was entirely covered in liquid gold.

He grasped the handle of the door, but there was no need, the door knew who he was and with the faintest breeze, opened and turned into a pile of golden dust. The dust floated into the air surrounding Jason's body, and became a part of him. As he walked into the house, the sturdy oak door splintered and the brick walls crumbled. The detritus that remained was reborn into gold. As Jason walked down the main hallway, everything he passed, the molding of the threshold, tables, pictures, light fixtures, rugs and floor boards transformed into gold, and melded to his being.

Jason's golden hand extended to open the door at the end of the hall. In his room, he saw the outline of a man leaning over a small, empty bed. Jason let out a sigh of relief that had been imprisoned within him for much too long.

Everything was right again. Jason's hand pressed against his chest and his body cracked around him like a shattering golden shell. He glimpsed down, and found he had the body of a small child. He ran across the room to take his place in the bed, and to listen to his father's powerful voice lull him to sleep with stories and songs. He opened his mouth to call out "Dad!" but something was wrong. The man's eyes were correct in color and shape, but they weren't his father's. They looked at him differently, as if Jason was a stranger. The mouth opened to speak, but the voice wasn't his father's. A guttural sound emanated instead, and Jason's body began to burn.

The giant approached, and though his arms never moved and his hands didn't lift a finger, Jason felt the apparition prying him apart, searching for something, burning him from within. Invisible tendrils enwrapped Jason's mind, and countless images from his life descended like a hurricane, almost faster than he could perceive. From beyond the burning cinder of his body, he could barely hear the horrible voice:

"Gggggggrrruuuuugggggggggchhhhadgggggggguuuuur"

The creature was upon him. Strong hands reached into the fire of Jason's mind, into the swirling nebula of all things he'd ever known, down to every sub-atomic particle, and ripped Jason apart. Just when he was sure death was upon him and the monster wanted to break his soul, the burning ceased and the mental touch became supremely gentle. Jason peered up at what he'd believed cruel, and saw only benevolent curiosity. He had so many questions, but they would have to wait, because the-specter-that-was-not-his-father opened its mouth to speak:

"Wake up."

Arms flailed without purpose, bleary eyes searched in all directions for a voice he couldn't find. As Jason's mind came to him, his dream faded into the obscuring mists of feeble recall. The only image that remained was an endless violet sky.

Chapter 5: Slightly Out of the Ordinary

Jason resembled a bag of potatoes sulking over his bike handles as he headed towards school, until the sound of furious peddling made him twist his head to see Daniel racing towards him.

"Jason! Wait up!" Daniel huffed. Jason clutched his brakes hard and his bike skidded to a stop, leaving a rubber trace on the asphalt.

"Daniel, what's going on? Are you all right?"

"Jason," Daniel squeaked, out of breath. "Nothing's wrong... nothing's wrong," he repeated with a wagging hand. "It's just that on my whole bike ride home yesterday I tried to think of something great to do and prove you wrong about this town. You know, 'cause you think it's really boring."

"Geez Daniel, you scared the hell out of me!"

"Sorry, I didn't mean to," Daniel apologized as he sipped little gasps of air.

"It's all right. Did you think of something fun to do?" Jason asked with genuine hope. Between making his mom cry, and a restless night's sleep full of strange-but-forgotten dreams, Jason figured he could stand a little fun.

Daniel caught his breath, "It's not what I thought of--it's what I saw!"

"You saw something fun that we can do?"

Daniel stood as straight and as tall as his short frame allowed.

"Well... I guess it's not something we can technically do per se, but it was really amazing!"

"What was it?"

"A shooting star!" Daniel exclaimed, his eyes wide.

Jason's fledgling enthusiasm died like a patient on an operating table. "That's it?"

"That's it?" Daniel shot back. "A shooting star is a meteorite being burned up in Earth's atmosphere!"

Jason waved his hand dismissively. "Yeah, I know that. So what?"

"Well... Don't you think that's amazing?" Daniel shot back.

Jason considered for a moment, "I guess, but we can't do anything with a shooting star."

"But-"

"And also, it's in outer-freakin' space! It's not something in Ashton!"

"*I* was in Ashton when I saw it yesterday afternoon," Daniel retorted.

Jason wasn't sure how that made any difference. "Fine, you were in Ashton when you saw it... but I didn't think you could see shooting stars in the middle of the day."

"You think I'm making it up? I probably know way more about science than you do," Daniel objected. Jason threw his classmate an annoyed glance. *What did I do to deserve this?* he thought. *No wonder he doesn't have any friends.* Jason was about to point this out when he noticed a cringe of regret on Daniel's face.

"Sorry, I didn't mean to be a jerk. I'm sure you're really good at science, too. I thought you would think it was cool and I swear I saw it!" Daniel pleaded.

"Okay, fine, I believe you," Jason said, trying to pacify Daniel, who seemed like he was on the verge of tears. Jason didn't think he could take being responsible for making two people cry within a twenty-four-hour period.

"I *do* think it's cool," Jason pressed on, "but why did you race across town to tell me that? We were going to see each other in like, fifteen minutes."

"I wanted to be the first to tell you," Daniel said, with a

diplomatic air of modesty. "That's all."

Jason gave him a confused glare. "I don't know if you've noticed this or not, but the other kids don't tell me very much. They probably wouldn't have mentioned seeing a giant ball of light flying across the sky during the middle of the day, even if they thought it was an alien."

Daniel tried not to be so angry with himself, but the pitying expression on Jason's face made him feel stupid. He knew a shooting star wasn't all that incredible, but he hadn't been able to think of anything to do and he knew that if he didn't say anything, Jason would forget all about him. After all, Jason probably had lots of friends in Chicago. He didn't know what living in a place your whole life and being totally surrounded with people who wanted to do things all the time, but never with him, felt like. Daniel supposed he was trying too hard, but he didn't have much of a choice, in his estimation. All the other kids already knew him; they'd grown up together and they'd chosen to either make fun of him or ignore him. *What's so bad about me?* he wondered.

"I just thought that since you're new here, you and I could…"

Jason didn't hear the end of Daniel's sentence. He was distracted by a strange movement in his periphery. He could've sworn he saw the entire landscape sort of, well, "shimmer" was the best word to describe it. Everything had vibrated for a moment: the air, the trees, the grass, the concrete sidewalks and the asphalt street, as if dancing in rhythm to an unheard melody.

Jason spun back to Daniel with a perplexed look. "Did you just see that?" he asked, wondering what he'd really seen himself.

Daniel eyed Jason questioningly. "No… I said I saw it yesterday, late in the afternoon."

Jason shook his hands. "No, no not the shooting star. I mean, did you just see the…" He was at a loss for words.

"Did I see what?"

"The, that whole kind of area to my right… just sort of

shimmered, I mean, wiggled? Something like that."

Daniel glared at him sternly. "Were you listening to anything I said?"

Jason gazed back blankly.

"Fine," Daniel pronounced to empty air.

"Fine what, what's fine?"

"Are you okay, Jason?"

"What? Yeah, I'm fine... Are you sure you didn't just see everything kind of...shimmer...right over there?" Jason pointed in the direction of the mysterious movement.

Daniel's face revealed that this was no doubt the oddest conversation the boy ever had.

"Are you messing with me?" Daniel tested.

"No I swear, it was... I guess it's gone now."

"Let's just go to school," Daniel stated, and began pedaling away before realizing that Jason hadn't followed. He pivoted on his seat to see Jason staring off into the park. "Aren't you coming?" Daniel shouted.

"Huh?" Jason could have sworn he heard someone talking to him, but the strange shimmering had returned.

"Yeah, I'll catch up with you later," Jason said to nobody in particular as he pedaled towards the strange sight.

"Fine, you don't want to be my friend, that's fine!" Daniel yelled. "You could just say it, you don't have to pretend!"

But Jason didn't respond. "What an ass," Daniel muttered as he furiously rode away.

Jason crept to the edge of Circle Park, a pristine green acre surrounded by tall birch trees in the middle of a roundabout. He walked through the birch trees about a quarter of the way to the center of the park, but there was nothing out of the ordinary. The birches swaying in the cool October breeze seemed to mock him as he surveyed an empty field of grass and a couple of swing sets in disrepair.

"I swear I saw something," Jason whispered.

He closed his eyes and began to laugh, disappointed and a little sad. There was nothing. He started to head back to his bike, glancing up once at the top of the trees, and allowed himself a faint smile. After all, it was a very nice day, even for Ashton.

But then "Hello" whispered in his head.

Jason stopped short and felt his face flush as beads of sweat brushed his forehead. Standing statue still, he peered into the trees. The peaceful blue day became at once eerie and unwelcome as he backed towards his bike.

"Turn around," the whisper inside his head ordered.

Half of Jason wanted to grab his bike and ride as fast as he could through the park, down the wide winding streets back to his house, leap under the covers of his bed and wait there until his mom came home from work. The other half of him was intrigued.

Jason's right foot found grounding on the wet grass and led his body, which was fighting the urge to run, to about face. He wasn't sure what he expected to find waiting, and only knew that what he saw was something he never imagined: a robotic being, perhaps half a foot taller than him.

There were no blinking lights, or socket hinges connecting awkward limbs. There were no antennas, buttons, or any of the other innards and outards that a robot was supposed to have. The being was made of a metal so black, Jason thought he was staring into an abyss, and yet the surface of the metal also gleamed in a translucent blue-and-white sheen that moved like lazy sand, as if the abyss was wrapped in a faint, cloudy sky.

The being had no arms, but Jason could see symmetric, covered compartments along both sides of its body. Below the conical abdomen was a tripod of leg-like jointed shafts, ending in spheres covered in countless tiny chords wiggling around.

Jason brought his eyes up. He saw no jaw or mouth, no ears or eyes, but rather four visor-like crystal protrusions jutting from the base of a smooth, oblong head. Each visor shone with a different luminescent display. The colors changed, slowly at first, but then faster, until Jason couldn't comprehend their speed. Suddenly, all four visors stopped shifting and appeared empty.

"There is no need to be scared," the whisper in Jason's mind returned.

He felt himself shaking, and the half of him that didn't want to run, had no idea what to do.

"How...how are you in my head?" he managed to squeak. "How can--"

"Explanation will follow shortly. Please come with me to my ship."

Jason didn't speak; he couldn't take his eyes off of the being's exterior, which reminded him of a swirling midnight dream. The whisper didn't return. Finally, Jason responded, "Ship? You mean, like a spaceship?"

"Not exactly," the whisper replied. "Follow me and I will show you."

Jason's eyes diminished into slits and his posture stiffened. Alien abduction wasn't the way he wanted to escape Ashton. He studied the being as it cocked its head slightly to the side. Could it sense that he was scared? And if so, how?

"Can you read my thoughts?"

"No, I cannot," the whisper remarked.

"How do I know you're telling the truth?" he probed, eyes squinting in deliberation.

"You do not," the whisper replied, in a tone as if meeting intelligent life from other planets was just another day at the office. "I anticipated your fear, but trying to decide whether to trust me is pointless. You have no evidence to support whether I am a threat to you or not. It is not my mission to convince you of either. There are others who suit the needs of the Archive; it does not have to be you."

The words simmered in Jason's head. Though he felt fear pulsing through his body, he couldn't push off the idea that this would be one of those chances that, if refused, he'd regret for the rest of his life.

"No! I mean, I'll go with you, but first, can you make me one promise?"

"No, I cannot," the whisper countered. "I am an archivist. What you want to know, or what you might demand, is not necessarily within my bounds to tell, or to offer."

"What do you mean you're an archivist? What is this Archive you're talking about?"

"Come with me to the ship. I will tell you."

The alien being's strange politeness made the unhelpful responses to Jason's questions seem sensible somehow. Despite his better instincts, Jason grew more confident. His fear dissipated, and his inquisitive inner soul emerged. He took a small step towards the robotic being and noticed it wasn't as tall as he'd first thought, nor quite so imposing. The swirling cloudy sky that flowed seamlessly over the alien's body lulled Jason into a sense of calm.

"Okay," he declared. "Show me the ship."

Two small oval indentations appeared in the Archivist's abdomen, like objects coming to the surface of a body of water. Equidistant compartments in the middle of the conical body emerged, and the black metal dissipated around the indentations. Two, foot-long panel doors slid open, revealing two more, apparently empty, crystal visors. They soon spirited to life however, shooting through a vast array of colors, until they glistened as one solid color Jason couldn't really describe, which then promptly disappeared.

"What happened to the colors?" Jason asked

"My visors give commands. Some are given in wavelengths of electromagnetic radiation your eyes can see, many are not. To activate 'Esan's Eyes,' the command is given in the visible light spectrum. To use Esan's Eyes, the command is given using radio waves."

"What's eyes?" Jason asked.

"Esan's Eyes. That is the name of the store-houses of power on each side of my body."

"So that's your name, Esan?"

"No, it is not."

"But that's how you see?" Jason inquired.

"No, it is not."

Jason let out a flustered huff. "So what do they do?"

"I use them to locate things. Things I would not be able to find otherwise," the whisper in Jason's head said. "Place them in your hands; they will take us to the ship."

Before he thought better, Jason grasped Esan's Eyes, and as he stared into the blank expression of the four visors on the front of the being's head, he found himself unsure in that moment, if he'd made the right decision, after all.

Chapter 6: An Unlikely Invitation

Touching the crystal protrusions the alien being called Esan's Eyes was the last thing Jason remembered. He'd expected them to feel smooth, like glass, and was surprised to find they felt like trying to grasp water running from a faucet. When he touched them, the vibrating world he'd seen while talking to Daniel, spread out to surround him like a shell. Then he was standing in a clearing surrounded by elm trees, as if whatever moment was necessary to connect two distinct pieces of time hadn't occurred. The world was still. The strange robotic being stood next to him, and the two panels on its abdomen were closed.

"Where are we?" Jason asked. "I thought you were taking us to your ship?"

"We are in the woods beyond your house, and the ship is right in front of you," the whisper replied.

"All I see is--"

The four visors on the being's face glowed a soft blue, and a huge grey horseshoe-shaped object about the size of Jason's house appeared. His eyes opened wide. "Whoa…cloaking."

"I am not sure what that means," the whisper interjected. "The ship was built with the ability to absorb, rather than reflect, different wavelengths of light, if circumstances warrant. Generally, this is the case in planetary systems with intelligent life."

"Right… that is sweet. But the ship is…well…"

"What?" the whisper asked.

Jason felt a bit disappointed. He'd imagined a galactic war vessel, or a space cruiser like in science-fiction movies. All the amazing cosmic appliances were missing!

"Nothing, it's…great," Jason muttered, not wanting to anger the alien being. He walked around the perimeter to examine the exterior, but couldn't find any doors or hatches. "How do we get in this thing?"

"There are no visible openings if that is what you are trying to find. I will take us into the ship, but before that, I must explain my presence here to you, as demanded by the Protocol of the Shantar Anar."

"The what of the what?" Jason asked, as he walked back towards the alien being wondering where all his fear had gone. There was something about the encounter that smacked of a familiarity Jason couldn't name or understand, almost as if they'd met before.

Ignoring Jason's question, the whisper in his head continued.

"Firstly, I am required to disclose that my planet of origin is not your own."

Jason crooked his eyebrow. "Right, I kind of figured that out."

"My name is Nierion Eindru Ebenin Shantar Anar. I am the Archivist for this Sub-Section of the universe. My objective is to study planetary systems that contain life, both intelligent and non-intelligent. My objective on this planet was to study eighteen forms of life and among these, human beings. You are the human I studied."

It sounds like it's reading off a telemarketer's script. Then Jason realized the being just spoke in the past tense, as if all of its objectives had already been accomplished.

"Now that I have disclosed the reason for my presence, the Protocol states I must show you the interior of the ship."

"What is this 'Protocol' you keep talking about?" Jason asked.

"The Protocol of the Shantar Anar, I have told you this already."

Jason shook his head. "But that doesn't mean anything to me. Can't you tell me about it?"

"It is the rule of action set forth by the Shantar Anar."

Jason thought he understood. "And you're one of them, Nierion of the Shantar Anar?"

"No. As I stated, I am only an archivist, one of their 'Ebenin,' which you might translate as 'creation'."

"The Shantar Anar made you?" Jason asked, his voice heavy with awe.

"Yes," the whisper answered.

"Wow… what are they? What do they look like? Where are they from? Is one of them here with you? Is that Esan guy that gave you your eyes a Shantar Anar?"

The Archivist stared at Jason as if speaking to a small child, "Esan is not a 'guy,' or a girl for that matter. But yes, Esan is Shantar Anar."

"And?" Jason asked, pleading with his eyes for more.

"And, under the Protocol, the rest is not required to be disclosed," the whisper in Jason's head stated as a matter-of-fact.

"They sent you here for me, didn't they? You can't tell me anything about them?"

"That is not my purpose."

"What are they like? How did they make you?" Jason pondered, ignoring the Archivist's abruptness.

"Once you have seen the interior the ship," Nierion continued, ignoring Jason's questions, "the Protocol states I must inform you of how we are able to communicate with one another."

As soon as he heard the words in his head, Jason wondered how he'd neglected to question their method of communication himself, but there was something about the presence of the Archivist in his mind that felt so natural.

Nierion moved effortlessly along the clearing in the woods towards the horseshoe-shaped ship. The countless, undulating chords attached to the spheres at the bottom of each of its tripod legs pushed its bulk over the grass like a swan skimming the surface of a lake. Jason watched, amazed, and wondered what kind of beings the Shantar Anar must be in order to create such a thing. *They must be really smart and powerful. If that's the case, maybe they can tell me what happened to my dad,* he thought sarcastically.

The Archivist stood ten feet from the ship and Jason watched as a sinuous coil emerged from another hidden compartment in its abdomen. The coil was made of the same black metal, covered in the distinctive blue-and-white sheen. At the end of the coil, a circular dial unfolded, which looked like the palm of a large hand. Jason could barely make out that the dial's outer rim seemed a thin, silky substance. Suddenly, he heard a pleasant hum inside his head, like a barely audible orchestra channeling their instruments into a vast ocean of sound.

The hum reached through Jason's mind, gliding over every neuron in his brain. The locked doors that separated him from the rest of the world, its energy, light and magnificence opened a tiny crack. He closed his eyes and in his mind saw, for only a moment, a vision of his own self which resembled him in a way, but wasn't, for the vision was so much more than he knew himself to be. But almost as soon as the door opened, it creaked closed. Jason opened his eyes and saw the Archivist's coil retract into its body. He gazed up at the ship, and saw a circular opening on the side of the solid grey mass, the center of which was level with his eyes.

"Whoa," Jason peeped. He walked towards Nierion, trying to feast his senses on every minute detail of his strange new companion and its ship; afraid he might discover in the next moment that he was only dreaming. He was unable to mask the wide smile that crept across his face as he followed the Archivist towards the opening. He wasn't sure why, but he felt no worry, no anger, no fear.

For an instant, he thought he should tell his mom where he was going, and he started to pull his cell phone from his pocket, but that seemed silly for some reason and his hand drifted back to his side. He never even thought to use the stupid thing to take a picture.

Beyond was darkness.

Chapter 7: Among the Billions

The new surroundings astonished Jason as he followed Nierion down a half-lit corridor. The interior of the ship was starkly contrasted with its monotone exterior. It was made of the same pitch-black metal as the Archivist, though the blue-and-white sheen was absent. However, the walls were covered in strange symbols Jason couldn't decipher. They ranged from simple, solitary shapes to complex, interconnected designs. What Jason found most wondrous about them, was that they weren't actually attached to the walls, but rather hung suspended, as if by invisible spindles of web. He craned his neck to see how far the designs extended, and noticed that the ceiling was covered in strips of phosphorescent gases, trapped behind glass-like, sheath cut-outs. He returned to the symbols and leaned in closely, trying to figure out how they were suspended, but there was nothing obvious.

"What are these things?" Jason asked, pointing at the symbols.

"They are the Arcon Drei," the whisper in his head replied, as if Jason was supposed to have any idea what that meant.

"Okay... what do they do?"

"Each one has a specific function. In aggregate, they control the ship."

Jason moved closer to one until it almost touched his nose. The Arcon Drei glowed in a soft blue hue. Suddenly, Jason felt like he was hit with a minor electric jolt. He examined his hands, which glimmered with the same blue light. Soon the light spread across his entire body, filling him with ticklish warmth. Within a moment, the glow retracted into his hands, and then disappeared, along with the feeling of warmth. The Arcon Drei grew brighter for a second, and then the light extinguished.

Jason spun around to find Nierion and its four empty visors staring at him.

"What just happened?" Jason asked innocently. But the whisper was not quick to return. When it did, for the first time, the Archivist's voice seemed unsure.

"I... I have never... what did you do to it?" The alien asked in faint accusation.

"I didn't do anything, I swear!" Jason pleaded, "I just turned and it started--"

"Never mind," the whisper cut him off. "Continue to follow me, and stay close."

But Jason didn't understand. "Why are you showing me all of this?"

"I am following the Protocol," the whisper replied, having reclaimed its emotionless confidence.

"You told me that already. That doesn't mean anything to me. Am I supposed to be learning something, doing something?" Jason asked. The Archivist's reaction to the Arcon Drei unnerved him and he didn't want to do anything to make the robotic being mad.

"The Protocol does not demand you learn or do anything."

This simple response prompted Jason to press further, but carefully: "So why did-"

"I am an archivist. It is not my job to know the motives of the Shantar Anar," the whisper stated, cutting Jason off.

The boy was utterly confused. If he wasn't supposed to learn anything, and Nierion wouldn't tell him anything, then what was the point of all of this? He wanted to find out what was really going on, but felt like he was walking on eggshells. The best thing to do, he figured, was to keep quiet. He meekly followed the Archivist down the corridor, hoping some kind of answer awaited him in another part of the ship.

With each step Jason let his mind wander, imagining what the Shantar Anar might look like, and who or what they really were. He was torn from his daydream by the startling insight that he was in the quietest place he'd ever been. Even the most vast silence he'd ever known, deep in the static grip of night, was still full of whooshing breezy air, and the stretching of old floor boards. He'd never before considered how full of sound the world was.

Jason shouted out "Hello!" just to make sure his own voice worked, and let out a sigh of relief as the word carried through the hallway. That was important; he remembered from science class that sound needed a medium, like air, to travel, and he realized he was breathing normally. But surely Nierion didn't breathe oxygen... which meant the atmosphere was there for him. Yet another indication that he was on the ship for a special reason, but what?

His eyes darted from the glowing ceiling to the floating symbols, and he felt like he might explode with questions. The fact that the Archivist wasn't interested in answering any of them made Jason afraid. He stopped for a moment and watched the alien being move through a dark threshold into another chamber in the ship. The feeling of familiarity with the Archivist was less comforting as the shadow outline of its form disappeared into the dim light beyond the entrance.

Too late to go back now, Jason thought, sure that there was no way for him to escape anyway.

The hallway opened into a large cabin with a dome-shaped ceiling. The first thing Jason noticed was that there were no Arcon Drei. In fact, the chamber was mostly bare of any detail, except for a hollow cylindrical totem in the center of the room. Affixed to the totem were four clear, empty orbs, which appeared to be made of the same crystal-like material as the Archivist's visors. The apparatus smacked of a mistake in engineering and looked to Jason like a chandelier some foolish alien architect had bolted to the floor instead of the ceiling. The rest of the chamber was similarly uninspiring, which Jason found just fine. There didn't appear to be any hideous tools or torture devices used for experimentation on abducted subjects, and he let out a sigh of relief. Nierion stood patiently beside the totem, as if entreating Jason to an examination. He walked to the cylinder, but saw nothing more than a hunk of metal and some ordinary looking, empty orbs.

"This is 'Esan's Heart.' It is the reason I was able to come to Earth to study you."

Jason bent towards the totem and scanned the surface for hidden details. "This Esan guy sure likes to name things after himself doesn't he… It, I mean."

"Esan's Heart has allowed my creators to learn much about the universe," the whisper related as the Archivist ignored Jason's comment.

"If the Shantar Anar are so powerful, how come you talk in a whisper? Couldn't they have given you a real voice?" Jason asked. He circled the totem, trying to figure out how the metal cylinder could possibly do what Nierion said.

"You should not be hearing me as a whisper." The Archivist became very still for a moment, then the voice returned.

"A minor error must have occurred last night when I formed our bond." Nierion's voice was now bright and clear.

Jason couldn't help but laugh. The mysterious whisper that spilled his blood into billions of tiny vessels of fear not an hour before had been nothing more than a volume dial set too low! His amusement was short-lived, as he realized what Nierion said. Jason felt a tingle of apprehension creep into his spine.

"What did you mean 'last night?' We just met."

"We did, in physical form. But in order for us to communicate, I had to instill you with 'Esan's Touch,' so you could understand my language and I could understand yours."

"Esan's Touch?" Jason exclaimed. "How many freaking things does Esan have?!"

"Many," the Archivist replied bluntly.

Jason was perplexed, "but you're speaking my language."

"I am not. Esan's Touch is translating my communications in a way you can understand."

"Are you *sure* you can't you read my mind?" he asked. The idea made him shiver.

"As I stated before, I cannot."

"Then how can-"

"Think of it this way," Nierion interrupted. "You are surrounded by ropes on all sides. Each rope represents a possibility of thought. I am holding the other end of one of an infinite number of ropes. I only feel the tension, and only know the rope is connected to you, when you tug on the single rope that I am holding. I have no power to influence or to interact with any of the other ropes that surround you."

"So that's Esan's Touch? Language software?" Jason asked.

"We needed a method of communication," the Archivist replied.

But why? Jason wondered. *Why did we need to talk, and why me?* There are billions of people on Earth… Why did Nierion pick him? Aliens and space ships and far off mysterious beings infiltrating his mind; who was he? *Nobody, I'm nobody,* Jason concluded, lowering his head morosely.

Then he glared at Nierion straight on. "What exactly did you do to me last night?"

The Archivist responded with a hint of annoyance. "I have told you this already. I instilled you with Esan's Touch. You felt my presence, though you didn't know exactly what I was. The beginning of the process can be uncomfortable, and for that, the Protocol insists I explain that the initial discomfort is essential to the process of connection."

"You mean my dream? That was you?" Jason asked, the memory pouring back to him. The eagle wings, the canyon, the river, the house, the great feeling of elation as he finally reached the door, the smell of home, the figure in the dark. He'd found his father again, and then, the gift of re-discovery was ripped away by the icy touch of strangeness. The incredible pain he felt as he'd been torn apart, and then the stillness, the gentle touch, the sense of understanding. The vision had been so vivid, so wonderful to find his father again. The idea that he'd been used as an emotional ragdoll without a choice by this... creature enraged him.

"You screwed with me just so we could talk to each-other?! Why? Why me?"

"You misunderstand," the Archivist remarked, oblivious to Jason's pain. "Communication is a proximate reason for using Esan's Touch; the ultimate was so that I could study you."

"Study me? It was just a dream. If you want to know stuff about me, ask me now. What do you need to know; what I eat, stuff like that?"

"You have misunderstood my purpose."

"What is there to understand? You won't tell me any-thing!"

"I was not sent here to study your eating habits. I was sent to study your physiology. Everything I needed to know, I learned last night."

Jason stared at Nierion with a blank expression as the truth dawned on him. His anger became sadness. There was nothing to this encounter other than a great coincidence after all. He wasn't a long lost hero of an alien prophecy. Any idiot with a skeleton would've done as well.

"So that's it? You came all the way to Earth just to study my body? You don't want to know anything else? I know I'm young but I'm... I'm not stupid. You don't have to keep se-crets from me!"

The Archivist's cold glare fell on him, no sense of com-passion evident in the empty visors.

"I have no questions for you. I am ordered by the Proto-col to reveal my existence, show you the ship, and inform you, since you are a sentient life form, of the invasive process I was required to use in order to do this, and the purpose of its intent. That is all, our meeting is concluded."

"What do you mean it's concluded?" Jason pleaded.

Nierion didn't respond as its visors erupted with color,

flipping rapidly through blues and reds, shifting faster and faster. Jason felt a sharp, twisting pain inside of him, like something he hadn't even known was there was being ripped away. A crushing emptiness flooded the space the unnamed essence had inhabited, and left a chilling void. He clutched at his chest like a wounded soldier trying to hold in the exposed gore of his guts with trembling hands.

"No!" Jason shouted. "No, you don't have to do this, not yet! Don't take it from me! Please!"

The Archivist was shocked and frightened as the human writhed in pain. Nierion had removed Esan's Touch tens of thousands of times in its long life, but this was the first time it had ever seen the extraction cause this… result. But there was no time to figure out what was different. The sequence could not be interrupted or the human would die.

Two panels in the Archivist's chest burst open. The inner visors of Esan's Eyes shot forth, reaching out like two inter-locking arms surrounding Jason and the space around him began to shimmer.

"Wait, please wait!" Nierion heard the human croak, Jason's body a rag doll in the grip of the inter-locking arms. The Archivist watched the human's flickering body fade away and felt distinctly unsettled. This anomaly was definitely going to have to be in the report.

Chapter 8: Where Did the Time Go?

The vast Pacific Ocean captured his spirit as Jason leaned against the window of the rental car rolling along the coast highway. He marveled at the blue green waves with streaks of white crusting their tops. The waves stretched in all directions, long past the horizon, and Jason imagined them all the way across the world, meeting the shores of distant lands.

Jason rolled down his window to breathe the cool, briny air. Droplets of mist danced around his face and settled on his cheeks, as refreshing as a frosty glass of lemonade. With the window down, he heard the humbling sound the waves made as they crashed against the giant rock cliffs of the central California coast. He was awed by their brutal power even more than the roaring thunder of Mid-West summer storms. And yet, he found something eternally peaceful in the crashing of the waves against the cliffs. He felt a part of the ocean's vastness, a part of the breeze, a part of the waves.

A picture, that's what he needed! He patted the seat next to him, while peering out the window, for his camera, but it was missing.

"Dad?" he directed at the passenger-side front-seat, where his father was dreamily staring outside. "Do you know where my camera is?"

Without taking his eyes from the view, his father replied, "I threw it into the ocean."

"What?!" Jason shrieked, "Why did you do that?"

"No pictures, no moments, no memories," he lulled the words.

"Why not?"

His father gazed at him amused. "Because none of this is real."

"What isn't real?" Jason asked.

"The whole world," his father said dreamily, "but it's nice to be a part of something. Nice to have something to believe in, at least for a little while."

"I don't understand," Jason heard himself say from somewhere beyond. "Why are you acting so strange, Dad? Can't you be normal again?"

His father's eyes looked sad. "I'm sorry... I can't go back. But you could join me if you wanted to."

"But you're right here, what do you mean-"

"Jason!"

His eyes shot open and Jason surged back to reality. Mr. Baker's bumbling frame towered like an awkward giant over his desk. The class snickered loudly, everyone was laughing at him. Everyone except for Daniel and Ashlyn, who looked concerned. Jason barely had a moment to think about what was happening, but he couldn't remember even getting to class.

"Are you feeling all right?" Mr. Baker inquired, stressing each vowel.

Jason tried to stealthily rub the sleep from the corner of his eyelids. "Uh, yeah, why do you ask?"

Mr. Baker stared at him as if being taken for a fool. "Mainly because you were snoring rather loudly."

Chortling laughter filled Jason's ears. He was beyond embarrassed.

"Are you sure you're okay?" Mr. Baker asked again, this time with genuine concern. Jason couldn't believe how oblivious his teacher was. Didn't the man know he was making the situation worse by drawing attention to him? He saw expressions of sarcastic concern on the faces of some of his classmates, and sighed.

"Yes Mr. Baker, I'm sure. I'm sorry," he said, lowering his eyes apologetically, hoping Mr. Baker would leave him alone. His reply seemed to have the intended effect, as Mr. Baker shrugged his shoulders, and walked back to the white board to continue illustrating diagrams.

Apparently, the class was learning about the lunar gravitational effect on tides. A few giggles resonated here and there as Jason tried desperately to remember when he'd fallen asleep. But to his chagrin, the last thing he recalled was talking to Daniel by the park before school. Mr. Baker's class was the last of the day.

Why can't I remember anything?! he wondered nervously. Jason's hands felt clammy, his mouth dry. He glanced at the clock and saw that, sure enough, the hands read 2:10 in the afternoon, five minutes before the end of school.

"Impossible!" Jason whispered. He surveyed the room nervously, but his classmates had already forgotten his embarrassment. Only Daniel still gazed fixedly at him.

The clock struck 2:15 and the end-of-day bell rang. Dizzyingly fast hands put away pens and books. Backpacks were slung over shoulders with immense speed, and though Mr. Baker tried to finish his explanation over the bell's blaring, the effort was futile. His words sank to the bottom of a linoleum-floor sea, trampled upon by a herd of thirteen-year-olds rushing for the door.

Jason hadn't even gotten out of his seat, but saw Ashlyn eying him as she left the classroom. There was something else beyond worry, a brief moment in which it looked to Jason like she was trying to decide what to do about him. He was about to get up to catch her -- at least to thank her for the other day -- when he saw, to his dismay, that Daniel still sat next to him, trying to peer into his soul with narrowed eyes.

The two boys studied each other with shared expressions of suspicion and inquisitiveness. They got up in unison and walked towards the hallway step for step. Mr. Baker's bellow stopped them in their tracks: "Jason, would you come here for a moment?"

Jason sighed, turned around and marched to a solitary chair beside the teacher's desk. He sat down meekly. *Time for my punishment.* Mr. Baker motioned with a casual wave of his hand for Daniel to leave and close to the door behind him.

Jason waited for the scold that never came.

"Just us now, so you can be honest. Is everything all right?" Baker asked.

No, everything is not all right, but Jason didn't dare share with his teacher that he simply couldn't remember either way.

"Yeah everything is okay, Mr. Baker. I guess I was distracted for a minute, that's all."

"It wasn't a minute, Jason. You looked like a zombie the entire class."

The description of his behavior frightened Jason. He focused all his energy on trying to remember where he'd been and what had happened to him, but he ran into a wall inside his mind. He tried to climb over, run around, push through, but the wall stood firm. The more he tried to tear the wall down, the stronger it became. The more he focused on the wall, the hazier it became, until he almost forgot it was there at all. But, when he was about to forget the wall entirely, a tiny Spark flashed in his mind, illuminating the dark surrounding the wall. For an instant, Jason clearly saw that the wall was preventing him from knowing something, but the Spark vanished for some reason and the darkness returned. He had to get home to the safety of his room and try to figure out what was going on.

"I'm sorry Mr. Baker; I didn't sleep well last night. That's all," Jason said, attempting to hide the fear glistening in his eyes.

"That's okay. I moved to a new place when I was a few years younger than you and had a difficult time sleeping myself. It can be very stressful. Some people like to count sheep, but I liked to count elephants. They have droopy eyes that make them look sleepy; it seemed to work."

Apparently there was not going to be a punishment after all, just weird facts.

"Yeah… I'll try that tonight… Thanks for the advice. It won't happen again, I swear!"

Mr. Baker sighed deeply, but relented. "Just take it easy,

try not to be too hard on yourself."

"Okay, don't be too hard on myself, got it," Jason repeat-ed, hoping he was more convincing than he sounded.

Mr. Baker waved his paw-like hand towards the door and Jason sighed a little in relief. He opened the door and peeked back towards Mr. Baker, but his teacher had already content-ed himself with reviewing material for the next day. He ap-preciated the man's concern, but somehow Jason didn't think counting elephants was going to bring his memory back.

"What happened to you?" Daniel blurted, not a nose-length away from Jason's ear as he walked through the door. Jason jumped back in fright, which quickly turned to annoy-ance when he saw his classmate.

"Holy crap! What are you still doing here?!"

"What happened to you?" Daniel repeated, standing, his arms crossed. "This morning I thought you were just ignoring me, so I left, but then you didn't show up to school! You didn't come until fourth period and then you just walked around like you were in a trance!"

Daniel sucked air back into his body as Jason keyed in on a piece of his tenacious classmate's rant.

"We did talk this morning, I remember that."

"Of course we did! You kept being distracted by some-thing."

"What?"

"I have no idea! You asked me if I saw something in the park."

"Why, what was in the park?" Jason asked.

Daniel frowned. "Are you messing with me? Trees and a freaking swing-set!"

Jason tried to remember what he'd seen. He closed his eyes and sought the answer, which he thought should have been easy to find, but when he searched, he found the same daunting wall looming in the wispy mist of his mind. He tried to break the wall apart again, hurling all the mental strength he could muster, but the force of his will did nothing.

"What are you doing?" Daniel asked, his hot breath brushing Jason's face.

"Be quiet, I'm trying to concentrate!" Jason barked, shooting Daniel a threatening glare.

He took a deep breath, disregarded Daniel's scowl, and tried to relax. He closed his eyes and found the wall again. *New strategy:* instead of trying to destroy the wall, he tried to imagine it didn't exist. The tiny Spark emerged again from unknown depths. The Spark, like the wall, felt foreign, like something that wasn't quite him, floating through his mind. The Spark infused itself into tiny cracks in the wall and light spread out across it, making the wall almost translucent. For a brief moment, Jason could see hazy images on the other side.

"What happened to you?!" Daniel asked.

The light, the wall, everything Jason had focused on disappeared. He opened his eyes and glared at Daniel.

"What do you want from me?" Jason roared.

"To know what happened," the small boy pleaded.

"I don't know what happened! Why do you care?!" Jason yelled.

Daniel was taken aback, but he knew the reason. "Because... you seem really lonely. I know what that's like, it can make you crazy. I just... wanted to help. If you don't want to tell me what happened, that's fine, but you don't have to lie!"

Jason watched Daniel's face smolder with anger. Seeing Daniel's rage stilled his own. He didn't know why Daniel cared so much, but he seemed to be the only one who did.

"I'm not lying," Jason said softly.

"I don't believe you," Daniel bristled.

"Were you lying to me about the shooting star?"

"No, of course not, I told you I wasn't."

"And I swear I'm not lying to you now. I really don't know what happened to me."

"Really?" Daniel asked.

"Really," Jason answered. "Something is blocking my memory."

"That's pretty weird," Daniel replied.

"Thanks, I know that," Jason snapped, "Maybe if you tell

me everything you remember from this morning, it will jolt something."

"Okay, let me think." Daniel casually tapped his right foot as a sea of students passed back and forth beside them in the hallway, talking loudly, ignoring their tiny universe. "Wait, do you have a cell phone?"

"Yeah, why?"

Jason's innocent question was rewarded with a blank expression from Daniel. Apparently the answer was very obvious. "Maybe you took some pictures."

"Oh!" Jason had his phone half way out of his pocket when Daniel's eyes grew very wide.

"Holy crap! Is that the ninth generation Axiom Plus?" Daniel asked, like an escaped prisoner who had found a buried treasure.

Jason glanced at his phone to make sure they were looking at the same thing. "Uh... I guess."

"I'm so jealous! My mom won't let me have a cell phone," Daniel sighed.

Jason tried to mask his total disinterest and opened the phone's camera pics.

"Anything?" Daniel chirped.

But to Jason's disappointment, the last picture he'd taken was of his mom unpacking on the day they moved to Ashton. She wore a small, indecipherable smile, half hidden by matted hair, sweaty from the effort of lifting heavy boxes. Jason stared at the picture bitterly before slipping his phone back into his pocket. "Nothing."

Daniel's shoulders slumped. "Well, it was worth a shot."

Jason nodded weakly in return. "So, do you remember what we were talking about this morning?"

"I was telling you about the shooting star," Daniel finally related.

Jason confirmed with a slight nod.

"Then, you asked if I'd seen something...shimmer, I think, in the park."

"Shimmer?" Jason asked.

Daniel looked up as if searching the surrounding air to make sure he was absolutely right. "That's what you said. You seemed fixated, like you didn't even know I was there."

"Then what?" Jason prodded.

"I tried to get you to come with me to school, but you wouldn't budge. You just kept staring at the park, but I couldn't see anything there."

"That's pretty strange, don't you think?"

Daniel repaid the question with an annoyed tweak of his lip. "Are you making fun of me or something? Of course it's strange!"

"I think I should check out the park, maybe there's some kind of clue," Jason reasoned.

"Maybe something is wrong with your brain," Daniel countered.

"Thanks."

But Daniel wasn't joking, "I'm serious! You were acting really oddly."

Jason feared that Daniel might be right, but he wasn't ready to call himself crazy.

"I'm going to the park," Jason said with resolve.

"Then I'm going with you," Daniel touted.

"Daniel, you don't-"

"I'm going with you in case something happens again," the smaller boy said firmly.

Not such a terrible idea, Jason thought, then felt the heavy weight of his backpack across his shoulders. "Fine, but this could take a while. I don't want to lug my books around with me. Let's put our stuff in our lockers, we'll come back and get them later."

"What about our homework?"

"We'll do it later. Do you want to help me or not?" Jason asked. He could tell the idea of leaving books behind was killing Daniel. *Hasn't he ever not done his homework?*

"Fine," Daniel said, though Jason could hear the waver in his voice. He didn't give Daniel time to rethink the decision. He grabbed Daniel's arm and led him down the hallway.

Chapter 9: A Fire Inside

The two boys navigated through the mob of students crowding the hall. They pushed their way out the front, double-doors of the school, and ran to the bike racks where more kids lounged, gossiping and making plans. Jason glanced at the boys and girls who filled Ashton, of whom he knew so little, and imagined how simple and perfect their lives must be. Suppressing a sigh, he walked through the racks.

"Where's your bike?" Daniel asked.

"I… I don't see it anywhere."

Daniel swiveled his head. "Where did you lock it up?"

"I don't remember! Remember?!" Jason barked.

Daniel stopped searching. "Oh, right. Well, maybe--"

"Someone stole my bike!" Jason shouted into the crowd of students. Strange faces quieted their chatter and stared at him.

"Calm down!" Daniel warned, but Jason wasn't deterred. "Somebody stole my bike!"

"How do you know you even rode it here?!" Daniel asked, throwing up his hands.

Jason stepped forward menacingly, but then softened his stance. "I… then how did I get to school?"

"I have no idea!" Daniel cried. "That's what we're trying to figure out. We can take my bike to the park. Maybe you left it there."

"Why would I have done that?!" Jason asked, taking his turn to throw his arms into the air.

Daniel continued flailing about in response, until the two of them resembled agitated monkeys.

"I don't know! Stop shouting!"

"You stop shouting!" Jason countered, but Daniel wouldn't let him have the last word.

"Fine! We'll both stop shouting!"

All the students by the bike racks were engrossed; watching the boys argue like it was late-night television. Before Jason could say anything else, Daniel grabbed his arm and pulled him out of the growing crowd, over to where he'd locked up his bike. Jason immediately recognized the light blue, perfectly maintained bicycle. Seeing Daniel's bike that morning was one of the last things he remembered. Two sparkling pegs jutted from the back of the bike's frame. Daniel took off the chain lock and tried to get onto his seat, but Jason grabbed his arm.

"I'm driving," Jason said, insistent.

Daniel's eyes went wide. "What? It's my bike!"

"I'm six inches taller than you," Jason replied as he scientifically layered his hands showing their difference in height. "I'm not riding on those pegs; I'll fall off."

Daniel wasn't convinced. "I can't hand over control of this vehicle to you given the-"

But Jason was done arguing. He threw his leg over the seat, then spun back at Daniel and cast the smaller boy a menacing glare. Daniel growled in annoyance, but stepped onto the pegs and gripped Jason's shoulders.

Pedaling the bike to the crest of the school's long driveway was hard work with Daniel weighing on the rear, but once Jason reached the downward slope, he heaved them forward with one last churn of the pedals and they shot off.

Jason's legs churned like pistons as he raced through the streets of Ashton. He swerved around other bikes, narrowly missed cars jerking away to avoid them, and cringed as Daniel's fingers hooked into his flesh.

"Slow down!" Daniel shouted into the wind. "You're going to kill us!"

"Stop worrying so much!" Jason shouted back, in thick, huffing breaths.

The park came into view and was fast approaching as they careened down the road. Jason gave his legs a much needed rest and let momentum carry them to the entrance.

When the bike finally came to a screeching halt, Daniel leapt backwards off the pegs. He breathed a great sigh of relief that he was still alive, and none the worse for wear other than the trembling in his knees.

"Have you lost your mind?" he asked with a shaky voice.

Jason spun the bike away from the hot track of rubber he'd left on the street, and lifted himself off of the seat. "Yes, and you're supposed to be helping me find it!"

"And I will, but I can't if I'm dead!" Daniel growled.

"I... sorry, you're right," Jason conceded and drew a deep breath. "I don't know what got into me."

"That's okay," Daniel said. His heart had started to slow its steady pounding. "Let's just focus on the task at hand."

The two boys walked into the park and immediately saw Jason's bicycle lying undamaged on its side. The sight was disconcerting. "Why would I have left it here?! How did I get to school then, how can--"

"Jason, calm down! Daniel implored.

"Fine, then *you* tell me what we should do!" Jason hadn't meant to snap, but he was afraid. No, terrified. Seeing his bike filled him with indescribable dread. First his father, then his friends, and now his memory; what else was he going to lose?

"What we have to do," Daniel said, ignoring Jason's flaring temper, "is collect evidence and develop a hypothesis."

"This isn't science class," Jason snapped.

"Wrong," Daniel retorted, "that's exactly what it is. We develop a hypothesis with the fewest assumptions possible, and then we attempt to -"

"I don't have time for this!" Jason ran into the park, leaving Daniel in his dust. Jason almost felt bad, but Daniel didn't understand what was at stake; Daniel could play detective on his own time.

Jason stood above his bike and tried not to cry. There

were no clues he could see. He ran from one end of the park to the other studying trees and grass, park benches and the empty swing set, but there were no clues at all. *What happened to me?!*

As Daniel watched Jason run into the park he supposed he should be angry, but instead he felt sad. He'd believed Jason was serious about needing his help, and that he'd actually listen to Daniel's advice. But now that fantasy was dispelled, and Daniel was left to wonder why making a friend was so hard. He fondly recalled a time when he had a best friend, but that seemed so long ago. Then, he was sure the friendship would last a lifetime, but Ashlyn Bluent made sure it didn't. He was still angry with her, and now he could tell that she liked Jason, too. He wondered if he really even liked Jason, or if he was just trying to keep him from Ashlyn. And what if he really was crazy; what did Daniel know about him, other than that he was from Chicago and seemed really mopey most of the time? But Daniel supposed none of that mattered, he'd made a promise, and Daniel never broke his word.

Blades of grass rubbed against Jason's jeans. He could've sworn he felt their maddening itchiness through the fabric as he sat beside his bike, chin resting in his hands. The surge of adrenaline that pushed him to his limit on the bike, and running through the park, had passed, and he felt defeated and drained. He caught Daniel staring at him and regretted agreeing to let his classmate help. But maybe Daniel was right, the answer to all of this was simpler than he wanted: no conspiracy, just something wrong with his head.

Jason closed his eyes, took a deep breath and tried to calm down. With his sight cut off, he had a vision in his mind of his father holding out his hand. Before Jason reached out to grab the hand, the skin and muscle burned away, until only bone remained. The bones split apart and reformed into a familiar wall. Jason screamed. His anger drove him further down, into the hidden depths in his mind. And there, he found the Spark, floating like a shining beacon adrift in a stormy sea. He touched the Spark with his mind's eye. The

Spark touched him back, and blossomed into a tempest of fire.

An intense power, unlike any Jason had ever felt, coursed through his body. The power devoured his sadness, awakened his mind and radiated through him. His heart beat like a blacksmith's hammer, his hands tingled as trillions of nitrogen and oxygen atoms brushed against them. His nostrils flared as the scents of grass, birch trees and pollen swimming through the air overwhelmed him. The burning ache in his leg muscles disappeared, replaced by lightness and strength he couldn't have imagined.

A blazing storm of power stretched through his blood and organs, into his cells, spreading through the mitochondria and nucleic acids, enveloping even the subatomic particles that comprised what he was. The power rejuvenated him, made him whole. Jason sought out the wall of bone, and found that it was very small and weak. If he reached out with a single finger...

Daniel stood in awe. He'd watched Jason slump in the grass and was about to try to comfort him, maybe even get the stubborn kid to listen to his suggestions, but then... At first Daniel thought he imagined the ripple in the air around Jason. But then, as if seeping from Jason's skin, a fog of blue and white surrounded his body, flowing over him like... *clouds skimming across the sky,* was all Daniel could think of. In an instant, the fog was gone and Jason was standing tall and firm, like a statue.

The wall collapsed. Jason was nearly crushed by the trapped memories that poured back into him like a surge of water bursting a dam. In a single moment, the impossible events of the day reasserted themselves as part of an unthinkable reality.

A shimmering world, a whisper in my head, a black-metal being, crystal visors staring through me, a horseshoe-shaped ship.

Names returned as well.

Nierion, Shantar Anar, Arcon Drei, Esan.

He remembered the immense pain he felt when the Archivist tried to break their bond, Esan's Touch it was called. Yet Jason was sure the Spark that was still inside him was somehow connected to the bond, which meant Nierion had failed. All of his unanswered questions poured back into him like sand falling through a sieve. He had to find the Archivist!

Suddenly, he felt his body being tugged. He turned, expecting to see Daniel leaning over him, but his classmate was standing thirty feet off, staring at him with mouth agape. The tugging grew stronger, and Jason also sensed something calling him: not a voice, but a pulsing wave of energy. When he focused on the wave, he found he could actually see a line of oscillating light emanating from him and leading off in the direction... of his house. Without further thought, Jason picked up his bike, jumped onto the seat and followed the glowing path. He was vaguely aware that somewhere behind him, Daniel was desperately trying to keep up.

–◑⇧Ƨ–

Ashlyn watched curiously from a little ways off as Jason rode down Tote Street with Daniel in tow. She could've sworn she saw something strange happen to Jason for an instant, like he'd changed colors slightly, or something weird like that, but she figured it was her imagination. *Maybe Daniel saw something,* she wondered.

What was Daniel's deal anyway? She could tell he didn't like her, but she had no idea why. At any rate, Ashlyn supposed Daniel keeping an eye on Jason was a good thing since he'd been acting so strangely during school. She wanted to ask Jason what was wrong, but she wasn't able to get him alone. Now that Ashlyn had the chance to find out what was going on, a little voice in her head said to go straight home to help with the grocery shopping, and *if she was late again...* or so her mother had warned. But maybe she'd caught every red light on the way home? *Not too bad of an excuse,* Ashlyn reasoned. Good enough to follow the boys a little farther.

Chapter 10: Unintended Consequences

The world effervesced with color and the buzz of life. All hues from red to violet shone brightly from flowers, front lawns and brick houses. Even the sidewalk sparkled like a cement sky of stars as he whirled past. How had Jason missed all this? The brisk October air felt like hummingbirds fluttering against his skin as he sliced through the invisible currents swirling in mad dance around him. The thermal heat from reflected sunlight bounced off the countless points of space around him and energized his legs, until they felt like pistons firing at a thousand revolutions per minute. The Earth spoke to him, and he spoke back.

Why had he never felt like this before? What had the Archivist done to him? The flame of full awareness billowed from its tiny Spark as Jason followed the pulsing stream of light, which eventually led to his house. For a moment, the intense sensations that gripped his spirit dimmed as he peered through the front window into the dark carcass of the living room, and he almost forgot what he was doing. He almost opened the front door to wait for his mom so he could tell her everything. If only he could make his mother believe him about the alien encounter, together they'd figure out what it all meant. But the incessant chord of light pulled him harder, and his focus was stripped of all but one endeavor: to find the ship and the Archivist.

His bike dropped against the side gate of his house and he followed the rope of hypnotic light into his backyard. It continued past the back wall of chipping wooden stakes and into the woods beyond. The elm trees sang to him as his fingers brushed their bark. The song was carried on molecules of oxygen escaping from the breath of the trees. He sang back to them with molecules of carbon dioxide, which the trees joyously inhaled. He could even hear the heartbeats and circulating rivers of blood flowing through small animals around him. But soon, the concert of life that surrounded him became too much to bear. The joy transformed into a terrible sensation of drowning in an ocean of feeling. He tried to block everything from his mind except the trail of light, but failed. Moving became difficult. He felt individual synapses firing from neurons sending instructions to every muscle in his body.

His heart beat faster; sweat poured down his face, and bubbled from his pores. He felt hot, much too hot for the temperate air, like he was a tiny star burning from within. The pulsing light wouldn't relent, and tugged him into a small meadow, where he sank to his knees and heaved in deep, exhaustive breaths. Jason closed his eyes, and a lucid vision of the symbol on the ship that glowed in his presence -- the Arcon Drei -- appeared. He could see the other end of the light trail tethered to the symbol, glowing a ghostly blue. The Arcon Drei was calling him.

Jason's eyes shot open, and there in the clearing was the ship. His memories poured back even clearer than before, including the fact that he should not have been able to find the ship without Esan's Eyes.

Relief filled him as a piece of the puzzle was found, but the trail of light seemed to mock Jason as he remembered there were no doors or hatches. Only Esan's Eyes enabled Jason and the Archivist to enter. Then, the calm trail of light crackled with violent electricity, starting at the ship and spiraling outwards towards Jason. He didn't even have time to scream as the lightning bolt rushed at him. Instead of striking, however, the bolt split into hundreds of smaller whips of electric fury. The lightning quieted again into the calm light, and Jason found himself completely enveloped in a spherical shell of pale blue. The light expanded inwards from all directions, and Jason felt like he was being lifted from the world... then everything went blank.

When Jason's eyes focused, they stared at the black-metal, interior hallway of the ship. The trail of light, and the unbearable power of awareness that had erupted from the tiny Spark, were gone. Jason still felt the Spark, like the specter of a forgotten memory, hiding deep within him, but that was all that remained.

Without the Archivist at his side droning on about the Protocol of the Shantar Anar, the unnatural stillness of the ship was enhanced by eerie shadows cast by an otherworldly luminescence from above. The place felt larger, and more uninviting, than before. The Arcon Drei lining the walls were as silent as the dead, and Jason's skin prickled with fear. He wasn't supposed to be on board, and though the Archivist seemed friendly enough, Jason wasn't sure how the alien being would react to an uninvited guest. But his desperate resolve to find out what the alien had done to him pushed Jason down the ship's corridor towards the central chamber.

When he was within ten feet of the threshold, he felt a shift in the environmental pressure, like he was pushing through the membrane of a giant soap bubble. The sensation passed when he entered the chamber. The room looked as it had before, with one exception: locked within the cylinder that reminded Jason of a large chandelier, was the Archivist. The four visors formerly positioned on the front of its head, now formed a circle. Each visor pointed towards one of the empty, glass spheres and glowed in deep, rust orange. The orbs ascended perfectly in line, as if strands of silk connected them from floor to ceiling. When they were level with the visors they stopped, seemingly hypnotized by the rusty glow. Tiny lights emerged in the center of each glassy globe, flickering in-and-out like a watchtower in a heavy storm.

Jason was hypnotized as well. He stretched his neck and squinted his eyes to focus on the orange glow, but the rest of his body didn't receive the orders to march forward, and he stumbled to the ground. He let out a resounding "oof!" that filled the room. Before he could lift his head, he was stunned by a familiar voice that was itself eclipsed by intense surprise.

"Jason! How... how are you here?!"

The lights within the orbs vanished as the four spheres descended back into their holding places. The glow that emanated from the Archivist's visors fizzled out, and the building energy of the preceding moment was replaced by silence.

Cursing his clumsiness, Jason staggered to his feet and warily looked into the lifeless visors; all four again in line at the front of the being's head, and piercing him with a cold stare. And yet, despite Nierion's stone-like appearance, Jason could sense somehow, that the Archivist was actually very afraid.

A series of locking bands that held Nierion in the cylinder unraveled from its body, and shimmied quickly back into the cylinder itself.

"How are you here?" the Archivist demanded to know, its voice crackling with suspicion.

A clammy sweat creased Jason's brow and he backed away.

"I don't know, I swear!" he stammered.

The Archivist tore from the remains of its bonds and moved towards Jason at the far end of the room. The tiny chords at the bottom of its tripod of legs made Nierion appear to be levitating; an apparition of a far-off world hulking over him.

The visors emanated a buzzing violet light.

"Impossible." The word fell upon Jason like heavy frost. "You should not have remembered anything! You should not have been able to find the ship!"

Jason cowered beneath Nierion's penetrating gaze. The alien certainly didn't act afraid, and yet, as if he was a wolf smelling his prey's fear, Jason felt a creeping terror within the Archivist.

"I saw a wall in my head and I just... pushed past it, I guess, and everything came back: you, the ship, everything!" Jason spit out. But the same grating word met him. "Impossible!"

"Why do you keep saying that?!" Jason pleaded. "Why is it impossible?"

Nierion didn't answer, but continued its inquisition. "How did you find the ship? How did you get into the ship?!"

"I'm not lying," Jason cried. "It reached out to me! I didn't try to get inside, honest! I didn't mean to mess anything up, I swear! Just tell me how to get off and I'll go. You don't have to tell me anything!"

The Archivist retreated slightly; the violet glow dimmed. "What reached out to you?"

Jason fuddled through his head for a name on the tip of his tongue, "You know... the symbol."

"What symbol?"

"The Arcon-"

"Drei, an Arcon Drei?! How, which one?"

"That's what I'm trying to tell you!" Jason yelped. "When you brought me here one of the symbols reached out to me, remember? You thought I'd messed with it, but I hadn't done anything. When I pushed past the wall in my head I saw a rope of light, which led me here. I'm sure that symbol made the rope for me!"

Jason tried not to shiver as Nierion stared at him. Where he'd sensed fear before, was now a muddle of confusion, as if the alien being's grand understanding of the universe had shattered. But that seemed absurd.

"I'm sorry I messed up whatever you were doing, but you took away my memories! Why did you do that to me? Can't you at least tell me *that* before I go?"

The violet visors bored into him, but the light quickly disappeared.

"You have to follow me very quickly," the Archivist insisted. "We must get you a suit."

"A suit?" Jason asked. "You don't need to give me anything. I told you everything I know."

"What you know is of little concern at this moment."

Jason growled in frustration. "What *should* I be concerned

about?"

"Your life."

Jason shivered uncontrollably. "You don't need to tell me anything! Just let me go and I promise I won't bother you again."

"I cannot let you go."

Jason's heart was ready to explode. Why had he tried to get back to the ship?!

"I won't say anything about you! Nobody would believe me anyway, I'm just a kid!"

But the Archivist didn't approach him menacingly; it seemed to lack any desire for violence.

"You are not a prisoner. I cannot let you go because the ship is no longer on Earth," Nierion said.

The meaning of the words filtered through Jason's ears, but surely he'd misheard.

"What?! Take me back; I swear no one will ever know about you!" Jason sobbed.

"I cannot," the Archivist replied. "I do not control the ship. It is on a preset navigational path."

A deep, cold fear gripped Jason like a claw of rust and ice.

"What does that mean?" he whispered.

The visors glowed in a hazy light blue.

"It means that if you don't come with me now, you are going to die."

Chapter 11: The Price of Friendship

"Wait-up!" Daniel shouted at the streaking form half a block ahead of him. Jason didn't so much as turn around, and Daniel couldn't deny the possibility of his half-joking hypothesis: the kid might really be crazy. His classmate's strange behavior in the park was now compounded by the fact that Jason seemed completely lost in a world of his own creation. Daniel had been ignored enough times in his life to know that what he'd witnessed was something else; Jason seemed truly oblivious.

He wanted to help Jason figure out what had happened, and he wanted the reason for the lost memories to be easy and the solution to their restoration to be his. But as he watched Jason fly down the road, Daniel had to admit that this problem was beyond him; he needed to tell an adult what was happening.

Jason swerved into a driveway, and Daniel commanded his legs to slow from their breakneck speed. He gripped his brakes hard and swerved into the same driveway, only to see Jason's bike tossed aside, the backyard gate thrown open, and the sprinting legs of his would-be-friend again leaving Daniel in the dust.

"Damnit Jason, just stop for a second will you!" he huffed, but there was no indication that he'd been heard, or that Jason even knew he was there. Daniel ran as fast as he could to catch up, but when Jason effortlessly hopped the back fence and skittered into the woods beyond, Daniel lurched to a stop.

Chasing Jason down on his bike through familiar neighborhoods was one thing, but running off into the woods after a kid he barely knew and was probably crazy, was quite another. Daniel knew what he needed to do: he'd write a note and leave it on the doorstep for Jason's mother to see when she got home. He began crafting the note in his head...

Dear Mrs. Swann,

My name is Daniel Elliot, I go to school with Jason and I just wanted to let you know you should really consider getting your son psychiatric help...

As he thought about the letter, the imagined voice of Anne Swann scolded him.

Daniel, why did you stop to tell me this? You should've gone after him into the woods... Don't tell me you were frightened? Oh...that's it, isn't it? You were too frightened of trees and birds, and now you're handing me this useless note, when, at this very moment, horrible things could be happening to my son!

He was formulating a retort to his own imagination when he found that his arms and legs, without his consent, had already climbed the fence and taken him into the woods.

There must be some mistake, he thought, but continued walking. Daniel was pretty sure there were no dangerous animals, nothing to be frightened of except the penetrating silence of being completely alone. *How did this become my problem?* he lamented to an elm tree. The eeriness of the woods made him forget he'd practically begged Jason to let him help. At least Jason's path was easy to track. Tossed up dirt and broken sticks marked a trail from the entrance behind Jason's house all the way to a clearing beyond a cluster of trees, about a hundred paces ahead.

As Daniel approached he could make out a very large, dull-grey shape beyond the cluster. *Boulders,* he thought, but didn't quite believe, as he walked cautiously through the trees into a meadow. He found Jason and let out a sigh of relief, until he saw a giant grey object that was definitely *not* supposed to be in the Ashton Woods.

Daniel gaped in disbelief at the horseshoe-shaped machine. Once he'd processed what lay before him, a confident inner voice speculated that, despite the improbability, there was really only one thing the contraption could possibly be. In all the books he'd ever read, depictions of extraterrestrial life and of alien spaceships always made him laugh. Not because they were funny, but because authors often imagined life strictly from a human perspective. However, why should an alien's creations resemble anything humans would make?

This massive construct was something *truly* foreign, not built in a book by imaginary beings, but by something very much alive and real in the universe. He was filled with a sense of wonder that eclipsed the passing joy of fantasy, and a smile spread across his face.

The smile quickly disappeared when he realized Jason was not only transfixed as well, but his body was surrounded by a translucent shell of blue light, of which Daniel could see no source. Suddenly, a small section of the machine's exterior churned like honey winding around a spoon. The metal liquefied, but somehow retained its shape. A hint of blue and white materialized within the grey metal, as if a clear sky was peeking out from behind the cover of storm clouds.

Then the fluid metal opened like a giant mouth, leaving a hole ten feet in diameter. Daniel saw nothing but darkness within. A streak of blue lightning shot out from the darkness and struck the shell of light surrounding Jason. The shell grew brighter, and lifted from the ground...

"Get out of the way!" Daniel shouted, but Jason was in a trance.

"Snap out of it! You have to move!" Daniel yelled at the top of his lungs, but Jason remained still. Daniel sprinted towards him and leapt through the air, praying the blue light wouldn't hurt him. But as Daniel's hand breached the sheet of light to grab his classmate, the momentum careening him forward was gently halted. He was pulled by an unseen force into the shell. He saw a flash of brilliant light, and then the world faded from view.

Daniel's eyelids opened sluggishly. He stared up at strange glowing lights and realized he was flat on his back. He felt like he'd been punched, but managed to prop himself up on his elbows, where he was facing a long, dark corridor. The lights above cast mottled shadows upon hundreds of floating symbols that lined the walls. He scrambled to his feet, heart pounding, and spun in every direction, but there was no sign of anyone else.

"Jason?" Daniel squeaked. The only reply was a faint echo that seemed distorted. He stood still and listened for any indication of a living presence, but all he heard was unnerving silence. He tried to draw a deep breath, but the air felt thin and the dark quiet of the corridor stirred his imagination, reminding him of the hallway in his own house in the middle of the night. He'd stand outside the threshold of his door, staring into what seemed an infinite passage of dim shadow. But of course that was only at night, and in the light of day, the fifteen feet from his bedroom to the bathroom was no journey at all.

If only there was more light, he wished. The ship didn't indulge his desire, however, so Daniel collected his courage and stepped delicately down the corridor. He kept his ears open and his eyes alert for any sign of Jason.

Though the trek felt like an eternity, after only a few steps, Daniel heard the weak sound of a familiar voice up ahead. He started to run, but quickly stopped himself and moved forward cautiously instead. Daniel prepared himself for what he might see, but there was little point if there was a real-life alien. Also, if Jason was in trouble, barging in with no plan of attack would do little good.

Jason's voice led Daniel to the threshold of a large chamber. Daniel crouched and pressed himself flat against the wall beside the doorway. He peeked through and saw Jason having a far-too-casual conversation with a robotic being made of metal blacker than a starless night. Daniel sucked in his breath and held the air tightly in his chest. He tried not to gasp as he realized that swirling over the black metal was a haze of blue and white that looked like lazy clouds floating in the sky. He'd seen that haze before, on Jason in the park!

"Oh my god," Daniel whispered, so frightened he could hardly move. The sneaking around, the coy, elusive answers to his questions, the strange behavior in the backyard, and now this! There was only one conclusion: *Jason is an alien!*

He turned to flee, but remembered there was nowhere to go; he'd seen no doors, no hatches, and no obvious escape of any kind from the clutches of the ship. Daniel was trapped. He'd been tricked into walking through the woods alone, and tricked into trying to rescue someone he thought could be a friend. No doubt, Daniel reasoned with horror, what he'd thought was a human named Jason, was talking with the other alien being about what they were going to do with *him*. Interrogation, dissection, torture! Sheer terror brought Daniel to his feet, but also left him off-balance and he tumbled to the ground uttering a great "oof" as he struck the floor.

Daniel winced in pain and looked up hesitantly to find both alien creatures staring at him. Jason appeared positively stunned. The other being was harder to read. Then an odd event transpired: Jason began talking to himself.

"How should I know, I don't even know how I got on board!"

"Yeah I know him, he's in my class but…"

Oh my god, the thought struck Daniel like thunder, he's communicating telepathically with that robot!

Any hope that Daniel had been wrong disappeared from his head; Jason was an alien, there's no doubt. Daniel pressed his hands together in a pleading motion, and began to sob. "How can you do this to me, after I tried to help you?!"

The Creature-Formerly-Known-as-Jason looked stunned. "*Me*, what the hell did I do?!"

"You tricked me!" Daniel cringed as Jason rushed to him and grabbed his shoulders.

"What's wrong with you? Stop fighting! Calm down!"

Daniel tried to scramble from the larger 'boy's' grasp.

"Get away from me Jason…or whatever your real name is! Let me go!"

Jason loosened his grip and squinted at Daniel.

"Whatever my real name is? What are you talking about?!"

The eyes looked so honestly perplexed, that Daniel almost believed he'd been mistaken, but not quite.

"Stay away from me... I saw you!"

"You saw me what?!" Jason asked in mounting disbelief.

"Talking to that thing; you're an-"

Jason restored his hold on Daniel and jerked him forward.

"Shut up and listen to me! We're both in serious danger. I don't know how you got here, but we need to go with the Archiv... that thing over there, right now!"

Daniel remained in his defensive crouch and tried to break away from Jason, but he was too strong.

"Please don't dissect me!"

Jason's grip fell limp. "Holy crap, you think *I'm* an alien?"

"Aren't you?" Daniel asked.

"Have you freaking lost your mind?!" Jason shouted, and Daniel suddenly found himself on the defensive.

"No! You're the one who supposedly lost his mind, re-member? I was the one-"

The Jason-like being's grip tightened again and yanked Daniel to his feet.

"We don't have time for this; we're running out of air!"

Daniel felt powerless as the creature-in-human-disguise pulled him towards the robotic entity.

"We need to go with the Archivist right now or we're both dead!"

Daniel wasn't sure which thought was more distressing: that he'd been right, or that Jason was Jason after all, and he was going to die horribly anyway. He let himself be dragged to the larger alien as he pondered over which fate was worse. Of course he wanted Jason to be human, but the idea he was going to die from lack of oxygen in a weird alien ship, just because he wanted a friend seemed as bad as Jason being an alien.

From somewhere beyond his own terrifying thoughts, he heard Jason speak.

"Nierion, please tell me you have two suits."

Chapter 12: Tailor-Made

Jason gripped Daniel's wrist and tugged his classmate along as he followed the Archivist down a passageway on the other side of the ship's central chamber. Daniel appeared lost in his own thoughts and was content to be led. Thankfully he'd seen the sense in delaying more debate about Jason's motivations until after they received the so-called "suits." Nierion glided over the ship's floor, like a blade on ice. Jason almost bumped into its back as the Archivist stopped suddenly, next to a rectangular pattern of Arcon Drei that lined an otherwise inconspicuous section of wall. It began a careful scrutiny of the symbols for a reason Jason couldn't begin to fathom. The alien being's meticulous examination wasn't very long, but with every passing second, Jason swore he felt the air around him thinning; his breath became short and wheezy. He squeezed Daniel's hand hoping to get some kind of reaction from his companion. He wasn't used to Daniel being so quiet, and the lack of commentary did nothing to ease Jason's nerves.

"Nierion, what's taking so long?"

The Archivist didn't respond directly, but a compartment, similar to the ones containing Esan's Eyes, opened in its abdomen and a thin coil of black metal unraveled. A tiny blue light that looked like the bulb of an anglerfish marked the coil's end. The coil sinuously approached the symbols like a swaying cobra. The tiny bulb touched the symbols in a specific order, briefly lighting the Arcon Drei in a shade of the same ghostly blue. The symbols melded into the wall and a slim rectangular outline formed, like a laser was burning the shape from the other side.

The rectangular face shot down into an invisible slit, exposing a cavity perhaps three feet deep. Inside were eight, thin rectangular sheets of black metal. Each sheet was suspended by a brace attached to the top of the compartment. The tiny bulb at the end of the Archivist's coil gently touched the locking brace of two of the metal sheets. The braces released and the two sheets, as if moving along a magnetic track, exited the cavity and came to rest flat on the ground before the two boys. Jason studied the sheets, puzzled, but heard Nierion's voice in his head.

"Jason, you and the other human must step onto the sheets."

"I thought you said we needed space suits?"

"These are the suits," the Archivist replied.

Jason looked again at the lifeless sheets of metal on the ground. He shot Nierion an incredulous glare.

"Daniel, Nier… the Archi… the alien says we have to step onto the metal things on the ground."

Jason sensed suspicion oozing from Daniel's eyes.

"For god's sake, I'm not an alien!" Jason cried. "This thing," he continued, pointing at the Archivist with an accusatory finger, "invaded my mind in a dream and did something to me so that I can talk to it. I promise I'll tell you everything once we aren't dead."

He didn't wait for Daniel's reply, but stepped onto the metal sheet, as curious as he was frightened as to how this was going to keep him alive. Almost instantaneously, Jason's feet felt warm, like he'd dipped into a temperate bath. He looked down to discover that the flat sheet of solid metal had liquefied into a large blob, held together by surface tension. The fluid snaked its way up his body, conforming to his shape, but Jason felt no foreign material or any added weight.

Then, without warning, the liquid metal poured into his mouth and down his throat. Jason gagged and flailed about as he felt the metal fill him from within. Though there was no heat scalding his innards, he was aware of the substance like an itch he had no power to scratch. The sensation intensified, and Jason clawed at his mouth to pry away the viscid metal. Just when the itch became intolerable, the sensation abated, leaving a dull heaviness he couldn't describe.

A voice that sounded like rustling leaves spoke to Jason from within, though it wasn't the Archivist. There was a bizarre intelligence to the voice, and he knew as surely as his brain was hearing understandable words, his other organs, muscle and bone where being talked to in languages that they too could interpret.

"What do you need?" the voice asked, like a doctor examining a patient. He tried to answer, but was stopped by a gentle clenching of the substance on the exterior of his body. The answer instead emerged from his organs and blood, his sinew and bone, and deeper still to the elements and molecules that made these things: water, oxygen, proteins, enzymes, triglycerides, polypeptides, amino acids, metabolized energy…

The essential needs of his existence emanated from him as an interlocking code of sensations, instructing the suit that now surrounded him inside and out, on how to keep him alive. The answer was received, and the flowing metal slowed until it was solid again, then faded from sight. But the suit was there, keeping him alive, an atom-thin shell of alien life-support. Jason drew a deep breath, and was surprised and elated to feel a generous serving of oxygen fill his lungs. He nimbly spun about, laughing; all the while feeling nothing of the amazing apparatus that had been assigned his protector. "Awes-"

"Incredible!"

Jason saw Daniel beaming with scientific curiosity. His companion looked no different; certainly no sign of an interstellar space suit was apparent.

Daniel took several breaths, and sighed in contentment at the sweetness of the air.

"It's like this thing is building new elements from the stuff around us!"

Jason didn't care how the suit worked so long as it did, but he didn't want to dour Daniel's improved mood. He took the opportunity to set things straight.

"Now I can tell you what happened. I can prove that I'm not an alien and-"

"Good, the suits have taken form," the Archivist spoke with a clear, placid voice that sounded like wind spinning through a ceiling fan. The voice, however, was not in Jason's head.

Jason's eyes opened wide as dinner plates.

"You can talk?!"

"I have an audible means of communication," Nierion stated, "though not one capable of being detected in your range of hearing; nor understood, for that matter. Were it not for the suit, you would not be able to hear or understand me."

"I'd also be dead."

"Yes, you would be."

Jason blanched at the Archivist's bluntness.

"Why do you even care? I'm only some nobody you came to study, right? Why didn't you let me die?" Jason tried to bite back his anger, but the emotion rippled through his accusation.

"That you found yourself in this situation is a direct result of my actions… I know what you think I am, but you do not understand. Thankfully, the suits worked, I have never used them before."

"Can someone please tell me what's going on?" Daniel chirped.

"You've never used them before?!" Jason asked, stunned, ignoring Daniel's plea.

"No, it has never been necessary."

"Then why are they on the ship?" Daniel queried, causing Jason to cast his companion an annoyed glance, he should be the one asking the questions.

"To keep you alive outside of Earth's atmosphere and to allow us to communicate," Nierion replied.

Jason scratched his head. "But I thought you never take anyone with you."

"That is… correct," the Archivist stated, stumbling over its words.

"So why-"

The Archivist interrupted Jason with a consideration.

"I was instructed in what the suits do but… not why they are on board. Strange, I never really thought about it before."

"Jason, can you please tell me what's going on now?!" Daniel begged.

Jason faced his classmate and drew a deep breath.

"Daniel, this is Nierion, he works for these super-powerful aliens called the Shantar Anar. He made some sort of mind-link with me and then tried to erase my memory… Only it didn't work like it was supposed to, which I guess is a really big deal for some reason, and now we're stuck. And anyway, what are *you* doing here?"

"What do you mean what am *I* doing here?" Daniel asked.

Jason felt an undercurrent of ice in the words.

"You started acting loopy once you found your bike in the park. You wouldn't listen to me and took off. I followed you into the woods behind your house to make sure you were okay. You were GLOWING BLUE, and then the ship reached out to take you, so I tried to save you, but when I touched you everything went black, and I ended up here and saw you talking to a freaking alien! That's what I'm doing here! And what do you mean we're stuck?!"

"The ship is no longer on Earth," the Archivist interjected. "I am not empowered to return there."

Jason watched in disbelief as his small, gentle companion lunged towards him and gripped his shoulders with surprising strength.

"What did you get me into?! Make this thing take us back!"

"Daniel, calm down I can-"

"Why did I ever try to be your friend?!"

Jason felt the hysterical strength of Daniel's grip fade, and watched his arms fall limp against his sides as tears welled in his eyes. Jason grabbed Daniel and hugged him tightly.

"You have to calm down. I promise we'll figure out a way to get home."

Daniel pushed him away. Jason peered into Daniel's eyes and saw that he wasn't going to be forgiven so easily. *How is this my fault?* Jason wondered. He felt overcome with hope-lessness as he was struck by the hollowness of his vow. He had no plan at all. Daniel shuffled to the Archivist. They examined each other intently, as if seeing the other for the first time.

"Your name is Nierion?" Daniel asked.

"Yes," the Archivist replied.

Daniel nodded briefly.

"Nierion, if we're not on Earth, where are we?"

"In a kind of stasis, outside three-dimensional space," the Archivist answered. "The coordinates were pre-set for my next assignment, and the ship is currently building the power to make the journey."

"Can't you change the coordinates back to Earth?" Daniel inquired.

"I cannot; I do not control the ship."

"Isn't there an override or something?" Daniel posited. "There must be a way to take us back. It's *extremely* important that I get home before dinner."

The Archivist didn't respond immediately and Jason winced at Daniel's forthrightness. This kid got an F for street smarts in Jason's estimation.

"There is a way," the Archivist finally replied, and Jason felt the momentary lightness of renewed hope.

"What is it?!" Jason pressed.

"I can return you both to Earth if it is in the interest of the Shantar Anar to return you."

"Well, what are you waiting for then?" Jason asked jovial-ly. "Just call that Esan guy, tell him you messed up, and that you need to take us back home."

"Who's Esan?" Daniel asked.

"Esan Shantar Anar," Nierion responded, "is my creator, and unfortunately, Jason, your suggestion is not that simple. The Shantar Anar are not like you. They are motivated by different forces than human beings, and their lives last eons longer than yours. If I sent a transmission this instant, there is no guarantee I would receive a response in either of your lifetimes."

Jason was furious. "So what are we supposed to do, just wait on this ship until we die?!"

"No," the Archivist replied sternly, but without malice. "You will both travel with me to the next planetary system, and I will send a transmission to my supervisor relaying the events that have transpired. You cannot understand this from your limited perspective, but the very fact that you both are here is an incredible anomaly; one that might be great enough to demand quick resolution from the Shantar Anar."

Jason met Daniel's gaze and saw a glimmer of hope in his eyes. As for himself, he had no faith in any destiny other than to be spirited away to the stars. Jason suddenly longed for the quaint streets of Ashton. He felt an arresting fear that he wouldn't see them again. He wouldn't see his mother either or have a chance to make things better between them.

And he would never find out why his father had died.

Chapter 13: The Prodding Power

The Archivist had re-entered the central cylinder and was preparing the ship for its travel sequence. Jason leaned against the wall of the chamber and watched Daniel with wonder as his undersized companion buzzed around Nierion like a moth at a bright light. It seemed Daniel had already forgotten what a terrible mess they were in as he assaulted the Archivist with non-stop questions bilging from scientific curiosity.

Jason didn't care how the ship worked or how this did that and that did this. He sat, frowning at his bizarre surroundings, and sadly realized that there were no recognizable features of a human environment. At least the tree-lined streets of Ashton, boring as they were, tied him to a life where he could be reminded of everything he'd left behind. But on the ship, surrounded by nothing other than the products of alien minds, the weight of Jason's grief suddenly felt very light. If he wasn't careful, he'd be swept away like a grain of dust in a cosmic sea.

An even more horrible thought entered Jason's head: How could he possibly let his mom know he was okay? She probably thought he'd run away and that it was her fault. His stomach lurched as he pictured his mom alone in a dark house waiting for him to come home, and when he didn't, she'd assume the worst had happened to him!

He tried to push this horror down, but he was too angry with himself to do so. Jason desperately wanted some way to contact her, even if only to tell her he'd never come home again. He checked his cell phone in vain, hoping for a signal, but was quickly reminded by a clever graphic of an "x" that yes, whatever rip in the fabric of time and space he now inhabited was decidedly out-of-network.

I should never have gone with it, Jason pined as he cast cold eyes at the Archivist. *It didn't even have to be me! Any stupid human would have worked.* What did that matter? Nierion had chosen him and now he was here. There was nothing he could do. *I'm sorry, Mom…*

"…so the Arcon Drei respond to sound as well as touch," Daniel said.

"That is correct," the Archivist replied as it busied itself with tasks unseen.

Daniel thought for a moment. "But what powers them?"

"A special element the Shantar Anar call 'Ziin,' which means 'life-force.' It is not an element found on Earth. The Shantar Anar transform Ziin in many ways using methods I do not comprehend. This element is the backbone of their creations…"

What are they talking about? Jason wondered. The voices coming from the center of the chamber sounded like chattering crickets. The flittering words tapped at Jason's temples like a hammer driving a nail. Self-directed anger oozed from his pores and captured Daniel in a sticky bog. *How could that idiot have thought I was an alien? Isn't he supposed to be smart? If he's so smart, why can't he figure out a way to get us back? Maybe he doesn't want to get back! That's what they must be talking about. He doesn't want to go home, he has no friends, he's a loser, he's a coward, he's a…*

"… precisely, Daniel. That is an astute observation. You should also consider the fact that…"

…Why is Daniel being so friendly? It's almost like they're old friends. How could he like that thing?! No compassion, doesn't care at all that it ruined my life! Doesn't care…

"…that is why the ship does not depend on travelling through space…"

…They're laughing at me. How could I have trusted either of them? There's no such thing…

"… travelling at speeds close to light…"

… Just lies, that's all people are good at. Doesn't matter who they

are, doesn't matter if they're supposed to love you and be honest. They just lie, that's all they do. They don't want to feel hurt, don't want to be sad, don't want to see things for what they are...

"... but if that's the case, then wouldn't..."

... Look at this ship, and at all the things Nierion can do. Of course it could take me home if it wanted to. That's not the plan, more lies, wants me to go with it, wants me to drown in secrets, never going to tell me anything. No one is ever going to be honest with me...

"...perspective changes, not in an illusory sense but physically..."

...I bet this happens every time, Nierion pretends to be surprised, never takes away the bond, always find the ship, always taken from home, not this time, not to me...

Jason rose to his feet. His heart pumped fury through his blood. The chamber dimmed into a den of mocking smiles hidden in the shadows. He couldn't distinguish between Daniel and the Archivist; there was no difference between them. His teeth shivered and his hands clenched into fists as he stepped forward...

"Jason, come over here and listen to what Nierion is telling me; it's fascinating!"

He met Daniel's calm eyes and welcoming smile. The lights in his head flipped back on and the shadows disappeared. He recalled the terrible thoughts of hate he'd had not a moment before, but couldn't understand why he'd had them. They were someone else's thoughts, surely not his. Daniel was in this mess because of him, not the other way around.

"What did Nierion tell you?" Jason asked benignly as he walked towards the center of the chamber.

"We're talking about the ship and the Shantar Anar," Daniel Replied.

Jason cast the Archivist a puzzled look. "How come you wouldn't tell me about them before?"

"Circumstances have changed," Nierion stated. "I have to admit that your presence here is... disconcerting, but I am sure there is a sensible explanation."

"Maybe it's not the first time it's happened," Daniel interjected. "Maybe that's why the suits are on the ship."

Daniel's hypothesis sounded reasonable enough to Jason, who added, "Right, the Shantar Anar must screw up some of the time, they probably just-"

"They do not," the Archivist interrupted. "There is… there *must* be another explanation."

Had Jason heard fear in Nierion's voice? Its visors glowed a soft violet, and he could have sworn this indicated relief. "The ship is now fully powered, we can commence our journey."

The bands that had earlier retreated into the central cylinder suddenly shot out of hidden compartments. He and Daniel jumped back as the bands looped around the Archivist. Nierion's visors shifted through a network of invisible slots until they formed a circle around the middle of the Archivist's head. The visor lights shifted from violet to blue. Their soft glow increased in brightness, and the four empty orbs beside the cylinder ascended. Tiny lights blinked into existence within them; they looked like flickering stars.

The lights expanded into perfect spheres, barely smaller than the orbs that contained them. They continued to grow in size and intensity, and consumed the orbs like glass melting in the center of a roaring inferno.

Jason retreated as four beams of blue light shot from Nierion's visors, like pinpointed lasers. They struck the miniature stars, and a shiver of lightning crackled around each beam emanating from the Archivist, like a fracturing wave. The entire chamber was ablaze as the four spheres were pulled inward, along the beams of blue light, until they reached Nierion and melded into one. The Archivist was like a molten metallic core at the center of a translucent sun. Jason had one moment to contemplate why he and Daniel weren't also consumed. Was the blinding light a figment of an event occurring somewhere else, very far away? Then, the space around him began to shimmer and contort.

Daniel felt crushed, and at the same time, stretched mercilessly like a rubber doll. He felt heavy as the densest stone, but at the same time, so light he couldn't ground himself to anything. His mind expanded past limitation, able to comprehend any set of data outside the bounds of human understanding, and yet simultaneously stunted into the primordial stupidity of ooze. He was separate and beside himself, while at the same time unable to escape the horrifying prison of being completely alone.

He tried to concentrate in the shifting world, and managed finally to balance each opposite perfectly against the other; though how he accomplished this, he couldn't say. With the greatest of effort he held apart the two connecting jaws of a mental trap, pushing back against his will. He knew if he let go, he'd be devoured. Then, at the very end of his strength, set between the two moments of his last defiance and ultimate defeat, the pain ceased. His eyes closed, and he found the welcoming peace of sleep.

–◑↑℥–

Jason couldn't believe how much he hurt. He saw the world shimmer around him, and then the entirety of his innards, as if upon the shaft of a blade, gored the cavity of his body and stabbed upwards into his brain, leaving the rest of him a void. He felt every infinitesimally small piece of matter enter his mind, drowning him in the growing bruise of his own genetic blueprint.

Visions of an old dream possessed him, and he soared through violet sky to the simple brick house he loved, and basked in its gentle presence. For an instant, he felt the tiny Spark, the remnant of the alien bond called Esan's Touch, resting in a lazy daze at the bottom of a subconscious sea. The Spark was waiting patiently for him to return, to open himself to its power.

Jason psychically reached into the sea, but the feeling passed, and the Spark disappeared as he was bludgeoned by the force of the components of his body re-asserting themselves. He lurched forward, clutching his chest for a minuscule comfort until, entirely exhausted and spent, he fell to the ground as darkness washed over him.

Chapter 14: A New Nightmare

Anne Swann pulled into her driveway and sighed in relief. She relished the peaceful purring of her car's engine at low idle, and then turned off the car, happy to be done with the vehicle for another day. She stretched her back against the seat, rolled her neck and let a smile overtake her face. She couldn't wait to spend the evening with Jason. His heart-breaking apology the night before convinced her that he was ready to hear the whole truth of her ignorance about Michael's death.

She wasn't sure why she had so much difficulty admitting what she didn't know, but she also didn't want tonight to be yet another disappointment to Jason. He sought a reason, an epiphany that would somehow bring an end to his grief. Anne knew their tragedy wasn't so simple; she'd held back, because full honesty would bring her son no relief. Maybe this admission couldn't dress the wound of his pain, but the time had come for them to move forward. Anne hoped they could do that together.

Her stomach felt flinty as she gathered client files and her laptop. She suddenly recalled empty valedictions her parents often told her to wrap up the complexities of life in a neat little bow, which always seemed to end in "that's just the way things are." Her insistence that maybe things didn't have to be a certain way was met with patronizing glowers from her mother and father. Lamenting their child's awareness was good parenting in their estimation.

Her father was an insurance agent, but before she was old enough to understand risk management, he liked to tell her he worked in a salt mine. Anne questioned him about the mine; he answered with a playfully evil smirk, telling her about serious conditions affecting the miners that day. He wasted no opportunity to insert ludicrous claims that she, a child without suspicion, took for fact. "Good fun," was how he described his deceptions to her many years later. But there was no fun for her to learn she'd been the butt of a cruel and ongoing joke, perpetrated to bring a little excitement to a deeply unhappy man who hated his job. He'd resigned himself to the fact that any remaining joy in his life could only be attained by abusing his daughter's naïve imagination.

How sad, she thought, these lies were likely the best part of his day.

She closed her car door with a swing of her hip and saw in a flash, another memory: Jason was four. She'd had a long day at work, and her son, god bless the little whirling cogs in his head, couldn't stop asking why to this, and why to that, and why to the answer to the answer to the answer. So she'd told a lie, a little one, to end his inquisition and enjoy the silence.

That same night, she couldn't sleep. She listened to her husband's rhythmic snoring and worried that Jason would resent her when he eventually found out she'd deceived him to shut him up.

But after Michael died, Anne found that she didn't have the energy to care about such petty things. Her life had become a wading through the shallow waters of a dream, and in a dream she didn't have to worry about how much television Jason watched and whether or not he did his homework. In a dream, it didn't matter if she lied to him to make her life a bit easier to endure. But when she awoke from the initial nightmare of grief and saw the evidence of her indifference, she became a harsh disciplinarian. She now felt more like the warden of a prison than a mother.

Time had made her sorrow, if not bearable, then duller. The long years transformed the bursting emotions of her tragic storm into the gentler buzz of fireflies flickering in glass bottles of memory. Despite this, Anne saw the specter of Michael's face staring at her in the windows of the shops she passed, and in the familiar avenues. She found no love, no soul in the face that gazed at her, only the empty husk of a time past, and a secret that he wouldn't share.

She opened her front door, strolled into the small foyer, and noticed immediately that no lights were on and the house was quiet. She figured Jason spent the afternoon moping in his room and hadn't noticed night descend.

"Jason, I'm home."

Her son didn't reply.

Anne sighed.

"Jason, can you come down here please; we need to talk about something." Only silence.

Why does he have to ignore me? Anne thought with annoyance. She took a deep breath and settled her frustration. *Not tonight.* She was halfway up the stairs when she detected something indescribable in the stillness that felt eerily different from the silence of Jason ignoring her. Anne hurried up the stairs, switched on the track lighting, and continued to Jason's bedroom.

"Jason?" She knocked. "Are you in there? Can I come in?" There was no response. She opened the door and fumbled for the light. No backpack, no scattered binders; nothing had changed since that morning.

Why didn't he call to tell me he wasn't going to be home? Anne wondered as she walked, irritated, to her bedroom to change out of her work clothes. She tried his cell phone, but the line kept ringing; she didn't even get his voicemail.

"Damnit Jason, I spent three hundred dollars on that phone, can't you at least keep it charged?!"

She was about to head downstairs when she noticed a blinking light on her bedroom phone, indicating a message. The number "4" blinked in-and-out on the tiny, digital display. She pressed the button next to the blinking light, leisurely waiting for an explanation from her son as to where he was.

"Hi Anne, this is Sharon Elliot, Daniel Elliot's mother. Daniel is a classmate of Jason's. Sorry to bother you at home, I hope you don't mind. I found your number in the school roster and I wanted to call because, to be honest, Jason is the only other student I ever hear Daniel talking about. I've never met him, I'm sure he's very nice... Anyway, I thought Daniel might be at your house since he never came home from school today, which is very unlike him-

"Hi Anne, Sharon again, sorry I think the machine cut me off. As I was saying, it's very unlike Daniel. I thought maybe he was at your house, which is fine, but could you please call me back because Charles and I, Charles is my husband, are beginning to worry since -

"Sorry, Sharon Elliot again; boy that machine doesn't give you very much time at all does it? Anyway, if Daniel's there please have him call me as soon as you can. If he's planning on having dinner at your house, which would be fine, I have to tell you that he is allergic to most wheat products. I make his sandwiches with spelt-based bread. Also, before he eats, I normally give him some dietary enzymes to help digestion, but I guess one time without would be-

"Cutoff again, would you please just call me when you get this? … End of messages."

No messages from Jason. Four messages from the mother of a friend of whom she'd never heard, calling to say *her* son was missing too. Anne picked up the phone to dial, but realized to her dismay she had no idea what the Elliots' number was. She set the phone down and replayed the messages, listening intently to each one. "You didn't leave your number, Sharon!" Anne barked at the phone.

She scrolled through the call history and found all four calls showed up as "Blocked Number."

"Oh for the love of....Where did I put that student roster? … Kitchen!" Anne ran down to the kitchen table, which was nestled in a cozy nook, swiped at the day-old newspapers on the surface and searched the corner for the roster. She didn't find the roster, but she did find a list of school contacts. The list was useless, as the school was closed, but clipped to the list was a Post-it that caught her eye. On the Post-it was the home number of one of Jason's teachers, John Baker. She grabbed the phone hanging on the kitchen wall and dialed his number. The phone rang several times before a voice answered with a curt, "Yes?"

"Is this Mr. Baker?" Anne asked, trying to ignore the man's perhaps unintended rudeness.

The voice on the other end was quiet for a moment, but then answered. "Yes, and who is this?"

"This is Anne Swann, I'm Jason's mother, I believe he's in your science class?"

"Oh...yes, he is. Thank you for calling; I was a bit worried about him today. He isn't the most talkative of students, but he always behaves himself in the classroom. I assume he explained to you what happened?"

Anne's heart sank. "No, actually he didn't. That's the reason I'm calling, Mr. Baker."

"John. Please call me John."

I don't care what your name is, just help me!

"Sure, that's why I'm calling, John. Jason isn't at home. I received several phone messages from Daniel Elliot's mother saying that Daniel isn't at home either. I need to call her back, but she didn't leave her number and I can't find my student roster. I saw your number next to my school contact list and I was hoping you might have the Elliots' contact information."

"Daniel is missing too?" Mr. Baker inquired in a slow drawl.

Can't he just listen and do what I ask? Anne thought furiously, but calmed her voice and responded as politely as she could. "I'm not sure if either boy is actually *missing*, they just both aren't at home. If you'd give me the number to the Elliots' house, I'd really appreciate it."

"Of course," Mr. Baker replied with a grave undertone, "give me a minute to look it up, I'll be right back."

He couldn't have been gone for more than twenty or thirty seconds, but the empty end of his receiver made Anne feel alone on the whole Earth. Her mind distorted the friendly shadows of her house into a theatrical nightmare of her own design. The ghosts of her own possessions mocked her with their lifelessness.

...If I lose them both...

"Anne, are you ready?"

She snapped back to life, "Huh?"

"Are you ready for the number?" Mr. Baker repeated.

"Oh, yes, sorry." She wrote down the number, thanked John Baker for his help and hung up before he had a chance to respond. She dialed the Elliots' number as her foot tapped uncontrollably on the linoleum floor. The phone rang only once, and a small but clear voice answered.

"Hello, this is Sharon Elliot of the Elliot residence. Whom may I ask is calling?"

She must have been standing right next to the phone... "Hi Sharon, this is Anne Swann, Jason's mother. I just got home from work and saw your message...messages, and I wanted to let you know-"

"Oh hi Anne, don't worry if Daniel has already eaten wheat. I didn't mean to scare you. He may develop some minor hives in the next couple days, but nothing to be overly concerned about."

Anne took a deep breath and closed her eyes, heavy with the knowledge that she was about to shatter a stranger's hope. "I'm sorry to have to tell you this," Anne said, finally exhaling, "but Daniel is not at my house."

"Oh," Sharon said. Anne could hear the anguish in the woman's voice. She sounded like a dying stone. "Thank you very much for calling me back Anne, and now I-"

"Wait Sharon, don't hang up! Jason isn't home either. I don't know where he is. He never called, which he always does, and I was about to go look for him."

"Jason is missing too?" Sharon asked.

"I don't want to say he's missing... but he's not home... and I don't know where he is."

"I see," Sharon responded. Anne detected coldness in

Sharon's voice. *Does she think Daniel's missing is Jason's fault?*

"Anne, why don't you come over to our house? My husband Charles will be home soon and we can call around town, and the police, if necessary. I'm sure somebody has seen them recently."

"What's your address?" Anne asked. Maybe the boys were together, though she'd never heard Jason mention any "Daniel." Then again, Jason didn't tell her very much about his life. For all she knew, the two boys were best friends.

But right then, she only wanted Jason to be safe, and home. She needed to talk to her son and walk forward together, away from tragic dreams.

Chapter 15: Who is Like God?

As she stood on the Elliots' front porch, Anne had the sensation of being watched. Not by a person, but by the empty streets of Ashton, and the countless stars that filled the sky. The world around her was so still she could hardly believe things had changed so quickly. There was no measure to the strangeness of life.

A slightly trembling finger rang the doorbell. Within seconds the door opened noiselessly, and Anne was greeted by a petite brunette in her mid-forties wearing a pressed white short-sleeve blouse and khaki capris. Anne glanced at her own sweat pants and tennis shoes.

"Hi Anne. Thank you for coming. Please come in," Sharon Elliot said graciously.

The house was painted in soft, earth tones. White crown molding lined the ceiling, and dark walnut covered the floor. A console table with an orchid and white candles rested against the wall to Anne's right. Through a large, arched entrance to a formal living room, Anne saw untouched couches and chairs. French Impressionist art books rested on a tasteful coffee table. A silver-framed family portrait sat on the mantle above the fireplace, and she could make out the stoic face and well groomed hair of child who clearly didn't want to be wearing a buttoned-down, collared shirt.

"I've been calling everyone I could think of, teachers, administrators, parents," Sharon said as she bid Anne follow her into the dining room. "Nobody has seen Daniel... or Jason, since school today. I think we should call the police."

"Already?" Anne was taken aback. "Don't you think we

should maybe try driving around for a little while, to see if we can find them?"

"I didn't mean file a missing-persons report, or anything like that," Sharon replied. "I was going to call Captain Willis at home."

"Who's Captain Willis?"

Sharon smiled neatly.

"An old friend," she replied, then briskly walked into her kitchen.

That doesn't really tell me very much, Anne thought.

"Look Sharon, are you sure you want to make this a police matter so quickly? What if the boys are just-"

"Don't worry about it," Sharon called from the kitchen. "It won't be a Police matter... unless Captain Willis thinks it should be."

Anne sighed. She could tell Sharon was politely informing her that the decision had already been made.

"Do you want something to drink? I was going to fix myself a cup of tea to settle my nerves."

Anne needed something stronger than tea but... "Some tea would be fine; thanks Sharon."

As Anne listened to calculated clatter coming from the kitchen, she felt perturbed. She didn't want control of the situation being taken out of her hands, and though she'd just met Sharon, Anne thought she was the type of person who thrived on taking control. If only she could get up from the table, sneak out of the pristine house and pretend she'd never called Sharon in the first place. Yet, something kept her there: a stubborn understanding that she shouldn't be refusing help. But she needed to step away for a minute to gather her wits.

"Do you mind if I use the restroom?" Anne asked the focused figure skittering about in the kitchen.

"Of course not," Sharon called back. "Go down the hall to the right, third door."

Anne headed down the hallway. There were two third doors, one to the right, and one to the left. *Right is right,* she reasoned and opened that door expecting to see an immaculate bathroom, but instead found a child's bedroom. *This must be Daniel's room*, she thought, and was about to close the door, but a wave of familiarity stopped her. Before she thought better, she'd entered and closed the door behind her.

The bed boasted a dark wood frame decorated with taped-on pictures of wonderful abstract designs. Next to the bed was a white bookshelf fat and replete with all kinds of stories. Anne fondly recognized some books she'd read to Jason when he was little, and was embarrassed to find others she'd always meant to read herself, of which she found many worn and dog-eared volumes. Next to the bookshelf was a desk, cluttered with glues and inks sitting on top of schematics and designs for inventions that surely had some profound purpose to Daniel. The walls were covered with framed maps of ancient empires and prints of masterpieces huddled next to posters of rock-bands.

The image of Daniel that now formed in her mind was different from the unhappy kid in the picture she'd seen. A grand soul resonated in this room. Anne was reminded of her own son, laughing, feet kicking up in the air, dirty socks hanging on for dear life as her husband knelt, tickling the daylights out of their child with a giant grin on his face. Even in this stranger's room, she couldn't escape. Everything she saw unleashed a current that drew her back to an old house, an old time…

–◉⋂ॐ–

Michael had awakened one day feeling unwell. He tried to describe the sensation as being… incomplete, as if something vital had been taken from him, but he had no idea what. A piece of his soul he said, though he'd laughed at how foolish that sounded. She told him he was working too hard. He was stressed out and needed a vacation; that would set him right. So they took a trip, but he felt worse, not better.

When they got home, Michael went to the doctor for a full physical. The blood-work showed nothing out the ordinary.

A battery of other tests revealed a perfectly healthy man in his mid-thirties. Anne had hoped that confirmation would make her husband feel better, but he was more confused. He knew something wasn't right. Months passed with good days becoming less and less common.

Ever more frequently he'd stare into space at the dinner table, like he lived in a different place all together. The smallest things made him glow with anger. He would yell at her and Jason for reasons he couldn't say.

Michael maintained his face as best he could for the outside world, at work, parties, and family gatherings. But at home, he stopped reading to Jason before bed. He stopped playing with him when he got home from work. He stopped admiring Anne and Jason with any love in his eyes. He was drifting away. He couldn't tell Anne why he felt so different, why he was losing himself.

Anne found out he'd contacted doctors and healers off the beaten path, anyone who would listen to him without rolling an eye. Every answer was the same: yes, his problem could be serious, but the most important thing he had to acknowledge was that he didn't have a physical affliction. What he felt was in his head and could be conquered.

The momentum of life carried the two of them through the days, but only as the shells of friends, departing ghosts dwindling into the cavities of life. In the dead of night as they both lay wide awake, she studied his eyes, distorted by the mists of darkness, and wondered with an aching sadness, why the end had to be so different from the beginning. She closed her eyes, and let her mind wander to a much fonder time...

... *2 A.M., rain pelting against the glass doors of a tiny coffee shop... Only their first date, but the best she's ever had...*

"I think the world is actually a pretty simple place, despite all the clutter and mess."

His voice so sweet; his eyes so kind...

"It has rules you can learn and use to make all kinds of things. The best part is the rules always stay the same!"

He's so interesting, passionate...

"If we left anything we've created to time, it would eventually fail mechanically, fall apart due to wear and tear from atmospheric conditions. But there are rules for that too, why things fall apart more easily than they can be put together. It's like that for us too, don't you think?"

She nods, doesn't want him to stop talking. Third cup of coffee, she's sad, knows the sun is eventually going to come up. She wants the night to last forever.

"Every day we wake up, and trust that our arm will bend, and our legs will keep walking. All with an effort we aren't even aware of!"

His hand brushes against hers, the touch makes her shiver…

"There's a much more subtle elegance to our design than anything we can make. That's why I like my name."

"Michael?" she whispers.

"Exactly, Mi-Cha-El. Who is like God?"

"Not us, that's for sure," she says with a confident chuckle.

He takes her hand in his.

"And that's a beautiful thing…"

–◎↑§–

Anne closed the door to Daniel's room and stood with her hand on the knob for a moment. She then set resolutely down the hallway towards the kitchen. Now was not the time to indulge the past. Now was the time to be strong. She'd need more than melancholy memories to find her son.

She tried his cell phone again, hoping for anything other than an endless string of mocking rings.

Chapter 16: Transmissions Through the Stars

Jiarnu Sindru Ebenin Shantar Anar pondered the transmission it had received. As a Regional Supervisor for the Assembly of the Archive of the Shantar Anar, its job was to appropriately handle all incoming and outgoing transmissions of data for ten thousand archivists. Most transmissions were benign and inconsequential: coordinate mapping, sample retrievals, destination time stamps, but this one… A tiny moment of doubt bubbled up in Jiarnu. From everything it understood about the Protocol of the Shantar Anar, and about the resources of the archivists, *this* transmission should never have occurred.

The first instinct was to label it an error of the transmitting archivist and not an oversight of the Shantar Anar. But the exact message repeated several times, muting Jiarnu's desired reaction. This was something to be carefully examined, and rushing into rash decisions was not a character trait of the Shantar Anar, nor any of their creations. Jiarnu contemplated possible courses of action as it stared out the giant viewing ports of its station office into the vast cosmos beyond.

Each star was admired for its power and persistence. Jiarnu marveled that within the seemingly insignificant, far away lights, incredible quantities of hydrogen atoms were being converted into helium; while inside stars close to self-destruction, heavier elements, the rarer building blocks of the universe were being forged by immense, intra-stellar density. The starlight observed took eons to reach Jiarnu. Of course, the Shantar Anar knew there was no necessity to travel as light did throughout the universe. There were much faster ways to journey among the stars.

Jiarnu felt very young, and very unsure, as it gazed upon the ancient lights. It thought again about the improbable transmissions and wondered if this wasn't a test of some kind. Perhaps the transmissions had not really come from an archivist, but from one of the Shantar Anar. It processed the message again.

To: Jiarnu Sindru Ebenin Shantar Anar – Regional Supervisor of Section 347785112287311 of the Universe, for the Assembly of the Archive:

From: Nierion Eindru Ebenin Shantar Anar, Archivist for Sub-section 347785112287311-44765 of the Universe, for the Assembly of the Archive:

This transmission is to inform you that a sentient LIFE FORM from system A-AA-AAB-334233 was studied, and made aware of the study, according to the Protocol of the Shantar Anar. During the initial Travel Sequence to my next destination, this same life-form, known as "Jason," located and was granted entrance to my vessel, though I was not involved in restoring his memory or helping him to locate and enter the ship. I then discovered that another of the same species, known as "Daniel," had as well gained entrance to the vessel, although I suspect his admittance is related to Jason's, and is not a separate occurrence. My intention is to take these two with me for my study of the next planetary system, as I do not think leaving them unsupervised on the ship would be advisable.

Jiarnu reviewed billions of archived transmissions and found, as it suspected, the singularity of the matter. A reply to this incident was well beyond the authority of a Section Supervisor. There was only one place to forward the message.

FROM: JIARNU SINDRU EBENIN SHANTAR ANAR, REGIONAL SUPERVISOR OF SECTION 347785112287311 OF THE UNIVERSE, FOR THE ASSEMBLY OF THE ARCHIVE:

TO: ESAN SHANTAR ANAR...

Chapter 17: Alternatives to Space and Time

The dim light of the ship forced Daniel to strain his eyes to see. He'd woken up in the same place he'd fallen over in pure exhaustion. While he waited for his sight to adjust to the low visibility of the chamber, he wondered at how similar everything appeared in the dark. For a moment he swore he was back in his room, peeking out from the covers of his bed into unseen perimeters shrouded in the blanket of night. But when his eyes finally adjusted, there was no mistaking his surroundings. The cavernous central chamber looked ten times larger now, than when the four, blinding, tiny suns filled the room.

Where the *ship* actually was, now that was a better question, he wagered. Judging from how he'd felt before passing out, he would've guessed that the ship had flown directly into a Cuisinart. But he gave his body a once-over glance, and was relieved to find that he was, at least, still intact. Jason slept soundly about ten feet to his right, and the rhythmic bellows of his chest reassured Daniel that his companion had survived the ordeal as well.

Daniel leaned up on his forearms and hands, then pushed himself off the ground. He had no idea how long he'd been unconscious, but the muscles in his arms and legs ached like he'd been stuck in a hospital bed for a week. He tried to shake the fatigue out of his body, but forgot all about this discomfort as his eyes found the outline of the Archivist, locked into the cylinder at the center of the chamber. Nierion's visors were dim and the alien being's body was a solid mass of black; the hypnotic blue and white sheen was gone. Captivated, he stared at what he likened to the statue of an imagined god.

"What are you?" he whispered with wonder. He felt drawn to the Archivist, both to its physical appearance, and to the notion that the emptiness of space contained something so different from anything on Earth. He stepped lightly towards it, and found when he was close, that Nierion looked to be in a deep, exhaustive sleep. Daniel brushed his fingers against the metal surface of the Archivist's body, which was cool to the touch, as expected. But there was something else, the faint essence of life, surging beneath the exterior, like a quiet heartbeat. Daniel pulled his hand away and cast the Archivist a quizzical stare. He pressed his other hand against the metal body and felt the same, faint beating of life. *Appearances are so deceiving,* he thought. Clearly there was much more to this being than he could-

"Daniel."

He withdrew his hand and jumped back. But Nierion was still.

"Behind you."

He shot around to find Jason, not two feet away. "Was that really necessary?" Daniel wheezed.

"Sorry, I called your name like, five times but you didn't respond," Jason remarked.

Daniel peered at the Archivist. "I guess I was a little distracted."

"Why, did Nierion do something?" Jason asked.

Daniel leaned closer to the still, resting form. "No, it's just been sitting here. Why do you think it was on Earth?"

"To study stuff, at least that's what it told me," Jason said, glancing at Nierion coolly.

"In Ashton?" Daniel questioned.

"One place is as good as another, I guess," Jason concluded.

"Do you believe it?" Daniel followed.

"What do you mean? You think it lied to me?"

"I don't think it was lying," Daniel interjected, shaking his head. "It's not human; no reason to treat it like one. But something is bothering me."

Jason grunted. "Just *something* is bothering you about all of this?!" Daniel took an involuntary step back. "All I mean is, Nierion seems convinced you finding the ship and getting back on should have been impossible."

"Right…"

"'Cause the Shantar Anar never mess up."

"Yeah…"

Daniel put a contemplative finger to his lip. "Maybe they didn't mess up. Maybe you were *supposed* to find the ship again."

Jason waved his hand dismissively. "That's crazy, after everything Nierion did to take away my memories, send me back to school…"

"I'm just saying… maybe Nierion doesn't know the real reason it was sent to Earth."

"But that means-"

A sound like a spooling disk abruptly ended the boys' conversation. The Archivist's visors displayed a soft, grey light. A gentle hum emanated from its body, which glistened in the blue-white sheen.

"Jason," Daniel whispered. "I didn't have a chance to tell you earlier, but when you were in the park, you were surrounded in the same-"

"You are both alive," the Archivist declared as simple fact above the sound of the spooling. The bands that held Nierion in place retracted into the cylinder.

"Don't sound so excited," Jason replied. Daniel grimaced at the sarcasm dripping in the words. *Does he think being a jerk is going to help us somehow?!* But the Archivist seemed unaware of the intent.

"There was a possibility the effects of the Travel Sequence would be too much for your bodies to handle. I am glad to see that is not the case."

Daniel caught Jason shooting Nierion a venomous glance. He wondered how close to death he'd actually been.

"What happened to us?" Jason asked.

The Archivist explained. "A consequence of the way the ship travels. Your bodies were… unclear on how to respond to the change."

"What change?" Daniel questioned.

"Travelling through space is a very slow process, even at speeds close to that of light."

Daniel was shocked. "So the ship can go faster than light! I thought that was impossible!"

"No, the ship travels by avoiding the drawbacks of three-dimensional space altogether. The passage from the third into the fourth dimension is tricky, especially for beings used to living in three dimensions."

The fourth dimension! Daniel was awed.

"How does that help the ship go faster?" Jason snipped. Daniel could almost see Jason's frustration pouring from him like sweat.

As far as Daniel could tell, Nierion was oblivious to Jason's scorn. *Maybe it has a lot more patience than we do,* he reasoned.

"Consider this," the Archivist suggested. "If you did not have the ability to move in the direction up, no matter how hard you tried to reach a location just an inch above you, you would never be able to go there. But, if you could move in the direction up, as you are able to do in three-dimensional space, then the journey is a very simple task.

"This ship works on the same principle. Distances that are, for all intents and purposes, impossible to travel in three-dimensional space, are as simple as reaching an inch above you, in a different dimension."

"How far did we go then?" Daniel asked. His hands felt clammy. In Ashton, Chicago seemed a huge distance away.

"Approximately four hundred thousand light-years from Earth," the Archivist replied, "but in a matter of moments." Daniel had to steady himself; the distance was too ridiculous to contemplate.

"How does the ship-"

"Who cares?!" Jason shouted. "It doesn't matter, none of this is going to help us get home!"

"It might!" Daniel shouted back, surprising himself. "Who knows what might be useful? We should find out as much as we can!"

Jason fumed. "There's only one way we're getting home, and that's not ever going to happen! Don't you get it? THEY DON'T CARE ABOUT US! Not Nierion, not the stupid Shantar Anar!"

"That is not true Jason," the Archivist replied. Daniel was surprised by the conviction in Nierion's voice. The emotion made him think of the life he'd felt beneath the alien being's cold exterior. "I have already sent a transmission to my supervisor. It is aware of our predicament and... we just have to wait for now."

Daniel cringed as Jason threw his hands up and sulked away to a corner of the chamber. Daniel wasn't sure why, but he felt the need to defend his friend. "I'm sorry Nierion, I-"

"No, I am sorry, Daniel," the Archivist interrupted. "This is the first time in my existence when I have felt unsure. I do not like it, but there is nothing more I can do."

"But there is. Tell me how the ship works."

"My knowledge of that is incomplete; I am not an engineer, just an archivist."

"What *do* you know?" Daniel prodded.

The Archivist considered for a moment, then spoke slowly. "The move between dimensions takes an incredible amount of energy, far more than even nuclear fusion harnessed safely would generate. There are only two things of which I am aware that can produce this power: the first is gravitational energy, for example the accretion disk created by matter falling towards a massive black hole. But harnessing that energy is beyond the abilities of even the Shantar Anar. The second is the controlled elemental decay of Ziin."

"That's the stuff you said the Shantar Anar mine on their planet?"

"Correct."

"What makes Ziin so special?" Daniel asked.

"It has properties of many different kinds of elements. For example, the suit that I-"

"Stop!" Jason bellowed. He stood up and lumbered back to Daniel. "I can't take this anymore! Just tell us where we are and what we have to do."

Daniel barely kept himself from strangling his classmate. He was sure Nierion was about to reveal something important.

"Very well," Nierion said. To his dismay, Daniel could tell that his conversation with the Archivist was over.

"We are on the surface of a planet called Ranis Anjiran by the dominant species of sentient life, the Ranis Aun."

"What does that mean?" Daniel asked, ignoring Jason's impatient grunt.

The Archivist focused on Jason. "Ranis Anjiran means, World of Fragile Stone; Ranis Aun, Molders of the Stone. I do not know what the planet itself would like to be called."

The grey lights in Nierion's visors shifted into azure blue, the color of a bright Earth sky. Daniel clenched his teeth in anticipation of violence, but the Archivist did not strike.

"You cannot stay in the ship," It said, decisively.

"We have to go with you, like onto the planet?" Jason asked.

"Shouldn't we wait here?" Daniel interjected. "After all, if you get the order to take us home, it makes sense for us to stick close to the ship."

"The ship is not a safe place for you to be without me," the Archivist declared. "The Arcon Drei and other-"

"I get it," Jason said. "You don't trust us. YOU don't trust US!"

"Stop!" Daniel ordered. He understood Jason's anger, but his emotions were getting out of control. Why was he making everything harder?

Jason spun to face him, and Daniel at last could see the burning cinder of anger matted in Jason's eyes. "Don't tell me to stop. Don't ever tell me what to do you little-"

"Enough!" the Archivist boomed; the words sounded like thunder. Daniel turned ashen with fright and saw a similar look of terror etched on Jason's face.

Nierion towered over Jason. The light in its visors turned from blue to an intense violet that was difficult to behold. Jason shrank away and cringed. The Archivist's head lowered so that its visors were even with Jason's eyes. The violet light grew brighter, and the space around them buzzed like white noise. But again, there was no violence, and after another drawn-out moment, the Archivist backed away.

Nierion is searching for something, Daniel thought.

"We must depart," the Archivist stated, in a granite tone that assured obedience. The Archivist's abdomen opened, and four additional visors on long, metallic, black coils shot out of the hidden compartments. Daniel recoiled involuntarily. "What are those? What is this going to do?" He wanted to be prepared in case this "departure" was going to feel anything like the ship's Travel Sequence.

"Don't worry Daniel, this doesn't hurt," Jason replied. The sharpness of his voice had dulled. Daniel wasn't sure the Archivist had scared Jason straight, but his classmate appeared subdued, like the fire inside had been extinguished.

"Doesn't really feel like anything at all," Jason continued. "One second you're here, and the next second you're there."

Daniel winced. "It really doesn't hurt?"

"I promise," Jason said with a sincerity that surprised his companion.

The visors spirited through an array of colors far too fast for Daniel to make out individual hues. Soon they emptied of visible light, and Jason touched them without fear. Daniel did the same. The space around him shimmered, and then he was no longer on the ship.

Chapter 18: Cohev Senar

Slumped beside the Archivist's ship, Jason surveyed his surroundings. The surface of Ranis Anjiran was about the least inviting place he'd ever been. Everywhere he looked was endless brown and grey rock, interrupted by a mountain here and there on the horizon. The stars were hidden from sight, as the entire sky was covered by an impenetrable wall of menacing clouds that looked like a sea of pea-green vomit. The light that penetrated the putrid overcast gave the atmosphere a rusty, orange hue.

Rocks crunched under foot as Jason lumbered to the other side of the ship only to find the same scenery waiting for him there. As he surveyed the vast, unwelcoming terrain, he imagined living on this planet instead of Earth and frowned in dismay at the idea of spending his life wandering through the lifeless rock utterly alone. A thought occurred to him: *Where are the Ranis Aun?*

About twenty feet to Jason's left, Nierion held a rock the size of a fist in a coiled arm. Its visors glowed a soft turquoise. Daniel crouched next to the Archivist, apparently studying the rocks as well. The Archivist was calm again, utterly focused on something so mundane that Jason almost forgot the being's powerful command. The ferocity of Nierion's voice frightened him, and yet the fear diminished his anger. He peered at the Archivist with more cautious eyes. What had he been arguing? He couldn't even remember as he timidly approached. "I thought you were here to study the Ranis Aun?"

"Yes, I am," Nierion replied, and placed the sample of

rock into an abdominal compartment. "But I am also here to study other life-forms, and geological composition."

"For the same reason?"

"For the Assembly of the Archive."

"But I mean, the Ranis Aun, just to study their bodies, like with me?" Jason was surprised at how pouty he sounded, as if he'd been rejected by a girl he liked. The thought of the Archivist going through the same routine with another unsuspecting being made him far more sad than he would've imagined.

"Yes."

"Are you going to do the same thing to the Ranis Aun that you did to me?"

"Yes," the Archivist replied. "But, this time there will be no anomalies."

So that's all I am, huh, a mistake? Suffocating self-pity rose up within him. Though the tiny Spark-the remnant of Esan's touch- hiding deep inside didn't flat out tell him to be sorrowful, this emotional state seemed heightened by the Spark's presence. He hadn't recognized the connection before, but now Jason was sure that Esan's Touch had encouraged his terrible anger on the ship as well. Maybe he'd been wrong about all of this. There was no malicious intent; no alien mind implanted in him trying to control his every move. No, the Spark was a part of him as much as his pulse. Most of the time the Spark was barely noticeable, but it magnified strong emotional responses, just as it had enhanced his senses in the park.

"What are they anyway, the Ranis Aun, I mean?" Daniel asked the Archivist, "Are they like us?"

"In many ways they are. After all, both humans and Ranis Aun are Cohev Senar," Nierion answered.

Jason splayed his hands waiting for an explanation that didn't come. "...What does that mean?"

The Archivist continued analyzing samples and spoke in passing, "Cohev Senar is a species classification of the Shantar Anar. The rough translation is 'Young Builder,' but that does not capture the deeper meaning of the words."

"Builders of what?" Daniel wanted to know.

The Archivist took a moment to consider, then replied, "A synthetic environment."

"You mean like a city?" Jason asked.

"Yes, but much more than that. The term is not limited to things of so narrow a scope. There are thousands, perhaps millions of devices employed by human beings to create artificial environments for themselves. Most of these relate to survival, the acquisition of food and shelter. That human beings do all of these things is what makes you Cohev Senar."

"So 'Cohev Senar' is how the Shantar Anar describe intelligent life," Daniel replied. Jason noticed that his companion appeared very pleased with this assertion.

"Incorrect," the Archivist replied with absolute assurance. Daniel's smile faded, and Jason felt glad Daniel was wrong. *Smug...*

"There are many intelligent life forms that have been discovered by the Shantar Anar that are not Cohev Senar. Your planet alone houses an unquestionable quantity of life possessed of intelligence other than human intelligence. While they alter their natural environments to suit their needs, they do not have the power to Create, as do the Cohev Senar."

"How many kinds of Cohev Senar are there?" Daniel asked.

"As of now, the Shantar Anar have discovered four."

"Only four?" Jason asked.

"Yes."

"In how many life forms?" Daniel followed.

"Billions."

The boys looked at each other in amazement, and Jason let out a thin whistle.

"How long have the Shantar Anar been searching?" Daniel questioned further.

"Approximately two and a half billion years."

Jason's jaw dropped. "They must be like gods," he whispered.

"No," the Archivist responded. "They are only the Shantar Anar."

"Wait a minute," Daniel said. Jason noted a tinge of suspicion in his companion's voice. "Something doesn't make sense."

Why does Daniel care so much? Jason wondered. Couldn't he see their situation was hopeless? *Who cares what the Shantar Anar call stuff? It's all meaningless.* A smog of despair roiling in Jason's head fed these thoughts. He heard Daniel ask more questions, but his companion's voice sounded far away and inconsequential.

"Don't you think it's kind of weird you were assigned to study one species of Cohev Senar directly after another, Nierion?"

That did seem strange, Jason thought, but so what? The storm in his head echoed his thoughts: *Doesn't matter, so what… Why can't Daniel let it go?*

The Archivist seemed unalarmed, "The probability of the sequence of assignments is small but-"

"Think about this whole chain of events," Daniel prompted. "Something deeper is going on. Maybe the Shantar Anar-"

"You are wrong, Daniel," the Archivist said. "You are both here due to a failing of my own. I am… sure that is the case."

"For the first time ever?" Daniel queried. "I don't buy that. I bet the Shantar Anar-"

"You do not understand the motives of the Shantar Anar," the Archivist interrupted, its words heavy with dismissiveness. "You do not think the same way; you do not approach existence the same way. They are not human beings. You blink in and out of life like a flickering light. You simply cannot understand!"

Daniel averted his eyes from the penetrating gaze of the Archivist's visors, empty of light and compassion. A torrent of grief flooded Jason as he fixated on Daniel. He was sure now that the Touch allowed him to feel his friend's hurt as a swirling mist seeping through the dry brown rocks… like a thunderhead slowly gripping the tops of a mountain range. The physical sense of Daniel's pain intensified until Jason felt like he was drowning beneath a riptide. He gasped for breath and fought the rushing emotional current. He frowned at Daniel, afraid the boy's suffering would stretch across his face, but his companion hardly seemed affected, as if he'd already brushed aside the Archivist's hurtful words.

"If the Shantar Anar are so different from human beings," Daniel remarked, "then why aren't...

Jason couldn't hear Daniel's words as the punishing grief turned inwards. Visions flashed in his mind of terrible pasts and terrible futures... *His mother and father yelling at each other, fighting like they never had... His father looking at him without love, without recognition in his eyes... His mother crying at his father's grave... Strangers with thin hands and sweaty skin asking how he was doing; if he was okay.*

...His mother now alone in a dark house, his father gone and he's gone, too. She doesn't want to be there anymore either... He tries to tell her everything will be fine, but she can't hear him, she can't feel him, he's too far away... She doesn't want to be there anymore...

"NO!" he screamed, and shattered the night that enveloped him. The bleak surface of Ranis Anjiran returned. Daniel and the Archivist stared at him. Lines of worry matted Daniel's brow. "'No' what, Jason?" Daniel asked in almost a whisper.

Jason's mind was quiet. "No I..."

Daniel stepped close to him, "Are you okay, for real?"

"I think so." The words sounded hollow even to his own ears, and Jason knew Daniel didn't believe him. "Well... Nierion says we need to move on."

–◎∩ꙅ–

The three-beaked, giant rock slug of Ranis Anjiran was a one-meter long, slimy, spotted invertebrate that fed on a putrid, moss-like substance prevalent beneath shaded stone outcroppings. This was far more than Jason ever wanted to know about the creature. He listened to the Archivist relate these facts nonetheless as a black, metal coiled arm scooped residue off the slug's back. Jason cast a quick glance at Daniel, who positively beamed with excitement. Jason was trying to be patient, trying not to let anything make him angry, sad, or anything in between. That was hard to do because he felt like he'd been following the Archivist around for hours, but he could still see the ship!

How many things did Nierion need to study before it got to the Ranis Aun?! Jason stopped himself mid-thought; he was getting frustrated again. He took a deep breath, let the suit turn whatever molecules he was actually inhaling into the perfect mixture of mostly oxygen and nitrogen he rarely even noticed on Earth. He felt better, though he was slightly annoyed by the sight of Daniel gliding his finger against the slug's back, presumably for his own experimentation. Daniel barely stopped talking since they'd left the ship. *How many questions could this kid have?* Jason wondered.

"How do you know so much about us? Humans, I mean?"

"I am not the first archivist to visit Earth." Nierion was enjoying the conversation as much as Daniel, in Jason's estimation. *If we don't get back home, maybe Daniel can become an archivist too,* Jason thought sourly.

A deep hum emanated from Nierion's interior as the slug residue was deposited into a hidden compartment by the coiled arm. "Other archivists have studied human culture and history. This is done on a relatively frequent basis to ensure that any mutations, or societal alterations, which may require updating in the Archive, are captured. "

"Who was studied before me?" Jason asked, suddenly curious.

"I am not sure…" the Archivist paused, as if remembering something strange. "I can check for you once we return to the ship, if you are still curious."

"More importantly, what can you tell us about this planet?" Daniel chirped. Jason shot him a menacing glare, which went unnoticed. The Archivist was happy to oblige.

"Ranis Anjiran is an interesting planetary specimen. The planet is too far away from the binary star system it orbits to be warm enough for most of the planet's life-forms to inhabit the surface; this slug being one of the exceptions. The energy the Ranis Aun rely on to thrive comes from a super-heated and large, molten-iron core that dissipates heat throughout fissures within a couple miles of the surface. The Ranis Aun built a vast subterranean network around these fissures, connecting their civilization across the entire planet."

"Mole people," Daniel remarked, matter-of-factly. Jason frowned in confusion and was rewarded with a shock of surprise from Daniel. "Come on Jason, you should know this."

"Know what?"

Daniel sucked in his breath, "Issue fifteen of Lava Man!"

"I never got into that comic," Jason said, apparently far too casually. Tremendous effort was required not to be angered by Daniel's visible despair. *Breathe in, breathe out, breathe in, breathe out...*

"Never got into Lava Man, the greatest graphic novel of the last twenty years?"

"Sorry, I never read it."

"We'll have to rectify that when we get home," Daniel pronounced, more to himself than to Jason. "Anyway, in issue fifteen, Lava Man travels to a planet where he's supposed to meet an ancient oracle, and he gets there and the place is deserted. There's no one anywhere. He meditates, slowing down all of his bodily functions, and sinks into 'Lava Mind.' He realizes that the reason the planet seems abandoned is that everybody lives underground, because the surface is too harsh for everyone EXCEPT LAVA MAN!

"He uses 'Lava Strike' to burrow into the ground and discovers a vast civilization of creatures that are smart like humans, but look like giant moles, Mole People, and Lava Man finds out that the oracle was imprisoned because she kept saying stuff some of the other moles didn't like and-"

"Moles are small, blind mammals on Earth, correct?" the Archivist asked.

"Yes," Daniel replied. "As I was saying, the other moles didn't like what the oracle had to say so-"

"Then, no, the Ranis Aun are nothing like moles."

"What are they like?" Jason asked. He tried to ignore Daniel's crossed arms and the dour expression on his face. *Breathe in, breathe out...*

The Archivist replied, "Ranis Aun society is approximately nine million years old. Their lengthy gestational periods and rapid metabolic state has prevented over-population through low-birth rates and relatively short life spans, roughly two times the normal, human life expectancy. Ample food and building materials have assured relatively easy and sustainable lifestyles. In spite of all this, they have long been engaged in vicious wars. The most recent occurred an estimated one hundred years after the last archivist was active on this planet."

"What were they fighting about?" Daniel asked.

"Architectural disputes."

"They fought over how to make buildings?" Jason asked, his head dipping into a perplexed tilt.

"Amongst other trivial matters. I admit it is bewildering, but all of the Cohev Senar have acted confusingly at times. I cannot give you precise reasoning for irrational and counter-productive acts. But each innovative species has been brutal to their own kind, and to the planets they inhabit."

"Are we even safe here?" Daniel asked. The anxiety in his voice matched Jason's feelings. Nierion appeared unconcerned.

"Currently, yes. As such, I am required to locate a Ranis Aun named Laushtee, selected at random by my supervisor, as in your case, Jason. Once I have completed this task, we will be on our way to our next destination."

"What if you have the same problem again?" Daniel asked.

"I will not!" Nierion snapped, and then regained its calm. "The process will work; I assure you."

But Jason didn't care about assurances, "What do you mean our next destination? You said you were going to at least try to take us home!"

"I am sorry Jason, but I cannot do so without a direct command to the ship, and I have not received any reply to my transmissions. I suspect, given the magnitude of the issue, that the matter has already moved on."

Daniel scrunched his eyebrows, "To where?"

"One of the Shantar Anar probably. As I said, to my understanding, this has never happened before, and certainly not in my lifetime."

Jason saw the Archivist in a new light.

"How old are you?"

"Much older than any human being. In fact, I am older than human beings."

Jason stood in silent awe of the realization.

"You look pretty good for a couple million years old," Daniel remarked.

Now he wants to be funny?! Jason tried to ignore the comment. *Breathe in, breathe out...*

"But once the Shantar Anar read your messages, they'll change the ship's preset coordinates, and then you can take us home, right?" Jason pressed. The Archivist turned the blank stare of its visors, which Jason was beginning to detest, in his direction.

"...right?"

"Perhaps," Nierion finally said, "But there is a chance the Shantar Anar will want to know what went wrong, and why."

"What does that mean?" he asked with a lump in his throat, though he had an idea Nierion's comment had something to do with him and the Touch.

The Archivist was silent for a time, but then admitted, "They may want me to bring you to them."

"And you would do that? What did we ever do to you! Can't you try to find a way to work the ship?! Please, I have to get home!!" *Breathe in, breathe out...*

"Don't be frightened," Nierion pleaded, "They are not evil. They will treat you fairly."

There was true conviction in the Archivist's voice, but Jason didn't care. "No, you don't understand…"

Another vision entered Jason's mind; his mother back on Earth, totally alone. What would she do if she thought he'd left her too? *What was she capable of?* he wondered with sharp terror. The horrible possibility that he would somehow get home, only to find himself deprived of his mother… that he would be completely lost, without any of his family, sent a shiver of fear through him so cold he thought his heart would turn to ice and stop beating.

His hand wouldn't stop shaking as he pulled his phone from his pocket, suddenly desperate to see her familiar face. He stared at the picture of his mother moving boxes, which before had produced nothing but bitterness, and saw for the first time that her secret smile, which he'd taken for undeserved happiness, didn't match the aching pain now so clear to him within her eyes.

His fingers brushed against the smooth, dead surface of his phone, lingering over the million pixels of his mother's hair before the battery died completely, and the screen went blank.

Chapter 19: Just Breathe

The grey-brown rocks beneath Jason's feet scattered as he paced back and forth like a disgruntled soldier. Every so often, he paused to look at the Archivist. Nierion was in a sitting position: its tripod of leg-like appendages splayed out perpendicular to its body. The Archivist's visors had shifted and rotated until two sat parallel on each side of the metallic head. They faintly glowed in a dark, murky green. Each time Jason caught a glimpse of the alien being, he imagined Nierion sitting just so, but on Earth, burrowing into his mind, infiltrating his dreams.

Daniel sat close by and Jason thought his classmate seemed content, sifting through the rocks, like there was no place he'd rather be. Jason tried not to let the sight of Daniel happily working away bother him, but he was infuriated. The pulsing Spark within him assured that this was a reasonable feeling, and maybe not strong enough. His life was ruined, he had to remember that! He wasn't sure if he was angrier with the Archivist or Daniel; both were driving him crazy, but what could he do? There was nowhere to go; he wasn't even... A curious thought entered his head and momentarily soothed his brooding angst. He went to Daniel and peered over the small boy's shoulder. *What was so damn interesting about those rocks?!*

"Daniel."

He received no response other than a muted grunt of acknowledgement. Jason bent down until his mouth was poised next to Daniel's ear.

"Daniel!"

Rocks flew out of Daniel's hands as he jumped to his feet. "What?! What's wrong?"

"Are you hungry?"

"No, of course I'm not hungry. Weren't you listening?"

"To what?"

"To Nierion!"

Jason glanced at the still motionless Archivist.

Daniel groaned at Jason's inattentiveness. "Not now. Before, on the ship... the suits."

Jason was incredulous. "The suits are feeding us?"

"I don't know how, but they must be," Daniel asserted. "I doubt the Shantar Anar were gonna stock their ships with roast-beef sandwiches."

"I know that Daniel! Do you think I'm stupid?!"

Daniel was defiant. "No, I don't. All I know is that since we got the suits I haven't felt hungry, and I haven't had to go to the bathroom. I'm sure the suit's doing a whole bunch of other things I wouldn't even know to think about."

The hypothesis concerned Jason. "That's a good point; who knows what Nierion programmed the suits to do," he peeped in a conspiratorial whisper as he eyed the Archivist.

The murky green emanating from Nierion's visors made Jason think of drowning. He shuddered, then shifted squarely back to Daniel.

"We need to figure out how to get out of here. Nierion brought us to this place to die, I know it!"

"Get a grip!" Daniel said fiercely. "Nierion didn't have to give us the suits; we would have died then anyway."

"That's my point!" Jason countered. The words grated against his tongue as he realized what must be happening. "Nierion didn't want us to die before we got the suits. They must be doing something to us, something bad, for the Shantar Anar!"

"Jason... You sound crazy."

"I'm *crazy* now, huh?" Jason lurched back his shoulders and dropped his arms to his sides. He felt tension clatter through his shoulder blades, down his arms and into every bone in his fingers.

"It's just an expression!" Daniel appealed. "You have to calm down… Try taking some deep breaths."

Breathe in, breathe out. Breathe in, breathe out… He's going to tell me how to do that now too?

"What do you know?" Jason growled. "You're just playing in the sand!"

Daniel stood up to meet Jason's stare.

"I'm examining," he said through gritted teeth.

Jason glared down at Daniel with a condescending gaze.

"A bunch of rocks?"

Daniel met Jason right back in the eyes.

"They're a lot more than that, but I wouldn't expect you to understand!"

"Oh, I forgot I was talking to a real scientist! So what are they?" Jason stepped into Daniel's space.

The tension had spread to his entire body. Every part of him felt strained, like he was going to burst if he didn't vent the pressure.

"What's your problem?! Why are you being such a jerk?!" Daniel yelled.

"I'll show you a jerk!" Jason yelled back, and kicked the rocks and pebbles at his feet, sending a cloud of dust up into Daniel's face.

The violence of the act helped release some of the mercilessly squeezing tension. Letting his anger flood through him felt so good. The Spark blossomed. Last time, it had enhanced all of his senses, let him see the path of light leading to the Arcon Drei, but not this time. The only thing he felt now was intolerable rage. Everything around him was closing in to hurt him, to beat him down. He had to protect himself from the motives of every single atom surrounding him. They'd taken shape, made rocks, metals, and flesh. They all wanted him to die. He grabbed Daniel's arms in a vice-like grip, squeezing his fingers tight, like claws gripping prey. Salty spit dripped from his mouth. His eyes burned.

"Stop it! You're hurting me!" Daniel cried.

"Make me!" Jason shouted back, and clasped the smaller boy's arms even harder. His right arm released its grip and lunged for Daniel's neck. Jason wanted to pull the puny boy down and grind Daniel's face into the rocks.

Daniel saw the hate brewing in Jason's eyes. Their gaze was so intense that Daniel almost missed the shimmer of blue and white percolating around Jason's body. This was no coincidence. *What did Nierion do to you?* Daniel could see the Archivist over Jason's shoulder. Nierion was still motionless, and oblivious to Jason's actions.

Daniel felt clammy fingers clamp around his neck. *He's going to kill me,* Daniel thought. The strength of desperation shot down his shoulders, past Jason's grip, and down into the hand of his free arm where his fingers became a tight fist of knuckle and protruding bone. Daniel swung with a quick jolt, striking Jason square in the jaw.

Jason never even saw Daniel's fist as the knuckles cracked against his chin. Jason's eyes rolled back, the tension faded away, and the anger that had consumed him wilted like dead leaves. Jason hit the ground, calm, at peace, and lay on his back staring up at Daniel, riddled with guilt. Again, the memory of fury percolated, but the motivation was gone and impossible to understand.

"I'm sorry!" Daniel knelt over his companion's fallen body. Jason let out a long sigh of relief.

"Don't worry, I deserved that."

"It happened again!" Daniel spoke fearfully holding out a hand to help Jason to his feet.

Jason grabbed Daniel's hand and lurched to standing. He held his jaw, maneuvering back and forth and was rewarded with a satisfying crack.

"I know, I got super angry again. I honestly don't know what's wrong with me."

Daniel shook his head vigorously.

"That's not what I mean! When you were grabbing me, I saw the blue and white shimmering around your body. Like in the park... Like on Nierion!"

Jason blanched. He checked his skin to see if there was any trace of the effect, but saw nothing.

Daniel put a speculative finger to his lip.

"Maybe Nierion can teach you to control whatever it did to you."

Jason peeked over his shoulder at the silent figure of the Archivist.

"I don't think that's a good idea…"

"You should have seen yourself! You need help!"

Jason met Daniel's eyes.

"I know, but I don't want to ask Nierion for help."

Daniel was perplexed. "Why not?"

"'Cause I think you're right. Something about all of this doesn't fit. I'm not sure I trust everything Nierion is telling us."

Jason's lack of faith made Daniel grimace. "I really don't think we should be treating Nierion like a human."

"What if you're wrong, Daniel? What if Nierion *does* control the ship? What if there's no such thing as the Shantar Anar. What if-"

"We don't know either way, so let's not make assumptions," Daniel implored. "But I understand why you don't want Nierion's help. We'll figure out a way to control whatever is wrong with you… together." Daniel held out his hand. Jason hesitated for a moment, but then grasped it firmly.

"So… what were you trying to find in the rocks?" Jason asked.

"Connections," Daniel remarked as he surveyed the surface of Ranis Anjiran.

Jason frowned. "What connections?"

"When I examine the rocks," Daniel continued, "I'm trying to look deeper, to see the ways the rock is connected to the planet, and to me, I guess. I come up with my best ideas when I focus on connections. I'm not thrilled about leaving our fate up to Nierion either, and I'm trying to think of alternatives."

"Any ideas?" Before Daniel could respond, Jason saw the

green light emanating from the Archivist's visors blink out. After a moment, the tripod of legs pushed against the ground, lifting Nierion's body up to rest at full height. The Archivist faced the boys. Then the uncountable moving chords beneath it, carried it like a silent specter over the jagged ground.

"There is a problem." The Archivist sounded deeply bothered as it approached.

"What kind of problem?" Jason asked.

The Archivist didn't immediately answer.

"I… I don't understand," the alien finally managed to blurt out.

"Don't understand what?" Daniel asked.

Nierion continued, speaking more for its own benefit than the humans.

"Until my encounter with Jason, I had never experienced a deviation beyond the infinitesimally small tolerance of allowable change set forth in the Protocol, between every task that has been set before me, and my ability to complete this task."

"So what's the problem?" Jason pressed. He was scared. What if the Archivist had seen his outburst? What if *he* was the problem?!

"There is a second deviation," Nierion said. Jason heard an awful stress in the words, but he was also relieved. "I cannot locate Laushtee!"

"The Ranis Aun?" Jason asked.

"Why don't you try again in a little bit?" Daniel suggested.

"You do not understand, Daniel. Esan's Eyes have the ability to locate an energy source to a very specific level, regardless of spatial coordinates. Wherever Laushtee is, I should have been able to locate the Ranis Aun's energy source."

"Maybe Esan's Eyes aren't working right now," Jason followed.

The Archivist glided nervously back and forth under the shadow of the ship.

"That is a possibility, but they have never malfunctioned before. I can only think of two plausible explanations. One, the source of energy is being hidden in some unknown way; or two, the source no longer exists."

"You mean like the Ranis Aun is dead," Daniel announced flatly.

"Yes," the Archivist replied.

"Can't you choose another one? You said they have short lives, compared to you. Maybe Laushtee was just old."

"That is the bigger problem. I cannot locate *any* of the Ranis Aun!"

Jason saw a glimmer of hope. "Then you're done here, right? We can go back to the ship and you can follow up with whoever you need to about getting us back to Earth?"

"It is not that simple," the Archivist reminded him, and Jason's heart sank. Nierion's voice was surprisingly full of passion. "I *must* find the reason for the deviation!"

"How are you going to do that?" Jason asked, dreading the answer.

"While Esan's Eyes could not locate the Ranis Aun, they did find an unexpected source of energy different than the surrounding environment and its life-forms. Perhaps this is a gateway into the network of cities beneath the planet. I will start there."

"What if you don't come back?" Jason exclaimed. "What are we supposed to do then, wait here until we die?!"

"Jason…" Daniel warned.

Jason steadied himself. *Breathe in, breathe out.* "Sorry… I… sorry."

"That is why you must both come with me. We are in this together!" Nierion continued.

Daniel almost gagged, "With you, you mean *underground?*"

"Yes. We must not be separated."

The thought of following the Archivist into the dark depths of the planet made Daniel shiver. He recalled Jason's piercing questions and imagined himself helpless and blind beneath the surface. *What if it does control the ship? What if there's no such thing as the Shantar Anar…*

Chapter 20: On the Case

Ashlyn Bluent sat in the corner of the Elliots' kitchen nook, hands folded in her lap and her lips tightly puckered, as she tried not to say anything. She'd been warned to keep silent by the very man she observed with her bright, green eyes. He'd been adamant in his request, which was fine with her. After all, staying quiet wasn't difficult while surrounded by adults. But if a detail was dropped, a fact glossed over, what was she supposed to do?

Coregon Willis, Ashton's police captain, wasn't like any of the other adults Ashlyn knew. He was patient, and waited to see things other people missed. He took time to listen when other people didn't bother. And he didn't assume she was stupid because she was thirteen. Of course, these keen skills meant he noticed, more often than Ashlyn liked, when she followed him to lend an "un-needed" hand, as he described it, with his police work.

Ashlyn didn't want to be a cop, but she had reasons for trying to learn from Coregon: he was good at solving puzzles, and that's exactly what Ashlyn needed to do. When Sharon Elliot called her parents to inquire about Daniel, Ashlyn *might* have been listening on the other end, and *may* have heard mention of calling Coregon. She *might* have climbed out her bedroom window, shimmied down a drain pipe, crept into the garage, unchained her bicycle, and rode over to the Elliots' house to be of service to her reluctant mentor. Ashlyn worried Coregon would call her parents and drive her home as soon as he saw her, but she knew that this time he'd have to let her stay; after all, apparently she was the last person to have seen Jason and Daniel.

With affection, she watched Coregon work. He possessed the ease of someone confident in his own abilities. His right hand rested on the small swell of his belly as his left wrote tirelessly, taking meticulous notes. Every detail that left Sharon Elliot's mouth--and people thought Ashlyn talked too much-- to describe Daniel's physical appearance and demeanor, was captured on the notepad. Coregon wore trim, wire-thin glasses that bordered his discerning, hazel eyes. His peppered, neatly trimmed hair and three-day beard, rounded out the face of a man who hid his pain well. But Ashlyn could see that clear as day; his pain mirrored her own.

She marveled at Captain Willis' patience as he waited for Sharon to stop talking. Daniel's mother must have explained--three times at least--why she didn't feel giving Daniel a cell phone was appropriate, and she defended her position vigorously, though the Captain hadn't taken arms against her decision. When she finally stopped talking, he politely reminded her that he'd met Daniel on several occasions, knew precisely what he looked like, and had been appraised often about why he didn't have a cell phone. He then reiterated the fact--one Anne had mentioned--that Jason's phone wasn't working, which meant locating the phone through GPS was out of the picture.

Ashlyn didn't miss the shiver of scorn that flashed across Sharon's face because the captain spent precious time inquiring about the other child. Anne swiftly produced a picture of Jason from her purse at the captain's request. She didn't say a word, and Ashlyn liked her immediately; she seemed kind. But just as Coregon tried to hide his pain, Ashlyn saw that Anne tried to hide her exhaustion. She'd seen that spaced expression before, on the face of a dear friend.

The fatigue wasn't the sign of a sleepless night, but rather evidence of a grinding heaviness that came from dealing with real life. She also felt sorry for Anne. Her parents worried when she got in any bit of trouble, or even came home late from school. Ashlyn couldn't imagine how they'd feel if she went missing for so many hours.

"Thank you Anne, that'll be fine." Coregon Willis said. He pulled Ashlyn from her reverie with his soft-but-deep rasp. "How long have the boys been gone?"

"I guess since after school, Officer-" Anne answered.

"Coregon, please."

"Sorry, so no more than six hours," she continued. "Mr. Baker-"

"John, please."

Ashlyn heard a tiny sigh escape from Anne's lips. Mr. Baker often made Ashlyn want to sigh as well. When she'd walked into the Elliots' house, she let out a panicked squeak the moment she saw her bumbling teacher. She suspected he was still sore with her over the volcano incident, but he barely noticed her other than a cordial hello. This puzzled Ashlyn until she figured he assumed she'd come at Coregon's request.

That's what adults did, they assumed. The older she got, the more she noticed when adults wanted to believe something was one way--even if it wasn't--they'd do anything to discredit the truth staring them in the face. Well, maybe not all adults were like that, but enough to make her weary. Like Mr. Baker, he *had* to have known she was messing with him during class, right? Maybe he just didn't give her unexpected intelligence deserving credit.

"John, sorry," Anne continued. "As *John* mentioned earlier *Coregon*, both boys were in his class, which is the last period of the day."

"I saw them too," Ashlyn added. She clasped her hands on the table and gave Coregon a quick, innocent look. *Missing detail...*

"Was anything out of the ordinary?" Coregon inquired.

Mr. Baker put a paw-like hand to his chin, and scrunched his eyebrows. Ashlyn knew that was a clue her teacher was thinking of the best way to say something difficult. He was a careful man, and she appreciated that, but she still had to stop herself from laughing--he reminded her of a fat owl.

"There is the fact that Jason fell asleep during class. But even before that, he seemed out of sorts, like he was in a daze. I talked to him afterwards, but he appeared okay then. That was 2:15."

"Ashlyn, you mentioned you saw Jason and Daniel at the bike racks after school?"

She turned to the captain, eyes wide.

"Am I allowed to talk?"

Coregon barely glanced up from his note-pad.

"Yes, you may speak now."

Ashlyn drew a breath and straightened her back.

"As I was getting my bike, I saw them at the racks and Jason looked fine. They both grabbed Daniel's bike. Jason hopped on the seat. He made Daniel ride on the pegs, which Daniel didn't seem very happy about." She snuck a glance at Sharon Elliot and wasn't surprised by the woman's poorly hidden sneer. "Then they went tearing off down the street."

"That's the last time you saw them?" Coregon asked.

Every face stared at her. Aside from Captain Willis, they were filled with tension and worry. But she saw something else in Sharon's eyes--distrust, anger--of what, Ashlyn didn't know. Sharon's gaze made Ashlyn feel exposed, like she was being blamed for something that wasn't her fault.

"That's... yes," she said finally, averting her eyes from Sharon's glare.

"I see," Coregon replied. Ashlyn tried to signal him to watch Sharon closely, but his attention remained with his notes.

Anne interjected, "If that's the last anyone saw them, we don't know whether the boys are even still together."

"True," Coregon replied. "But even if they're not together now, finding one of the boys will help us find the other."

"How long will it take you to find... them?" Sharon asked.

Am I the only one that heard the pause? Ashlyn wondered glancing stealthily around the room. She glowered at Sharon. She tried hard not to judge people harshly, but in Sharon's case... Oh, how Ashlyn hated her!

"We're dealing with a six-to-seven hour time-window and I don't want to waste any more time," Coregon said. "What I need from all of you, is cooperation. The first thing my department has to establish, before I can authorize various search channels is that the boys are actually missing by Police definition."

Sharon opened her mouth to protest but Coregon stayed her response with a brisk wave of his hand. "Sharon, I assure you from the description of the events I've been told and from what I understand of the nature of the boys, I will be able to make the determination quickly."

Heads nodded and Ashlyn knew they all wanted to trust Captain Willis so badly. They wanted to believe he'd find the boys soon. But he wasn't perfect; Ashlyn knew that better than most, though she wasn't supposed to admit it. Yet she wanted him to be as good as he could be, and hoped he'd find them. Not just because she liked Jason, but, well, she was frightened. She could feel that there was something truly odd about their disappearance.

"What do you need us to do, Coregon?" Sharon asked.

"Let me do my job."

Ashlyn loved the way he said things like that--just like in a movie-- no room for compromise. "Ashton is a nice place," the Captain pressed on, "and people like to think of themselves as being safe here. We don't need anybody stirred up over speculations."

Ashlyn caught Coregon's glance at Sharon Elliot.

"You want us to keep quiet?" Anne asked.

Sharon looked like she might explode.

"For how long? I'm going to put signs around town and organize concerned-citizen searches. I have to do something other than sit on my hands, Coregon."

"I'll let you know if citizen action is needed. But first, the Ashton Police will do everything we can to find them. We'll send email blasts and faxes to local and state media outlets, post a local area of alert, send out radio broadcasts to state law enforcement agencies to start, but we have to do it our way, by our protocol." The Captain cast an intelligent glance at Sharon. "I wish Charles had waited for me to get here, before going to search for Daniel."

She probably sent him out before Coregon got here on purpose, Ashlyn reasoned, noticing Sharon's blushed cheeks.

"There's a methodology to these situations," Coregon said. "We have to rule out certain benign possibilities, ascertain the potential for criminal action behind the disappearance. I know this isn't what you want to hear Sharon, but your cooperation is paramount."

This is going to be a tough case, Ashlyn thought. She peered at the disgruntled frown pursing Sharon's lips and cast Coregon a knowing look. *He's going to need me more than ever...*

–ⓞ⋀ⓢ–

Ashlyn assured Captain Willis she didn't need a ride home, and he definitely didn't need to call her parents. After he drove away, she waited in the shadows beside Anne's car. Jason's mother walked like a sulking ghost down the driveway, and Ashlyn's heart lurched. She didn't want to take her by surprise, and stepped into the light of a street lamp.

"Anne?"

"Oh... Ashlyn," Anne replied weakly.

"Can I talk to you for a minute?"

"Of course."

Ashlyn leaned closer, as if about to reveal a great secret. "It's about the way Jason was acting in class."

"What way?" Anne's face shone with a thirst for any helpful detail, and Ashlyn took the cue to press forward.

"Jason is, medically speaking, healthy?"

Jason's mother was taken aback. Clearly, this wasn't a question she expected.

"Yes... He's never had any serious health issues. Why?"

"'Cause he looked sick," Ashlyn continued. "Not throw-up-everywhere sick, like when my brother tried to drink an entire gallon of milk; more like, it's summer vacation so you're not faking sick to stay home from school, but you still don't want to hang out with friends or anything. That kind of sick."

"He was fine this morning," Anne replied.

Ashlyn could tell from the woman's listless voice how weary she felt.

"I didn't mean like a virus-sick -- more like -- I don't know... something different."

Ashlyn noted the doubt in Jason's mother's eyes, and knew what was coming. Anne was thinking of the nicest way to tell her she was just a kid, but not in those words.

"Ashlyn, it's really sweet of you to try and help out like this-"

"But you want me to stay out of it and leave it to professionals," Ashlyn said, finishing the inevitable conclusion of Anne's thought.

"No, I didn't mean that. I'll take all the help I can get!"

Ashlyn eyes widened as she saw the conviction in Anne's face. *She must be desperate.*

"Nothing dangerous, nothing that'll get you in trouble, but you can ask kids at school if they know anything. And maybe... ask around town, too."

The latter seemed like a clear violation of Coregon's final request. But Ashlyn couldn't shake the sympathy that filled her at the sight of Anne's haggard face. Ashlyn nodded resolutely; she couldn't let Anne down.

Chapter 21: A Clue of Desperation

The blackness of night was composed of tiny, moving crystals. There'd been many times in Chicago, Anne recalled, when she'd enjoyed losing herself in the fuzzy, comforting dark. She relished the soothing rhythm of Michael's breathing as she recalled childhood friends and first loves. A melancholy smile overtook her face as she admired how the briskly flowing current of time had taken a naïve child and turned her into a remembering woman. Could that innocent girl really have been her?

Night felt different without her husband's sturdy snores. She felt disoriented amidst shifting walls and slivers of dusty light peeking in from the street lamps outside. Time had become a sluggish fool. She tried to endure the torturous predawn hours, but each time she fell into a restless half-sleep, she imagined the door to Jason's room opening. She'd leap back to consciousness, her heart racing, but not daring to hope. The silence of the house that followed dispelled the dream, and she was left alone again.

Anne got out of bed and walked down the hall to peer into the dimness of Jason's room, to make absolutely sure. He was not there. She walked down the stairs, and went into the kitchen to get something to eat. She wasn't hungry, but needed something to take her mind off the lazy seconds.

Faced with the ghostly light of the open refrigerator, Anne forced herself to pull out a few ingredients. She carried them to the counter, and robotically made a sandwich. When she was done, she put the sandwich on the kitchen table and sat down at one of the creaky, wood-and-wicker chairs. But she couldn't muster the desire to take a bite. In the grey-pearl shade of the kitchen, she could think of nothing else to do; so she folded her arms on top of the table, laid her head upon them, and closed her eyes.

Anne came awake with a start. She wasn't sure how many times the doorbell had rung before she woke up. The dings and dongs continued in spirited procession as she wiped groggy sleep from her eyes.

"I'm coming!" she shouted, and scuttled towards to the front door. Anne swooped for the handle without bothering to ask who was there, but was prepared to lunge violently at whatever solicitor of goods, or unwanted religious doctrine, waited on the other side. She threw the door open, but all her anger melted away when she saw standing on her front steps, not the saintly smile of a phony, but the charming grin of a thirteen-year-old girl.

"Ashlyn!"

"I really like your doorbell," Ashlyn replied. "A lot of people try to make their doorbells too fancy. My brother's friend Tony's doorbell plays the "Mexican Hat Dance," which is cool the first time... I guess."

"What are you doing here?" Anne asked, trying to be polite.

"Oh right—Oh, your house is so pretty!" Ashlyn exclaimed, sliding past Anne and in through the front door without waiting for an invitation. Anne admired the girl's lack of forbearance. With almost anyone else, Anne would have been angered by the presumption to barge into her house. But as she watched Ashlyn examine pictures--and ceiling molding--with genuine interest, Anne had to smile.

"Thank you, Ashlyn. Now, can I help you with something?"

"I... I was wondering if Jason ever came home last night," the girl finally said, but Anne suspected that was not her main intent.

"No... he never did," Anne replied. Her words felt sharp

as a blade on her tongue.

"Oh," the girl mumbled, but she didn't move and Anne regarded her curiously.

"I appreciate you following up, but I haven't learned anything new since last night. Don't you need to go to school?"

The girl didn't move as she debated whether or not to say something.

"Look," Ashlyn said suddenly. Anne was taken aback by the stern tone in the girl's voice. "I really want to tell you something... important."

"Whatever it's about I-"

"But... I need to know it's just between us."

For a moment, Anne almost felt intimidated by the thirteen-year-old's emphatic glare.

"That depends on what you want to tell me," Anne replied.

Ashlyn blushed, and Anne thought she understood.

"Do you have a crush on Jason?"

"A crush? I don't think anybody calls it that anymore, Mrs. Swann. I do... like your son though."

Anne smiled. "That's nothing to be embarrassed about Ashlyn."

Anne thought she was being kind, but the girl responded bluntly.

"I know that. That's not the thing that has to be just-between-us."

Anne couldn't hide her confusion.

"So what do you need to tell me, what happened?"

"Well," Ashlyn replied, "I was supposed to go straight home after school yesterday to help my mom get groceries."

Anne felt her face flush. "But you didn't..."

"I... I was worried. You should've seen Jason in class; he was acting really weird! So...I followed him and Daniel-"

"What do you know?!" Anne uttered ferociously. Ashlyn took a step back. Fear radiated from the girl's face.

"I'm sorry! I didn't mean to snap at you. Please... please tell me what you know."

Anne held a hand out to Ashlyn, inviting her back from a defensive stance. The suspicion oozing from Ashlyn's eyes almost brought Anne to tears.

"Please Ashlyn."

The girl sighed, and stepped towards Anne.

"The bike racks weren't the last place I saw Jason and Daniel."

Anne's ears perked up like a wolf.

"I followed them to Circle Park," Ashlyn continued. "I guess Jason left his bike there in the morning. He must've been distracted by whoever he was talking to. I wonder how he got to school?"

Anne didn't understand.

"Yesterday morning? You saw him before school, too?"

"Not on purpose," Ashlyn countered. "I was passing the park on my way to school and heard him talking to someone."

"You mean Daniel? Was he talking to Daniel?"

"No... it wasn't Daniel," Ashlyn said. "He was there too, but not in the park."

Anne felt a cold sweat pierce her pores.

"So who was he talking to?"

"I couldn't really see through the trees," Ashlyn admitted. "I just heard Jason's voice. *Only* his, but I know he was talking to someone. But in the afternoon, after Jason found his bike, he came back here. Then he left his bike by the gate and-"

Anne couldn't believe what she'd heard. "His bike is here? He was *here* yesterday afternoon?!"

The girl glanced at her oddly, perhaps finding the admission hard to believe as well.

"He left it right inside the gate to your backyard. Didn't you see it?"

Anne felt like a fool. "No, I guess I... I haven't been outside since I got home last night."

"Oh, well, Daniel followed him here, too. I think he was trying to be all sneaky, and spy on what Jason was doing, but

I could see him clear as day. He's not very good at hiding. He's pretty clumsy, and he's always scrunching his eyebrows... like this," Ashlyn said, doing her best impression of Daniel's nervous face.

Anne was astonished. "Daniel was here, too?!"

"Yeah, his bike is right next to Jason's."

How had she missed the bikes?! Anne imagined how furious Sharon was going to be when she learned this information. But that wasn't important now.

"What did you say to them?" Anne asked.

"Nothing," Ashlyn replied. "I didn't get a chance. I was kind of watching them from afar at the park. Jason was just sitting in the grass by his bike, but then he must've remembered something important, because he just took off all of the sudden. Daniel went off after him, and I chased Daniel. By the time I caught them here, Jason was running into the woods and Daniel was trying to catch up."

"Into the woods?" Anne had to fight past the lump in her throat to get the words out.

"I couldn't follow him Mrs. Swann, I'm sorry! I was late and my mom would've *killed* me!"

Anne tried to take a deep breath.

"It's okay, Ashlyn. You don't have anything to be sorry for." She began pacing, trying to think of what she was missing.

"I thought it might have been this guy..." the girl suddenly said, disrupting Anne's concentration.

"What guy, you mean in the woods?"

"No, I meant yesterday morning-- Jason might have been talking to this guy in the park," Ashlyn answered.

"Who is he?" Anne asked. She tried to stay calm, but was sure her desperation was palpable.

"He's... he's no one."

The girl spoke too carefully for Anne's liking.

"Just somebody that hangs out in the park sometimes. My mom doesn't like me going to the park when he's there, but he's harmless."

Anne's mind was a flurry of movement. She had to call Captain Willis right away to tell him about the bikes and the woods. As for the mysterious person in the park, she had no evidence other than the hearsay of a thirteen-year-old. She was sure there was something Ashlyn wasn't telling her, but Anne didn't think that had anything to do with Jason. On the other hand, if she ignored the omission and it turned out to be something important, she'd never forgive herself. She had to be careful; this new information was a place to start.

"Thank you Ashlyn, you have no idea how helpful you've been," Anne said. She glanced around the room for her phone. Ashlyn followed her darting movement.

"You're welcome. By the way, I already told Captain Willis about the bikes and the woods. "

Anne was taken aback. Could the girl read her mind? "You did?"

"Yeah, he won't tell my mom I didn't go straight home. Neither will you, right?"

Anne shook her head in assurance.

"But if you already told Coregon, why are you telling me?"

A staunch expression took hold of Ashlyn's face.

"I know what it's like to be worried about someone you love. It's the worst feeling in the world."

Anne recognized a familiar pain etched on Ashlyn's face, but the girl was too young to know that agony, wasn't she?

"Thank you Ashlyn, I appreciate your kindness more than I can say."

The door to the Swann house closed behind her as Ashlyn walked to her bike. She felt good for helping, but why had she mentioned the guy in the park?! She'd let compassion cloud her judgment. Ashlyn glanced back at the closed door and tried to imagine what unseen action Anne was taking. She couldn't fight off a nagging feeling that she shouldn't have said anything at all.

Chapter 22: Darka Aravan

The back of Jason's head rested in the crook between the top of his shoulder blades. He couldn't bend his neck back any farther, but he still couldn't see the top of what he was looking at. The curvature of the planet kept the structure hidden beyond the horizon for the first half-mile of their journey from the ship. When it finally came into view, the surprise of seeing something so massive made him think it was an illusion, a magnificent oasis on the otherwise barren world. Now, as Jason stood beside its base, the sheer size of the wall was almost laughable.

He returned his head upright to ease the strain on his neck. Daniel stood only a few steps away, bending his neck into the same contortion. The wall rose so high, Jason couldn't see any distance between the top and the pea soup cloud belt. To his right and left, the barrier stretched from horizon to horizon, and made Chicago's imposing skyline look like a child's building blocks. He had no idea what the wall's purpose was, but from his perspective the construction almost looked like a bridge from the land to the cloud-filled sky.

"This is the most amazing thing I've ever seen."

"It's the most beautiful thing I've ever seen," Daniel replied.

The wall wasn't made of the rock that surrounded them on all sides, but rather a synthetic material that had a dark-grey sheen, like titanium. As far as Jason could tell, every inch of the wall's surface was intricately carved with images that revealed a vibrant life they hadn't yet found on the planet.

Directly in front of him, no less than forty feet across, and perhaps twenty feet from top-to-bottom, was a carving of a serpent-like being. The imposing, coiled body had four arms, each ending in giant hands. Each hand had nine, wide, blunt fingers. The creature had a huge, bullet-shaped head, featureless except for a giant eye that seemed to stare right into him. The more he stared back, the more he felt like something was alive within those eyes, watching him, examining him. His heart beat rapidly, and he broke the gaze.

He focused his attention on the flowing script that surrounded the entire carving. The script was in a language he couldn't understand, and reminded him of the incoherent scribbles of a three-year-old, rather than the carefully worked cursive of an advanced civilization.

"What is this?" Jason asked, turning to the Archivist. He found Nierion examining another carving of roughly the same size depicting a similar, but uncoiled, creature, surrounded by the same scribbled text.

"I... I am at a lost to explain it, Jason," the Archivist answered. "I recognize the composition as an ancient dialect of the Ranis Aun. The images are depictions of Ranis Aun, and the text suggests that each individual pictured was an important member of the species. Some date back more than five million years."

"There must be thousands of them," Daniel observed.

"Indeed," the Archivist agreed. "But I have no idea of its purpose. There is certainly no mention of this structure in the Archive."

Jason wasn't as puzzled.

"It's a wall. Usually that means keeping something out, or something in. Maybe it's the wall to a city."

That seemed sensible enough, but Daniel wasn't convinced.

"I thought the Ranis Aun lived underground. Why would they build a wall on the surface?"

"What does it matter why? It's here!" Jason barked. He caught a squint of concern on Daniel's face, and took a deep breath. "Sorry, all I meant was, we can guess all we want; but we're supposed to be looking for the energy source Nierion detected."

"It is close," the Archivist said. "Not more than a few hundred feet to our right."

Daniel barely noticed Jason take off in the direction Nierion mentioned. He couldn't tear his gaze from the single, hypnotic eye in the carving looming above him. It reminded him of a portrait he'd seen in a museum when he was much younger: no matter where he looked, no matter which side of the painting he stood, the man in the painting stared directly at *him*.

Daniel was frightened then, now he was just... unsettled. He wasn't sure why, but he sensed that the unmoving eye was trying to tell him something important--a spirit with a warning from an age long past. But the vital message was lost to five million years thrust in between. Daniel tore his gaze away and studied Nierion; though he couldn't read the being's emotions, its silence convinced him that the Archivist was baffled.

"Do you know what it's made of, Nierion?"

The Archivist slowly swiveled to face him. The alien being's visors held a faint, violet hue that winked out, leaving them empty.

"It is a metallic alloy created by the Ranis Aun noted in the Archive as the primary building material of their subterranean cities. How such a massive quantity was brought to the surface I-"

"Over here!" Jason shouted.

The Archivist left Daniel and glided over the landscape to see what Jason found.

"Wait, what were you going to say?" Daniel asked the empty air left in Nierion's wake. Either it hadn't heard him, or it was intentionally ignoring him. Daniel sighed, and scampered towards Jason.

His stomach churned when he saw what Jason called them to see; an intimidating, perfect circle, made of an ink-black substance, cut into the wall. Starting about a foot off the ground, the circle stretched at least fifty feet above him, surrounded by a series of concentric rings containing the script of the Ranis Aun. Daniel found the wall disquieting enough, but the pitch-black circle screamed "danger."

"I touched it, and my finger went right through," Jason remarked haphazardly.

"You touched it?!" Daniel cried.

Jason brushed Daniel's concern aside. "What's the big deal? It didn't do anything."

"You could have been... I don't know... Vaporized!" Daniel shot back.

Jason slowly turned towards Daniel. His shoulders tensed as he approached his classmate.

"Are you saying I'm stupid?" Jason asked with a cocked head, his eyes narrowed into slits.

Not now, Daniel thought.

"No! Jason, please... We just have to be careful okay?"

And it was a stupid thing to do! Daniel tried to keep his expression calm, but that was hard. Keeping Jason levelheaded was hard enough, but Daniel's brain was flashing warning signs from all directions. He blamed Jason for this anxiety, after all, *he* was the one spouting conspiracy theories. Daniel felt like he'd been read a ghost story just before going to bed, and standing between the Archivist and the ominous circle wasn't helping his nerves.

"I *was* being careful Daniel; I only put my finger in."

Jason's tone said he was itching for a fight, something that Daniel was desperate to avoid. He *had* to steer the conversation elsewhere.

"Nierion, do you know what the writing around the circle says?"

"Yes," the Archivist answered. "'This is the Way to Spiria Inan. This is the Way that made Ijiran Ranis Jarna Aun successor of Bana Ranis Jarna Aun, successor of...' It appears to include a long list of past rulers of the city Spiria Inan. The first name is Nisah Najarana Jarna Aun. The grammar and words are incomplete at various sections, as if they have been reworked several times."

"See," Jason butted in, "I told you it was the way to a city."

Daniel ignored him, and addressed the Archivist.

"Reworked intentionally?"

"Perhaps. It almost looks like each one was trying to take credit."

"For the city," Daniel followed.

"No... the language is very clear; they are taking credit for the Way itself."

"Why would they care about that?" Daniel asked.

Jason huffed.

"They're aliens Daniel, who knows what they care about? Can we just go to the city please?"

"I don't have a good feeling about this Jason; why are you in such a rush?"

Jason grabbed Daniel's arm and pulled him aside with a frighteningly familiar strength.

"Look," Jason said in a harsh whisper, "are you blind? Can you not see what the Ranis Aun can do? They probably have spaceships and scientists and doctors of their own! They can fix whatever's wrong with me! They can take us home. I have to get home!"

"Maybe they can," Daniel whispered back, "but we shouldn't go barging through dark portals in creepy walls without finding out a few facts first!"

The grip loosened, and Daniel was tossed aside like a moldy loaf of bread.

"You really are a coward."

Daniel fought back tears. *He doesn't mean it, he's sick. And I promised I'd help...*

"Does the writing say anything useful?" Jason asked the Archivist.

"Two words are repeated with mention of every name, 'Darka Aravan.'"

"What does that mean?"

"The closest I can translate into your language, is 'Night

Path.'"

"Like… you're only supposed to take it at night?" Daniel asked.

"Because it's black as night," Jason proposed without taking his eyes from the giant circle.

"It is not a literal meaning," the Archivist corrected. "The word Darka implies an adjustment of sight, a change in perspective. Aravan can also mean 'journey' in the proper context."

"A journey of perspective; what does that mean?" Daniel wondered.

"I do not know," the Archivist said, to Daniel's dismay. "I have never been here before."

"But one of you has, right?" Daniel asked. "You said archivists come to this planet all the time. You must know something about it."

"As I said, there has never been an issue with Esan's Eyes before. I doubt an archivist has ever seen any of this."

Daniel pondered Nierion's words as he walked up to Jason. Something didn't seem right, but he couldn't put his finger on precisely what. He raised his hand and pressed his palm against the surface of the perfect circle. Waves rippled outwards from where he touched it, like he'd gently placed his hand on the surface of a pool. The rippling waves moved to the edges of the giant circle, where they disappeared, as if absorbed into the surrounding wall. Daniel put his entire hand through, and felt a slight resistance, as though he was pushing against a thin organic membrane. After only a few inches, he felt his hand emerge on the other side. The sensation was little different, just a faint tug on his fingers by something unseen on the other side. Daniel pulled his hand back, and was relieved to find it intact.

"We can't walk into that thing without knowing what's on the other side."

"I share your apprehension," the Archivist responded. Daniel was stunned. He'd been expecting the alien to cajole him, if not just shove him through the entrance. "I have yet to determine why this... object is giving off such a unique energy signature. I think we should return to the ship. I have additional-"

"No!" Jason screamed. "We're so close!"

Daniel's face drained of blood. In an instant, Jason had gone from quiet to possessed.

"Close to what?"

"Are you kidding me? What's wrong with both of you, can't you feel it?!"

Nierion's visors burst to life. They shimmered in vibrant, azure blue.

"Jason, step away."

Jason turned his back to the circle and spread his legs in a defensive stance.

"No."

A coiled arm of black metal fired from a compartment in the Archivist's abdomen. It lunged for Jason, but was too late; Jason had leapt into the circle.

Undulating waves of black liquid spread out from his body, but they quickly stilled and relinquished any evidence that he'd been there a moment before.

"What just happened?!" Daniel cried.

The Archivist's visors were still blazoned in blue.

"How could I have missed it?!"

"Missed what? What's going on?!"

"The energy source... I should have recognized it in a dormant state, but how could it be here?!"

The fear in the Archivist's voice shook Daniel to the bone.

"What do you sense?"

"Jason activated it, I have no idea how! We have no choice, we have to follow him!"

Daniel wanted to cry, he wanted to scream, but his words came out meekly.

"What did he activate?"

"A Travel Sequence."

Daniel knew he'd heard wrong.

"You mean like on the ship, how can that be?!"

Nierion's visors dimmed. The Archivist had no answer for Daniel, and said nothing, but whirled back to the circular portal, and glided through.

Daniel was left staring at the giant, black pupil. He hoped for the briefest of moments that he was the butt of a bad joke. He waited for Jason and the Archivist to jump back out of the circle, laughing in good fun. But of course, they didn't.

If Nierion was right, they were already somewhere very far away.

Chapter 23: Follow the Butterflies

The giant black circle stared at Daniel. He forced himself to stare back. He almost leapt straight in after the Archivist, but he needed to prepare himself. If Nierion was correct about the Travel Sequence, then Daniel was in store for a great deal of pain. But there was no other choice; he had no hope of helping Jason, or getting back home, if he didn't follow. He stepped up to the portal and tried again to see what lay beyond, but the smooth surface betrayed nothing. He took a deep breath, shut his eyes tightly, and jumped through. *Like jumping into a pool,* Daniel thought as the black liquid enveloped him and supported his mass. *This isn't so-*

The pressure instantly intensified and he was squeezed, as if constricted by a giant snake. At the same time, his body was stretched; his muscles, organs and bones felt like they'd tear apart. Yet, he was also being pushed inward, pressed into a single point. A searing heat, so hot it felt more like ice than fire, penetrated him. He felt like he was drowning in a star. Memories and thoughts melted away, eradicating any trace of consciousness. But then everything stopped, and he was held tightly in a single, dark point. There was no space, there was no time; yet he could think clearly, could see himself clearly from the outside, like in a dream.

This is different, he thought. Then, from outside the single point of dark, a wonderful breeze, like on a crisp fall day, swept through his mind. His entire life flashed before him, and the breeze danced through each infinitesimally small moment, leaving traces like tiny droplets of water resting on a leaf. Yes, the unfathomable complexity of who he was made perfect sense to Daniel. He watched from outside himself, like a spirit of light. There were billions of leaves, a tiny droplet deposited on each. The leaves were attached to millions of branches; the branches to a sturdy trunk. The droplets spread out and connected to one-another. They multiplied until the whole tree was encapsulated in the crystal clarity of his existence.

Then the light dimmed and Daniel couldn't see the tree, couldn't see or feel anything but a terrible darkness. He tried to reach beyond the tiny point of dark, but nothing was there. *Please,* he begged, *please, I don't want to be stuck here forever, I want my body back. I want light!*

Slowly, things began to make sense again. The world expanded until he was once more just a tiny speck in an immeasurable universe. The darkness abated and Daniel found himself in an immense, circular room. There was no sign of the gateway through which he'd travelled.

The room was stark white, and the floor, walls and ceiling gave off a subtle glow of peaceful, directionless light, just like he'd wanted. Though everything seemed and felt solid, Daniel was struck by the odd notion that they weren't as solid as they could be, and that this lack was somehow his fault. The feeling made no sense and yet, he knew it was right. He crossed the room to the other side. The chamber was at least two hundred feet in diameter, and the ceiling appeared equally high. But there was nothing present other than the stark white walls; no doors, no portals, and no one else but him.

"Jason!" There was no reply, not even an echo.

"Jason, where are you? Nierion?" he shouted again into the cavernous room. "I don't understand, we went through the same portal, so where did he go, and where did Nierion go?!" Daniel whispered. He didn't want to admit that the answer was obvious: *Who knew? Maybe another dimension, maybe a room like this but light-years away, maybe they didn't survive the Travel Sequence.* There were infinite possibilities and Daniel had no answer. A drenching fear burrowed from his pores and his heart thumped against his rib cage. He closed his eyes from the dizzying emptiness of the massive room.

Daniel tried to calm down but couldn't focus. His thoughts wandered and carried him to old memories. He felt like a little ship riding the ebb and flow of ocean waves. They were so vivid; he reached out to touch one…

–◌⌒§–

…A CHILLY AND PLEASANT NIGHT. CUD-DLED AND WARM BENEATH THE COVERS OF HIS BED. SHE READS MY FAVORITE STORY. A YOUNG BOY LIKE ME, WHO TRAVELS TO FAR OFF LANDS AND SEES AMAZING THINGS. BUT I WONDER…

"IS THIS REAL?" I ASK HER, "THE STORY I MEAN."

MY MOTHER SMILES, I LOVE HER SMILE…

"OF COURSE IT'S REAL, IN YOUR IMAGI-NATION," SHE TELLS ME…

I'M DISAPPOINTED, I DON'T UNDERSTAND; IS SHE LYING? SHE ALWAYS SAYS I HAVE TO TELL THE TRUTH, WHY IS SHE LYING? "IMAGINATION ISN'T REAL," I TELL HER…

"YOU CAN'T TOUCH IT, YOU CAN'T TASTE IT, BUT IT'S REAL," SHE TELLS ME. HER EYES LOOK SO KIND, BUT I DON'T UNDERSTAND WHAT SHE MEANS… I'VE SEEN THINGS I THOUGHT WERE KIND BUT WEREN'T… WHY WON'T SHE TELL ME THE TRUTH? "WHAT DOES THAT MEAN?" I ASK HER…

SHE KISSES MY CHEEK, BRUSHES HER HAND THROUGH MY HAIR, AND PULLS THE COVERS UP TO MY NECK. SHE KNEELS DOWN, WHISPERS IN MY EAR… "YOU CAN'T TOUCH IT, YOU CAN'T TASTE IT, BUT IT'S REAL…"

–◌⌒§–

Daniel's eyelids burst open and he clutched at his chest, trying to calm his heaving lungs. After several deep breaths, he found the strength to move and wiped away the salty wetness from beneath his eyes. The memory was already fading. The shapes of the child and mother melted back into the fog of his mind. But it felt so real! He feared closing his eyes again; he didn't even want to blink. *Why was he in this room but not Jason or Nierion?* The stark white walls, faintly glowing held no answers.

Maybe they'd been here but already left. Maybe there was a way out that he couldn't see. Maybe the exit was hidden in the featureless walls and strange light that cast no shadows. Daniel scanned the room and felt exposed. He decided it was too bright, like being in a sweltering desert. The room suddenly dimmed, and the stark white of the walls fell under a cover of grey shadow.

Daniel stood very still. He wanted the room to be bright again, and the white walls returned. He imagined a starry night sky, and the ceiling dissolved into midnight blue. Twinkling dots of light trickled down, but there was something ephemeral about it all. Daniel's feeling, that everything here was not quite *real*, returned. He didn't like that the room seemed to read his thoughts. Under the starry sky he contemplated having everything he'd ever desired, but right now he only wanted a way out. He needed to find Jason; he needed to help his friend. In response, an empty frame appeared on the far wall.

"Of course!" Daniel said aloud, marveling at the simplicity. He just had to imagine a way to leave!

Daniel walked towards the frame. As he focused on finding Jason in his mind, he was reminded of another friend he'd left behind many years ago. *No, he left me!* With each step, the memory of that day opened like a fresh wound, and the sadness he'd thought gone, poured into the cut.

…Doesn't make sense, why won't he tell me where he's going?

Daniel had taken only a handful of steps when he noticed that the frame was considerably closer. With each step he took, the frame became larger and larger, but not the wall behind it. He realized that it wasn't actually attached to the wall, but was being pulled towards him as if by magnetic attraction.

...Says it's too dangerous for me, says I wouldn't understand. Understand what? Where does he have to go?

Ten more steps and the rectangular frame was about five feet away. He couldn't tell what it was made of under the dim sky. Daniel wondered what he was supposed to imagine within the frame, but sadness distracted him.

"... But you're my only friend," I tell him. He doesn't care, says that's not enough, says he's tired and has to leave. I want to go with him, under the midnight sky, just like an endless midnight sea...

Daniel took three large steps forward. The frame moved towards him as well; only a couple of feet left between them. He could now see details and sucked in his breath.

The frame was made of thousands of tiny creatures that resembled moon-jellyfish. They glowed in noctilucent blue and moved over each other like schools of fish on preordained paths. They called to him with gentle pulses of their bodies:

"THIS IS WHAT YOU WANT."

He stepped close to the frame and reached to touch the jellies. Reality as he knew it slowed down. The prior stillness of the room felt like a bursting carnival of light and energy; too much energy, everything moving too quickly. This was better. The beating of his heart felt like the measured pendulum swing of a grandfather clock. The chaotic blizzard of thought that always seemed so normal was replaced with a few faint snowflakes drifting in a breeze. He remembered having just been very sad, but couldn't remember why. The Jellies confirmed this with comforting pulses of their bodies:

"NO REASON TO BE SAD."

Time came to a stop and Daniel didn't miss it one bit. How had he ever endured the incessant progression of one moment to the next in the first place? He felt like every instance of his life had been spent flailing his arms in the rapids of a river. He wished to drift away and never worry about anything again. He needed to touch the Jellies, but something held him back. Daniel's hand met resistance, like he was pushing into a thick foam mattress.

"TRY AGAIN," THE JELLIES PULSED, "THIS IS WHAT YOU WANT."

Daniel pressed through the resistance, then felt soothed, as if being carried by a placid current, into nothingness…

– ◯ ⋔ Ⳬ –

HE WAS A PEBBLE FLOATING IN AN OCEAN, DRIFTING ON THE CURRENT, CARRIED BY THE OCEAN'S VAST FORCE. HE WAS SWALLOWED BY FISH AND DISCARDED, SWALLOWED AND DISCARDED, SWALLOWED AND DISCARDED. HE WAS NOTHING TO THEM-- NOT SUSTENANCE, NOT PROTECTION, NOT CAMOU-FLAGE --JUST A TINY PIECE OF A WORLD THEY COULDN'T ESCAPE. THE CURRENT SPILLED HIM ONTO A BEACH. THERE, SURROUNDED BY OTHER PEBBLES, HE FELT PURGED FROM THE ONLY WORLD HE'D KNOWN. EVERYTHING WAS DIFFERENT. HE'D NEVER BEEN OUTSIDE THE OCEAN BEFORE! HOW AMAZING TO DISCOVER THAT THE OCEAN WAS ONLY SO LARGE, ITS POWER ONLY SO GREAT, ITS DEPTHS ONLY SO DEEP AND PERHAPS HE WAS FINALLY FREE OF A PRISON HE NEVER SUSPECTED TO…

– ◯ ⋔ Ⳬ –

Daniel was jolted from his reverie by an unseen force. The stark white room and the midnight sky rushed back into him. His mass felt like lead chains; his mind exploded in a squall of jabbering thoughts. The cacophony of the silent room filled his ears with pain. And time, that horrible juggernaut, pushed against him with tremendous might. But in the next moment, his misery ended and everything seemed… normal.

He peered into the center of the frame, trying to discern

the outline of something invisible, but there was nothing to be seen. He stepped back, took a deep breath, and turned to observe the room. With a thought, he changed the ceiling back to how he'd first found it; stark, shadow-less white, with a faint glow of light. Gazing at the ceiling made him feel totally insignificant. He was so tired of being small.

… That's why I can't find you. I'm too small, no one takes me seriously. I wanted to talk to the policeman; he seemed kind, like he would listen, but no one would take me…

Daniel turned back to the frame, which was no longer made of the moon-jellies. Instead, countless, sea green butterflies covered in cotton-white dots danced and fluttered their wings. They flew counter-clockwise around the borders of the frame. As they moved, they shifted shape and became droplets of lavender rain. The droplets continued along the frame's path transforming back into butterflies on the other side.

To be a butterfly, Daniel thought, as he lost himself in the entrancing, rhythmic transformation. They twisted in and out of each other's flight paths, creating a moving helix.

…if I could fly like them, I could find you. If I could fly, I wouldn't feel so small.

Delicate wings sailed him across the cosmos. Galaxies blinked in and out of existence. His body expanded until he couldn't feel his beginning or his end. He flew so fast that particles of light seeped from the tips of his fingers and toes, to be gobbled up into a waiting universe. If he could only reach the butterflies; if he could only touch them, he knew he could fly forever and be free from the burden of being small-- the burden of being a child. Daniel pushed forward with all his might.

"YES," THE BUTTERFLIES WHISPERED WITH LITTLE FLIPS OF THEIR WINGS. "TRY HARDER."

But the closer he got, the stronger was the resistance. Daniel mustered his strength, his muscles contracted, and his skin tightened, but something kept him at bay. He gave one last, valiant push, but a deafening voice exploded in his head.

"Stop!"

The world suddenly slowed, and Daniel felt like he was trapped in slime. He could barely move. He pulled back his hand and shook off his trance. It was as if a boulder had fallen on his back and broken his wings. After a moment, the room returned to normal.

"This isn't what you're looking for..."

There was a familiarity to the voice, a sense of authority that reminded Daniel of something he'd almost forgotten; the alien thing keeping him alive.

The suit was speaking to him.

Chapter 24: The Way Things Could Be

I must be going crazy, Daniel thought. How could the suit tell him what to do? It was too much to take. What else was going to crawl up from the storehouses of the impossible?

"You need to step away," the inner voice implored.

Daniel complied. He took several steps back from the frame. With each step, he felt its call diminish. Eventually, as if sensing he no longer wanted what was offered, the frame dematerialized before Daniel's eyes. Part of him felt sad he hadn't touched the butterflies.

"You should not feel sad."

"You can... How can you talk?" Daniel found himself asking aloud. "What are you?"

"I am you... a deeper part."

"What do you mean you're me; you're the suit aren't you?"

"There is no difference now. We are the same."

Daniel threw his arms up in the air in disbelief. "I thought you were just supposed to keep me alive. Why did the Shantar Anar make you mind-link with me?"

The inner voice was silent.

"Well?!" Daniel asked.

"You do not know."

"Right, and you aren't the suit, you're just some deep part of me that the suit is... making louder."

"Correct."

"If you're me, then why did you try to stop me... us... whatever?"

"To save our life."

"From what, butterflies?"

"No, immense danger, imminent death."

"Death? What are you talking about? I wasn't going to die, just touch the-"

"You wanted to disappear. Whatever this place is, complied with your request."

"But I was just trying to figure a way out of here, not to die!"

"I know that is what you believe consciously, at the forefront of your mind. You are on a mission to rescue a friend, but you are a... conflicted creature, many broken strands leading in different directions. It is not your fault; you were not taught how to be more."

"I'm not conflicted!" Daniel retorted. He was getting tired of this preachy subconscious part of him. "I'm trying to find Jason. He needs my help!"

"Jason is here too, wherever here is."

"How do you... how do I know that?"

"You followed him through the portal. How could one door lead to many different places?"

"You tell me!" Daniel exclaimed.

"He is here; you can sense his presence."

"I can?"

"It is just a sensation, like knowing someone is behind you though you have not seen them. He is dim, like a distant, but blazing, fire."

"How do I get to him?"

"We must take the same path."

Couldn't he even get a straight answer from himself? Daniel didn't want to talk to this inner voice anymore. Did he know himself so poorly that something this cold and alien could really be part of him? He sighed deeply and sat on the floor of the colossal chamber.

"The same path?" he whispered.

"You made the sky night; you made the butterflies to carry you away..."

"So I can make a path to Jason?"

The inner voice didn't confirm his question.

Daniel concentrated on the floor and beheld a sea of conformity. There wasn't a single point different from the rest.

He'd made the ceiling into a starry night, and the moon-jellies and the butterflies. They'd all been his choices, but he hadn't given them much rational thought. They seemed rather creations of his raw emotions. But that wasn't going to help him find Jason. His friend was in trouble. He didn't need sadness, he needed courage and strength.

What did courageous Daniel look like? he wondered as he stared at the polished white floor. He imagined he had the power to undo whatever the Archivist had done to Jason. He'd place his hands on his friend and take away his pain. And why stop with Jason? He could help everyone he cared about! Daniel saw this vision clearly, like a projection against the floor.

–◐↑੪–

... SHE'S SO SAD ALL THE TIME. DON'T SEE THE SAME KINDNESS IN HER EYES. "I'M SORRY YOUR FRIEND DIED," I TELL HER. EXPECT HER TO KISS MY CHEEK, PUT HER ARMS AROUND ME... SHE GRABS MY SHOULDERS INSTEAD. "WHO TOLD YOU THAT?"

–◐↑੪–

In a large circle around Daniel, the floor changed color. The stark white darkened through deep shades of grey.

–◐↑੪–

...SHE TUCKS ME IN, BUT DOESN'T SING TO ME. I TELL HER JOKES, BUT SHE DOESN'T LAUGH. SITS NEXT TO DAD, BUT DOESN'T HOLD HIS HAND. "I'M SORRY YOUR FRIEND DIED", I TELL HER. SHE DOESN'T RESPOND, JUST MOVES THE VASE ON THE CONSOLE TABLE TWO INCHES TO THE LEFT. "IT'S IN THE WRONG SPOT," MY MOTHER TELLS ME...

–◎↑§–

The circle continued to darken until it was pitch-black.

–◎↑§–

...SHE SMILES ALL THE TIME, BUT I KNOW SHE DOESN'T MEAN IT. "I LOST A FRIEND TOO," I TELL HER. SHE DOESN'T CARE. " I'M GOING TO FIND A WAY TO MAKE YOUR SMILES REAL AGAIN," I TELL HER. SHE MOVES A DINING CHAIR THREE INCHES TO THE RIGHT...

–◎↑§–

He was sinking into the ground and found himself surrounded by another pitch-black circle. He didn't have time to scramble or scream. *Not again,* he barely managed to think, as he tucked himself into a ball. His body sank into the placid liquid.

This time, only a fraction of a second passed before he was through the portal. Not even enough time to recall what he'd felt. Daniel let out a sigh of relief for small victories.

He was standing in a corridor no more than seven or eight feet tall and ten feet wide. The walls, floor and ceiling were grainy, meteor grey with dull veins of orange cut through them. He could see about thirty feet ahead, then the corridor was shrouded in darkness. This confined space was a comforting change from the giant emptiness of the last chamber.

He turned and came face-to-face with a dead-end five feet away. There was no sign of the gateway that brought him there. There was also no sign of Jason.

"I don't understand! You were supposed to take me to Jason!"

Silence followed his outcry.

"Who am I talking to?" Daniel asked himself. "I'm going crazy!"

The veins of dull orange began to glow. Those in the ceiling and wall curved further down the path, until they converged with the veins in the floor. The glow pushed back the darkness in the corridor. Thankful for a little more visibility, Daniel walked along the orange path.

With each step, the blackness abated. He soon heard groaning in the distance. He crouched down, solid and still. The noise took him off guard, mostly because it sounded familiar. He heard the aching moan again, and there was no mistaking that the sounds of pain were human.

"Jason!" Daniel shouted, as he sprinted down the hallway. The groans grew louder. After running a minute, he came upon a terrifying sight: Jason, in agony, writhing on the ground.

Chapter 25: Oh, the Possibilities

An incredible futuristic city was supposed to be waiting on the other side of the black circle. But he found only agonizing pain. Jason recognized the feeling as the same as he'd experienced on the Archivist's ship during the Travel Sequence. As he formulated the thought that this conclusion made no sense, his mind and body were stretched like rubber. His organs churned and rumbled. He felt catastrophic breakdown at a cellular level, and was sure he'd reached the end of his short life. He imagined departing as a trail of fine mist that dispersed into the corners of a dimension he couldn't comprehend. His body burned from within, but the heat felt more like a blighted winter frost than a blazing bar of steel.

Almost as quickly as the burning started, the heat dissipated into habitable warmth that was rather soothing. But Jason realized he couldn't feel any distinct parts of himself, as if his whole being was just a single point of space. *This is strange*, he thought, and then felt a breeze, like he was strolling through a park as cool, rushing air brushed his skin.

The breeze enveloped him and passed through him. The flutter of air swirled within his body… then stopped, as if it was searching for something hidden inside him... and found it. A key opening a lock was Jason's best description. Suddenly, he was overwhelmed by flashing images that made no sense, but evoked unbearable fear. He wanted to get away… to be someplace safe… to figure things out… to not be so lost…

The terror was suddenly gone. Jason felt solid ground beneath him and opened his eyes to see a long, narrow passage made of a grey metallic substance. The surface of the material shone in dim light, though Jason couldn't tell from where it emanated. There was no sign of Daniel or the Archivist. He hoped his companions were dumb enough to jump into the portal after him, and he waited in the silent corridor for them to arrive. As he lingered, his skin crawled with the eerie sensation that he was being watched.

"Is anyone there?" he called. Jason's voice carried down the corridor, but did not return.

"Daniel?! Nierion?!" Jason cried, but there was no response. *They have to come for me, right? They have to!* But Jason had no way to know if they did. He had no way to know where he even was. *If that really was a Travel Sequence... I could be a billion miles from them.*

He waited for what felt like hours for Daniel and the Archivist, but they never appeared. He was overcome with despair.

"I'm sorry Daniel; I should have listened to you."

Too late, he thought. He'd never felt more alone.

After ten steps, Jason came to an intersection leading to the right and to the left. He peered down each branch, but both corridors were exactly the same as the path where he stood. Neither way felt right.

How can a path "feel" right? Jason wondered, as he continued down the main corridor. A flicker in his periphery made him shoot around, but all that greeted him was the empty corridor. He shivered.

This place is creepy, he thought as he turned back. After a few steps, another intersection gutted the right and left of the path. He peered down the grey metal passageways and again there were no distinctive details.

"Hello?" Jason called down the right passage. No reply, no echo. Another flicker made Jason spin around, and the quiet corridor seemed to be mocking him.

"Who's there?!" he shouted. No reply, no echo.

"Daniel, is that you?! Answer me!"

No reply, no echo. Jason continued on, this time unsurprised by a close, third set of corridors leading off from his path.

"What is this place?" he whispered as his brow beaded with sweat. He tiptoed down the corridor and kept his ears keen for any and all sounds, but he heard nothing. He noted with some hopefulness, though he wasn't sure why, that he had to walk several hundred feet before a new set of right left passageways cut through his path.

Jason consoled himself that at least the longer passage was *something* a little different. He gazed down the right corridor and then the left. His heart sank. He couldn't say how he knew that these were the first two corridors he'd passed, but he was eerily sure they were.

Down the right-hand corridor, a momentary flicker of light against the grey walls caught his attention. He left the path he was on and hurried towards the source of the light. When he arrived where he was sure he'd seen the flicker, nothing was there.

Disappointed, he turned to regain the main path, but hit a dead end.

"Stop it!" he yelled into the silence. "What do you want from me?"

No reply, no echo. Tears welled in his eyes. How could he have been so stupid?! Daniel warned him, but he didn't listen. Why hadn't he listened?!

"I'm sorry Daniel," he whispered.

The words dripped from his mouth and fell to a soft death on the ground. He walked in the only direction he could, and wasn't surprised when he soon came upon another set of right-and-left passageways. Jason slowly nodded at the cruel joke being played on him. He sank to his knees, cradled his chest and closed his eyes.

–◎↑ട–

He remembers being five years old, lost in downtown Chicago. The skyscrapers loom

ABOVE, BLOCKING THE SKY. HIS DAD TELLS HIM TO
STAY CLOSE; HE CARRIES SHOPPING BAGS AND CAN'T
ALSO HOLD JASON'S HAND. "DON'T LEAVE MY SIGHT
JASON," HE SAYS. BUT FLICKERING BLUE AND RED
LIGHTS DOWN A SIDE STREET CATCHES JASON'S
ATTENTION-- FIREWORKS?! HE RUNS OFF TO INVES-
TIGATE BUT THERE AREN'T ANY FIREWORKS...

... ANOTHER FLICKER OF LIGHT, DOWN ANOTHER
SIDE STREET: GLORIOUS REDS AND BLUES! HE RUNS,
TRYING TO CATCH THEM; UP ONE STREET AND DOWN
ANOTHER. BUT IT'S JUST REFLECTIONS OF LIGHT ON
RAINDROPS FALLING FROM A WOMAN'S RED-AND-BLUE
UMBRELLA. HE'S SO DISAPPOINTED. HE LOVES FIRE-
WORKS, AND HIS FATHER PROMISED THEY'D SEE THE
FIREWORKS THAT NIGHT AT NAVY PIER, BUT THE
SHOW WAS CANCELED BECAUSE OF THE RAIN. HE
TURNS TO GO BACK TO HIS DAD, BUT CAN'T REMEMBER
IF HE SHOULD GO RIGHT OR LEFT...

... HE TURNS RIGHT, AND RUNS DOWN THE STREET.
NOTHING LOOKS FAMILIAR. HIS FATHER ISN'T THERE.
HE LISTENS FOR HIS DAD'S VOICE; HE MUST BE
CALLING FOR HIM, BUT HE CAN'T HEAR ANYTHING BUT
RAINDROPS PATTERING AGAINST ASPHALT, AND CAR
TIRES SWOOSHING THROUGH THE PUDDLES ...

.... HE DOESN'T KNOW WHICH WAY TO TURN. HE'S
DRENCHED AND SO FRIGHTENED. WHY DIDN'T HE
LISTEN? WHY DIDN'T HE STAY CLOSE? NOW HE'S LOST
AND SOMETHING IS WRONG. HIS DAD'S SUPPOSED TO
FIND HIM 'CAUSE THAT'S WHAT HAPPENED WHEN HE
WAS FIVE: HIS DAD FINDS HIM, AND THOUGH HE'S
ANGRY HE HUGS JASON ALL THE SAME. HIS FATHER
LIFTS HIM UP AND CARRIES HIM HOME TO HIS MOTHER
WHO SQUEEZES HIM SO TIGHTLY HE CAN BARELY
BREATHE. YES, THAT'S WHAT REALLY HAPPENED, BUT
THIS TIME HIS FATHER ...

...*PLEASE! SOMEONE HELP ME!* HIS LITTLE VOICE

CALLS OUT, BUT IT'S CAPTURED BY THE WIND AND CARRIED FAR AWAY. NO ONE STOPS TO ASK IF HE'S OKAY. HE DOESN'T RECOGNIZE ANY OF THE FACES HE SEES. SLIVERS OF SUNRAYS BREAK THROUGH THE STORM CLOUDS, CUTTING THE SPACE BETWEEN THE BUILDINGS AND CASTING SHADOWY STREAKS ACROSS THE FACES. THEY LOOK TIRED; THEY LOOK AS LOST AS HE IS. THEY'RE DRENCHED IN TEARS AND RAIN…

…HE CAN'T MOVE. EACH STEP HE ATTEMPTS IS CUTOFF BY ANOTHER STRANGER, HURRYING TO A JOB, OR DINNER OR DEATH. HE DOESN'T KNOW WHAT TO DO. HE SITS ON THE WET CURB AND CRIES. THEN AN OLDER BOY APPROACHES. HE CAN'T BE MORE THAN THIRTEEN OR FOURTEEN. IT'S STRANGE, JASON HAS NEVER MET THIS BOY BEFORE, BUT HIS FACE IS FAMILIAR: A YOUNGER VERSION OF HIS MOTHER, OR AN OLDER VERSION OF HIMSELF. *"I'M LOST,"* HE TELLS THE OLDER BOY. *"I KNOW,"* THE OLDER BOY REPLIES. *"TAKE MY HAND; I'LL HELP YOU FIND THE WAY."* HE GRASPS THE OLDER BOY'S HAND. IT'S WARM AND SOOTHING. THE OLDER BOY HELPS HIM TO HIS FEET. *"LET'S GO HOME,"* THE OLDER BOY SAYS. SUDDENLY, THE OLDER BOY'S BODY GLOWS IN BLUE AND WHITE. IT'S SUBTLE AT FIRST, BUT SOON JASON CAN'T DISTINGUISH ANY FEATURE OF THE BOY'S FACE. HE PEERS AT HIS HAND. IT'S COVERED IN THE SAME BLUE-AND-WHITE GLOW. HE TRIES TO PULL HIS HAND AWAY, BUT CAN'T. THE LIGHT SLITHERS UP HIS ARM, THEN HIS NECK, AND INTO HIS HEAD. IT FINDS A TINY SPARK, SLEEPING DEEP INSIDE HIS MIND, AND WAKES IT…

–◉⋂ⵥ–

Jason's eyelids burst open. He found himself drenched in sweat and pressed against a corridor wall. The sounds of the rain and cars, and the prickling freeze of droplets against his skin, all gone. He glanced at his body. Daniel had said he'd seen a blue-and-white glow covering him in the park, but Jason didn't believe him. Now, all doubt was gone. He shimmered in a faint cloudy sky. He held up his hands and stared at them in awe. In the spaces between his fingers he saw that he wasn't the only thing glowing, the corridor shimmered in blue and white as well.

The Spark in his mind--the remnant of his bond with the Archivist, Esan's Touch--shone like a dazzling star. The feeling of power and awareness he'd felt in the park when the Arcon Drei called out to him was dull and lifeless in comparison. He wasn't sure why he only experienced the full glory of the Touch sometimes; most of the time it just made him feel strange and out-of-sorts, but Jason didn't care. He held the power now, far more than he imagined possible. If he reached out his hand, if he merely willed the possibility, he knew he could change the world! A wondrous smile spanned his face as he waved his arms in flowing arcs, like a conductor wielding a baton.

Tiny spheres of blue and white broke off from the grey walls. They floated in front of Jason. He summoned more to join the others before him. Millions of them congregated. With a hand gesture, he asked them to merge as one. They complied. The multitudes joined to form an amorphous liquid, shimmering in prisms of light. He commanded the shimmering fluid to solidify, and take a new shape; one he desperately missed.

The floating, liquid mass succumbed to his demand. Limbs, hands, fingers, a broad chest, sturdy legs and a face: a sweet face Jason thought he'd only see again in pictures. But he wasn't finished. He thrust arms out to his sides and the walls groaned. The corridor, glistening in blue and white, changed shape. It widened, and compressed. Jason was tired of being lost; he wanted to be home. The corridor understood.

The formerly mocking passages disappeared, the blue-and-white sheen subdued, and the grey metal transformed in color and shape until every detail was complete. Jason surveyed his work and laughed with joy. His old room looked just as he remembered it: the egg-shell colored bed-frame, the plastic containers of puzzles and toys, the bookshelf overflowing with stories he loved. It was perfect. And his father smiled warmly at him.

"Dad!" He knew it had all been a bad dream! Everyone kept telling him he had to move on, to look forward, to change. But Jason knew they were all wrong, and he knew they had no idea what a person had to do to change… to really change.

His father's hand, just as he remembered, reached out to caress his forehead. Yes, just as he pictured, perfect. Jason crawled under the covers of his bed. His father picked a story off the bookshelf, and sat down beside him.

"Read to me," Jason commanded. His father's hands opened the cover.

"Wait! Where's Mom? She should be here too, beside you."

His room shimmered in blue and white, and in an instant his mother and father were close, together, and in love. He smiled at the joy radiating from her face, but something was wrong. Her hair fell in a familiar pattern, from a picture he'd seen recently, yet as if in another life, taken from him by the blank screen of his cell phone.

The piece of Jason's soul that had soared, teetered back to ground as he was forced to confront the reality that his mother couldn't possibly be here. She was on Earth, in Ashton, wondering why he'd left her. What had she done to deserve him leaving, too?

Then who, or what, was standing before him?

Jason's smile disappeared when his father began to speak because the voice was too deep, like a small child's fantasy of a grown man talking.

"That's not right!" Jason scolded. Fissures of blue and white crackled along the walls, mirroring his frustration. His father spoke again, but the voice was still wrong.

"That's not what you sound like!" Jason barked.

His father's eyes locked on his own, and Jason saw that they were empty of life. He turned to his mother, but the same drooping emptiness, fragile as glass, looked back. He studied his room and realized to his dismay that everything was slightly off. His father reached out to touch him again, but Jason lurched away.

"What are you?!"

His father did not speak.

"Tell me what you are!" Jason commanded. The flesh in the man's face was pallid and flaky. Jason felt exhausted; it took a lot of energy to keep this lie intact.

"Tell me what *you* are," his 'father' replied, the voice now hoarse, yet faint.

He wasn't real. None of it was real! The cruel joke never ended. He wasn't powerful; he was weak, and he was alone.

Fury boiled within Jason, rising from the depths of his being. He bellowed out a scream. Blue and white lightning crackled around him, jumping from point to point in the cloud of energy that roiled about his body.

Jason screamed until his lungs were buried under the ash of his wrath. He fell to the ground gasping for air. When he stood up every trace of his creation was gone, as well as the grey metal corridor. Instead, he was in a massive, stark-white chamber.

"Where the hell am I?"

There was no reply. He tried to think about the situation rationally. Why would the entrance to a city take him here? And why had the strange power returned? Only one answer came to mind: somehow, the Shantar Anar were involved.

Daniel's skepticism about the Archivist's purpose on Earth flew to the forefront of Jason's mind. He was sure Daniel was on the right line, but he still couldn't understand why the alien beings went to all this trouble only to mess with his head. Maybe that's what they did. Maybe they were deeply evil and manipulative. They were probably laughing at his expense right now! But that didn't seem right, either. After all, like Daniel, Nierion warned him not to enter the portal.

Perhaps this was some kind of prison made by Ranis Aun. Maybe the Shantar Anar shared some of their technology long ago and the Ranis Aun used it to control their enemies. The Archivist had said that the Ranis Aun were as bad to each other as humans were.

Jason felt like he was onto something, but even if he figured out where he was, he still had no idea how to escape.

"Well?" he shouted at the walls of the massive room. "Aren't you going to say something?!"

Silence was again the reply. Jason was furious.

"Somebody talk to me!"

He was again overwhelmed by anger. The sight of the white walls boiled his blood.

They should have stopped me from jumping in! he reasoned. *This is their fault!*

"Can you hear me Daniel?! You should have stopped me! You and your stupid comic book stories, freaking Mole People and Lava Man!"

As soon as he said the words, Jason knew what he had to do: Lava Mind. Well, not Lava Mind exactly, but he remembered that in Circle Park his mind had cleared, and he needed that clarity now.

Jason sat on the white ground, took a deep breath and closed his eyes. But he was immediately dragged into another vivid memory. He opened his eyes, not wanting to be drawn in any further. He couldn't believe how real these imaginings seemed, like he was watching a dream being made from the inside out. The images were distracting, perhaps intentionally so. He closed his eyes again, but this time pushed past the storm of images that skimmed the edges of his mind.

"Lava Mind," he repeated over and over under his breath. "Lava Mind"… A vision of a friend's birthday tried to pull him in, but Jason resisted. He dove further down, past the frothing myriad of colorful distraction, and the lucid images began to fade. *Lava Mind…*

Jason let himself sink even more. He imagined the Spark illuminating a tiny piece of perfect dark. He pictured the

Spark blossoming, giving him the ability to calm his mind. What good was the power to change a world if it was only an illusion?

Nothing happened. He tried again, but the Spark was unresponsive. He felt the specters of memories and dreams trying to infiltrate the darkness. He concentrated on keeping them out, but the effort quickly exhausted him. He had to escape before he was captured in another nightmare, and shot open his eyes.

So much for Lava Mind, he thought dourly. But then he noticed a new doorway on the far side of the enormous room.

"It worked!" he shouted, and gave himself a once over to make sure he wasn't shimmering in blue and white. He was not.

"It's real!" Jason raced across the room. The doorway was a cutout in the wall and a dim light shone from beyond the threshold. He walked through and found himself in a large cave.

The ceiling was smooth, and illuminated in the dim turquoise light reflecting off of a glimmering pool in the middle of the cave. Jason stepped back to get a better view of the geography, but his foot hit rock where the entrance had just been. He spun to face a solid wall of smooth stone with protruding jagged edges.

"I didn't make this!" he yelled. No reply.

Jason slowly turned around, afraid of what he would see this time. The cave was much the same. The turquoise pool continued its eerie glow. He studied his surroundings and was struck by an odd feeling that the cave felt... less real somehow than the vision of his past he'd brought to life.

On the far side of the cave, the pool reflected shadows against the wall. At first, he assumed they were being cast by the stalagmites that sporadically jutted from the ground. But then the shadows began to move.

They transformed from lumps into serpentine beings that thrashed across the cave walls. The shadows seemed like they belonged to the creatures he'd seen carved into the great wall on the planet's surface, and they continued to flail as if in great pain.

He cautiously stepped forward, but the shadows seemed lost in their torture. Slowly, he walked to the edge of the turquoise pool, which was so murky he couldn't see past an inch.

Jason crouched to dip the tip of his finger into the liquid. He didn't notice the appearance of ripples in the middle of the pool.

Chapter 26: The Stranger

The car sailed over smooth streets of Ashton's outskirts. Anne's finicky right hand changed radio stations every couple seconds while her left hand tightly gripped the wheel. On any other day, the drive might've proved relaxing, the quiet streets lined with Spanish Oaks could've served as a pleasing soak for the soul. Today though, she had no comfort. Anne called Coregon right after Ashlyn left confirming that he knew the girl saw Jason head into the woods. The Captain assured Anne he'd investigate the woods himself.

She almost told him about the man Ashlyn mentioned, but Anne didn't want the police banging down someone's door based on the tales of a thirteen-year-old. Instead she asked her neighbors, who all gave her the same name: Dean Kipson. From the tone of their voices, she knew there was no love lost for the man. And everyone knew where he lived.

Anne expected Kipson's dwelling to be a dingy shack on the edge of town, surrounded by other hovels, broken weathervanes and perhaps an eerie wind that somehow haunted only that street. However, she passed neatly lined homes, boasting well-tended lawns, and pleasant picket fences.

The light-brown house at 565 Cedar Road had a shingle roof in good repair and a dark wood front door decorated with wrought-iron studs. A well-maintained, blue Ford truck rested in the driveway. *Oh good, someone's home.* She had tried waiting till evening in case Kipson was at work, but she was incapable of sitting still.

The tidy house calmed her nerves. The only thing out of the ordinary was that Dean Kipson's shades were all drawn, like the veils of grieving widows.

Anne got out of her car and walked to the door. She wasn't sure what she was going to say, but was confident something appropriate would come to her if she found the nerve to ring the bell. She knocked instead; it felt more personal. She stepped back and pinned an ear to the door to detect movement on the other side. She waited an endless fifteen or twenty seconds before knocking again, louder this time, her hands thudding against the wood. She heard no shuffle of feet, no creaking hardwood floors. With a disappointed sigh she turned to leave; the truck had teased her, no one was home. Then she heard the lock-bolt retreat.

The hinges squeaked as if they were tired. The door opened a slit, then wider until the penetrating eyes of a tall, almost gaunt, man appeared. He had disheveled salt-and-pepper hair, and a long, thin nose. Anne's skin prickled at the sight of him, and for a moment, she lost the power of speech. She tried to meet his eyes, but found herself looking at his stained white undershirt, and sun-stroked jeans.

"Yes?" answered a gruff voice that creaked through hardly moving lips.

Anne met his piercing grey irises.

"Are you Dean Kipson?"

The man didn't answer at first, as if trying to figure out why anyone would want to know.

"Yes," he finally replied.

"I… You don't know me," Anne stammered.

"I know." His words were chiseled from ice. "What do you want?"

For a moment she forgot why she was there. She was hypnotized by the painful sanity behind Kipson's eyes, and couldn't reply. He began to close the door, never taking his eyes off her. Anne grabbed the door suddenly and pushed it open.

Sunlight splashed the dim lit hallway behind him. Musty air from the interior of the house drenched Anne's nostrils. The smell reeked of misery.

"Wait, please… wait. My name is Anne Swann. I understand you like to spend time at Circle Park." She rebuilt her resolve, watching Kipson's face for any twitch.

"So?" His face betrayed nothing.

"My son…" she began, but Kipson closed his eyes as if focusing on a memory, or preparing for an accusation.

"My son Jason was in the park yesterday and now he's missing. I want to know if you saw him or talked to him."

Kipson widened his sharp eyes and Anne found herself gazing into them. There was nothing menacing, but she needed to see under the blank slate of his face.

"What does he look like?" he finally asked.

Anne fumbled in her pocket for the bent, yearbook 2"x 3" and placed it in Kipson's rough hand.

"Here."

Dean studied the photograph. Anne noticed his hand trembling. A fierce quiver appeared on his lip.

"Have you seen him, Dean?"

The man didn't answer, but desperately stared at the picture like he was trying to find something he'd lost. Anne saw the torment almost breach the wall of his tempered expression, but Dean fought the wave of emotion and returned to stone. He held out the picture for Anne to reclaim.

"Have you seen my son?" she asked again with chilling authority. She was fighting her instinct to either accuse or to scream. Dean merely peered through her, past the fallen leaves lining the ground, past the still, squat houses on the other side of the street. He seemed to be searching for something invisible.

Then he whispered, "I found him in a dead land."

"What?" Anne asked, but he didn't acknowledge her, as if he'd forgotten she was there.

"He asked me how I'd found him, said it wasn't my time to die."

"What does that mean?" Anne cried, but she was ignored.

"He put his hand to my eyes and closed them. I wasn't supposed to see what was happening, but I watched anyway.

Saw the Earth open its mouth like a splitting wound and swallow him whole. It took him somewhere I couldn't follow."

"Who... Jason? Are you talking about my son?!"

"He left me alone in a field of dried grass and a river of mud. Birds came--finches, wrens, crows--beating their wings, pecking the mud for the remains of suffocated fish. I asked the crows where his bones were. I wanted to hold them. They turned on me, tried to eat my heart, make a meal of my guts. Then I was pulled away, don't know how. I tried to find him again. I kept searching and searching, but I couldn't find the right path. I haven't seen him since... only in my dreams."

"What does that mean?!" Anne pleaded. "Are you talking about my son?!" Tears welled in her eyes.

The door began to close, shutting Dean's knowing eyes back into the dark prison of his home. Anne felt her strength diminish, her fingers fell away from the wooden frame. She was left staring at the wrought-iron studs, her face ashen, and her lips dry and cold. The fall breeze nipped at the clammy sweat on her palms.

"What does that mean?" she begged, but the door said nothing.

Chapter 27: Pandora's Jar

Coregon Willis usually liked watching his breath twist through the air on chilly days. He felt alive and interacting with the Earth, a conscious part of nature rather than just a set of thoughtless eyes watching trees die and be reborn in the spring. As the sun rose from slumber, and the streets were empty and silent in the dawn, he marveled at the advent of another day. He judged the burnt orange and red painted across the sky to be a good part of the world.

That morning, however, he took no comfort in his frosty breath as he stood, surrounded by the forest preserve. The missing child alert he'd broadcast to the media and law enforcement agencies hadn't turned up a single hint of a possibility as to what might've happened to the two boys. He had only one lead to follow: the abandoned bikes and Ashlyn's claim of seeing Jason and Daniel run off into the woods.

Thirty of Ashton's police officers were now searching those woods for the boys. Truth be told, he couldn't spare that many, but when children were missing, people's practicality strayed from common sense to the imagined monsters responsible for the assumed crime. The task of keeping the well-meaning public out of his way in those first critical days was never easy, which is why he tried to keep a tight lid on the situation, but emotions often overtook thought. He understood that.

Coregon told the officers on either side of him to go ahead. He did his best work alone. As he walked, he listened to the sticks and leaves crunching under his feet. They sounded like dried-out bones. The quiet woods gave no easy answers to his questions, and Coregon had to confess he found the boys disappearance very strange.

All his inquiries reached the same wall. Clearly, they'd both been at school at the end of the day. Their backpacks were found in their respective lockers. Apparently, Ashlyn saw them head into the woods behind Jason's house, where the police captain now found himself. Beyond that, there was no trace.

Even if the boys had run away intentionally, the woods were only so big; a thousand acres of state preserve, and maybe an hour or two walk to come out the other side into the next suburb. No one had seen them there, either.

Two scenarios came to mind: One, Jason and Daniel were in the woods hiding with the intention of either running away, or for some reason, playing a horrible prank. But he knew Daniel, and Coregon couldn't imagine the boy choosing these options. From what he could discern, Jason was good kid, although a little moody. However, Coregon was well acquainted with the psyche of runaways and in almost every case, some kind of abuse was involved. Hiding didn't fit. Two, the boys were expertly kidnapped in the middle of the day by either a single person or a group.

Unfortunately, that seemed the more plausible explanation, but still lacking. Only Ashlyn knew where they'd gone, so who'd been waiting in the woods? Or was some other nefarious activity going on? Did the boys stumble upon something dangerous? Maybe, but Coregon had lived in Ashton a long time and these woods weren't known for harboring criminals.

He needed to find some clue. He knew Sharon Elliot rested all her confidence on his abilities, but he'd failed before in a case too similar for his liking. Sharon knew that, too. And then there was Anne. He saw in her face that she'd known profound loss, but she was desperate to give life a second chance. What did she see when she looked at him? A savior, or another tragedy waiting to happen...

Up ahead, his officers huddled over something on the

ground. He rushed to them and emerged in a meadow that had been hidden by a thick grove of elms.

"Take a look at this," his burly sergeant said at the sound of the Coregon's approach. The captain knelt to get a better view. There was a large indentation, four or five feet wide, in the grass and wildflowers.

"We found another depression in the ground about fifty feet that way," a second officer chimed, pointing left.

Coregon walked next to the indentation, following its slightly curving arc for eighty or ninety feet. Then he turned directions walked perpendicular to the trough for another fifty feet, to where the officer had pointed to the second indentation. He followed the second indentation back the same distance. They were identical.

His sergeant acknowledged him vacantly. "What do you think made them?"

Coregon shook his head. They weren't vehicle tracks, there were no tread marks, and they were very far apart. The impressions could have been made by felled trees that had been removed by the forest service, but the hollows were curved, not straight. Could a tree leave a rounded demarcation as it fell? Perhaps, but two trees making the same curve in the same fashion, seemed impossible. The only sure piece of evidence he ascertained was that whatever made the markings was huge.

He knew he was missing something, and walked back to the edge of the grove to start over very slowly. He scanned the ground with keen, owlish eyes. In his periphery, he caught a glimpse of a shadow moving on the far side of the meadow. He scowled.

She's persistent; I have to give her that.

"Sergeant Jameson!" The stocky policeman glanced up. "Take Officer Park with you on a northern sweep of the woods. Radio the other officers to be on the lookout for more of these grooves. I'll sweep to the south and do the same. Call me if you find anything."

"Yes, Captain," the sergeant replied, and led the uniformed officer with him to the north.

Coregon watched until they were out of sight. He didn't know why he indulged the girl, but he admired her tenacity. She'd been that way since she'd lost her friend. He blamed himself for that, too.

"Ashlyn! Come on out now," he directed his voice towards the tree where he'd last seen the shadow.

A stifled grunt emerged, but not Ashlyn.

"You either come here, or I'll go there; your choice."

Ashlyn grunted again, but this time walked out from her hiding place. She pretended to examine the elm, then turned to face the Captain with feigned surprise. "Capitan Willis... What are you doing here?"

Who does she think she's fooling?

"The same thing you're doing; only *I'm* supposed to be here."

"You're studying elm bark, too? That's weird; I'm doing it for science class, what are you doing it for?"

"Ashlyn..."

She glanced around for anything else to pile onto her excuse.

"And... um and the meadow grass too, I have to... observe it... doing... stuff?"

Coregon met her eyes with a gaze of stone. The girl relented.

"Okay! But here's the thing, I wasn't following you, I swear! I came here on my own to see what I could find."

His eyes pierced the flimsy excuse.

"Fine!" Ashlyn exclaimed and crossed her arms defensively. "But I only started following you once you were already in the woods. And I didn't come here until school was over."

What was he going to do with her? She always had a story ready, but he wasn't in the mood. He'd have to drag her out of the woods and take her home, have a stern talk with her parents. She had to let go of her dream. Her missing friend was long gone or more likely, dead. She was chasing a ghost and Coregon knew that came with a heavy price. He didn't want that, he wanted her to move on with her life.

Ashlyn crossed the meadow towards Captain Willis. *Maybe she'll come willingly this time,* he thought, but she stopped suddenly and stared down with her mouth agape.

"What?" Coregon called.

"Footprints!" she shouted.

Coregon ran to her. Sure enough, patches of matted grass, side-by-side in the general shape of shoes dotted the ground.

"Shoe tracks, not foot prints," he remarked dismissively. He followed the path, and the distance between each step widened as if the person who'd made them had been running, but then stopped, not more than ten feet from one of the mysterious indentations. He found another set of shoe tracks, much closer together. The second set of tracks was slightly larger and deeper, like the person had been standing in the spot for a while. He knelt to take a measurement, and a picture of the track, when he felt Ashlyn's breath over his shoulder.

"That's Jason's shoe!"

"How can you tell?" he asked. "And don't scream."

"Sorry," Ashlyn said and then explained. "See the three dots and jagged line in the middle of the print, I mean, track?"

Coregon took a closer look. "I guess."

"That's the insignia for 'Tri-Dome Lightning!'" Ashlyn stated. "It's this really cool brand of shoes that I never saw anyone in class wearing, except for Jason!"

The girl was jubilant, like she'd cracked the entire case, but Coregon was subdued. Even if the shoe tracks belonged to Jason, they ended abruptly by the strange impressions. There wasn't a single track from either set beyond that point. It was as if the two boys had simply left the world behind.

–◯↑ဒ–

Anne didn't notice she'd been staring blankly at her kitchen wall until the phone rang. She was lost in a recollection of the strange and haunting story Dean Kipson told her. She understood why Ashlyn's parents warned the girl to stay away from him. The phone pulled Anne out of her daze. Sharon was calling to tell her that Captain Willis had some news about the boys. Anne had hung up the phone and was out the door before she realized she'd neglected to ask if the news was good or bad.

She barely saw the houses passing by, and couldn't recall making any turns, or stopping at traffic lights. When everything came back into focus, she was in the Elliots' driveway. Sharon's small but fierce form stood at the open front door. Sharon quickly ushered Anne into the living room, where Captain Willis sat. Anne wasn't sure why, but the sight of him was calming. She barely knew the man, but there was something in his shrewd eyes that told her he saw life differently than most, and was humbled by what he knew. Next to him, hands clasped, spine straight and legs pressed together, was Ashlyn. Anne cast a quizzical look, but the girl just smiled cheerily.

"Hi Anne!"

"Ashlyn, it's polite to address adults by their last name," Sharon chided as she stalked the living room, adjusting picture frames and checking furniture for traces of dust. She didn't notice Ashlyn narrow her eyes.

"It's fine, I don't mind," Anne replied.

Ashlyn enjoyed the flash of incredulity poxing Sharon's face, and helped herself to a secret smile. She liked Anne more every time she saw her.

"Hello Anne," Coregon said in an even voice. Then, an uncomfortable silence filled the room. Ashlyn could tell Anne wanted to ask about Jason, but she probably wasn't sure she wanted to hear what Captain Willis had to say, so she said nothing. And Captain Willis was too polite sometimes as far as Ashlyn was concerned, so he said nothing in return.

"You're probably wondering why I assembled this meeting," Ashlyn remarked.

Captain Willis threw daggers at her with his eyes.

"But I'm the one who found the clue!" she pleaded.

Anne pounced, "What clue?!"

Before Ashlyn could answer, Sharon interrupted as she emerged from the kitchen carrying a tray of drinks. Ashlyn hadn't even noticed the woman leave the room.

"Anne, I'm glad you could come over on such short notice, I apologize for the way it looks around here."

The house looked the same as far as Ashlyn could tell, but Sharon was a mess. Her clothes were neat like always, but she had dark rings under her eyes and loose strands of hair dangling from a bun at the top of her head.

"Would you like some iced tea?" Sharon queried.

Anne nodded, "Iced tea sounds fine."

Sharon held out the tray to the Captain. "Coregon?"

"No thank you. By the way, will Charles be home soon from his important... 'errand'? This is the second time I've missed him."

Ashlyn didn't miss the sly crook to the Captain's mouth as he drawled the word 'errand.' He probably suspected, as Ashlyn did, that Sharon sent her husband out to search for Daniel against the Captain's wishes, and yet he seemed so reserved about the obvious disregard for his request. *Why was he so easy on her...?*

"None for me Shar... Mrs. Elliot. I'll take a glass of orange juice if you have it, though," Ashlyn said as she tried to hide the smirk fighting its way to the corners of her mouth.

Sharon's mouth drooped open slightly as the woman decided how offended she should be by Ashlyn's tone. *Like you were going to offer me anything...*

Sharon pursed her lips, but returned to the kitchen with a measured stride.

"What clue did you find?" Anne asked the Captain.

Coregon fixed the position of his wire rim glasses with precision. "We didn't find the boys Anne."

"Oh," Anne said. She rubbed her hands like she was trying to relieve an old ache.

He was also too blunt, Ashlyn thought. Her heart dropped as a fledgling hope drained from Anne's face. *Too polite and too blunt, is that even possible?*

"You have to tell her the good part too, Captain Willis," Ashlyn butted in. The glare she got from the Captain was enough to still time.

He turned back to Anne.

"I did find evidence, however, that the boys were together in a clearing in the woods not far from your house."

"I... actually, Ashlyn found their shoe tracks leading to two large indentations in the grass that appear to have been made by something very large and heavy."

"Like a truck?" Anne asked.

"The markings are too far apart. Besides, there's no way to get a truck in there in the first place. It looked more like... like-"

Ashlyn finished the Captain's thought, "A giant machine had been there."

Anne shook her head in disbelief.

"That's all? Where else did the footprints lead?"

Coregon cringed.

"Nowhere else, they stop at the indentations. I had thirty officers do two complete searches of the woods. They combed the place north, south, east and west, but found no other sign of the boys. They aren't in the woods anymore."

Ashlyn saw tears budding in Anne's eyes when Sharon Elliott trotted back into the room with a glass of orange juice. She thrust the glass into Ashlyn's hand, then walked placidly to a stately leather chair, where she sat down and crossed her legs. Ashlyn regarded the glass despondently; she wanted Sharon to leave so she could talk to Anne alone with Captain Willis. She hated orange juice.

"I assume Captain Willis filled you in on what he found," Sharon said. "It's really very good news. Now that he knows where the boys went, it's only a matter of time before he finds them."

Coregon exhaled as he faced Daniel's mother. Ashlyn wondered for a moment if his eyes actually were made of steel.

"Sharon, that's not what I said. The facts are the facts; we can't read into them or they tell us things that aren't true."

"But you said-"

Captain Willis held up his hand for silence.

"I told you the trail ends cold. You insisted I come here to tell Anne the same. So I have. We will continue to do everything we can, but right now I'm afraid to say we don't have much to go on."

The glance of raw disdain Sharon tossed at the Captain made Ashlyn furious.

"I understand," followed the look. The woman's words were delivered through thin lips and dripped with scorn.

Ashlyn didn't deny that Sharon should be upset. She also didn't deny that Daniel's mother scared her. Ashlyn saw the worry and sadness bristling on the woman's face, but there was anger as well, crusted against her eye sockets, bleeding into her cheeks and the harsh crest of her lower jaw. Hate was fighting to break through, searching for someone to blame. She knew from experience, if Daniel wasn't found soon, Sharon would point fingers at the people trying to help.

Apparently, Anne sensed the hostility as well, because she changed the conversation. Her words sent a shock of dismay through Ashlyn.

"Sharon, do you happen to know the strange man that sometimes hangs around Circle Park, his name is Dean Kipson?"

Ashlyn flitted her eyes to Sharon and watched the woman's face turn to stone. *Oh no...*

"Why do you ask, Anne?" A deep loathing simmered beneath the surface of those words. Ashlyn turned to Captain Willis, hoping he could dispel the matter, and saw a hard inquisitive expression resting on the sharp angles of his face. *Why did I tell Anne about Dean?!*

"Oh...well...I went to speak to him today and it occurred to me that-"

"How do you know Dean?" Coregon interrupted.

Ashlyn peeped at the Captain, then at Anne, praying the woman would keep her promise. The wolfish frown on Sharon's face inspired more prayer.

"I was… told he hangs around Circle Park sometimes, and I thought maybe he'd seen the boys yesterday, since I know they'd been there in the morning."

To her credit, Anne didn't glance at Ashlyn; she wasn't going to give her away. Ashlyn let out a sigh louder than she anticipated, and lifted the glass of hated juice to her lips, gulping down the sickly sweet nectar and pulp with an uncontrollable shudder.

"I wish you'd told me before you went to see him… alone," Coregon said.

"Why?"

Ashlyn heard the shakiness in Anne's voice clear as day. *Oh god, what did he say to you?*

Coregon's voice was soft. "He isn't well."

Anne nodded as if she had no idea. "Is that right?"

The Captain pressed on. "What did he say?"

"Nothing… specific."

"Of course," Sharon crowed. "It all makes sense."

"What makes sense?" Anne asked.

Ashlyn groaned silently. She could almost see the winding gears in Sharon's head.

"Sharon, you can't go making assumptions like-"

"Like what, Coregon?" Sharon snapped, rising from her chair. "He has something to do with this, I know it! He should never have been allowed to stay in Ashton after what he did! I knew it was a mistake, a huge mistake, and I told you then, Coregon! So help me, I told you!"

"He didn't do anything!" Ashlyn blurted out. She knew she shouldn't have said anything, but she also knew no one else would defend him.

Sharon turned to face her, and Ashlyn shrank back into the couch.

"What would you know about it, little girl?"

"Stop it," Coregon ordered with subdued but furious

strength. "She doesn't know anything about it. You need to calm down right now."

"Oh do I?" Sharon goaded.

Captain Willis slowly rose from the couch and stood like the chiseled statue of an ancient god. His eyes shone with righteous fire as he gazed at the mix of wrath and sorrow mired upon Sharon Elliott's face.

"I'm telling you this as a keeper of the peace. You cannot accuse a man without evidence, no matter how you personally feel about him."

"What's going on?" Anne pleaded.

Sharon turned from the Captain's fury to focus on Anne.

"I'm sorry," Sharon said with honesty. "I didn't mean to come off as harsh. Thank god nothing bad happened to you, talking to that devil. I don't care what you have to say about it, Coregon. That's what he is."

"You can *think* whatever you want about him. But I'm not starting a damn witch-hunt because you miss your friend. That's the *end* of it. *I* will speak to him in the morning. *I* will find out if he knows anything. *You* will be patient!"

Ashlyn's heart was beating so fast she thought it would burst. She'd never heard the Captain speak so forcefully. He was like thunder on an open plain. She watched Sharon turn from his withering gaze to stare blankly out a bright window.

"Fine," Sharon whispered, then walked away, up the stairs, and soon Ashlyn heard a door slam. She couldn't make herself small enough. The room felt like it was sinking. *Why, oh why, did I say anything about Dean?!*

New lines of worry streaked Anne's face. "What was that about? What is going on?"

"Don't worry." Captain Willis said, though Ashlyn saw him scrutinizing Sharon's wake. "It doesn't have anything to do with Jason or Daniel."

"But what does-"

Coregon gently interrupted Anne.

"You know, in my line of work I've met a lot of dangerous people…" The fire in his eyes had extinguished, but Ashlyn saw a renewed hardness behind the hazel and flecks of gold.

"A lot of things make a person dangerous. It's rarely what you'd expect. Sometimes, the most dangerous person is a good person who feels betrayed by those who gave her hope. It's frightening; our need to cast blame doesn't accomplish anything except to put more fear into our hearts. If we can't find a way to be better to each other… then I just don't know what good can happen in this world."

He rested his hand on Anne's shoulder. "Don't believe everything Sharon tells you. She's a decent person deep down, but she holds the blade firm when it comes to people she loves."

Coregon peered down at the scared girl on the couch. He took his hand from Anne's shoulder and wrapped it warmly around Ashlyn's. He helped her stand and bade Anne goodnight as he slowly walked Ashlyn out the front door.

Left alone, Anne had a sinking feeling she was being taken, against her will, into the unknown tragedies of a stranger's life. All she desperately wanted was to get Jason back home, so she could find a small peace within her own.

Chapter 28: Song Spirit

Daniel ran towards Jason as fast as he could. The orange veins of light coursing through the walls and floor of the hallway marked the way. He knelt down beside the writhing body of his friend, reminded of pretend soldiers on giant screens in packed theaters. This closeness to real-life agony was far more intimate and horrifying.

"Jason, what's wrong?" Daniel cried, "What happened to you?!"

Jason couldn't respond with words, but Daniel saw the misery written across his face.

"Please, you have to tell me what's wrong!" But his friend rolled away, hunching his body into a fetal position.

Daniel's hands clenched in and out of fists uncontrollably. He found Jason by focusing on his desire to help, but could he heal Jason as easily as he'd changed the white room's ceiling? The idea seemed absurd, but in this insane place he didn't discount anything as foolish. He had to act; he couldn't lose his only friend… again.

He put his shaking hands on Jason's contorted body. Jason twisted like a serpent and gurgled barely audible pleas for help. *What does courageous Daniel look like… What does he do?*

Daniel closed his eyes and imagined the cause of Jason's torment as tiny black spheres. If he simply willed it, the spheres would ascend from Jason's body, pulled as if by magnetism. He imagined these ebony orbs contorting in shape, transforming into amorphous blobs cascading through the pores in his skin and then reforming. When these reached him, instead of bringing pain, they'd carry warmth and comfort. Daniel saw all this vividly in his mind's eye.

A tingling sensation in his arm made Daniel open his eyes. Just as he imagined, tiny black globules arose from Jason's body. Daniel was awed, not just by the spheres, but by his own power. The spheres contorted as they sailed up and around his arm, gracefully gliding to his chest, where they melted into him. They swam through his veins and arteries, energizing his blood. Daniel couldn't quite tell if the sensation was real or all in his head. He was again struck by the bizarre feeling that the black blobs were not as real as they could be. It was a feeling that couldn't be put into words, almost as if…

Jason's screams abated. Daniel left his doubts behind to look at his friend's face, which slowly but surely returned to peace. He continued with even sharper focus, pulling more pain-spheres from Jason's body and turning them into conveyers of gentleness.

As Jason's breathing slowed, his body rolled flat and his eyes opened. Daniel stared at his friend with relief and pride. Jason's hand clasped his own like a thankful brother. The embrace made Daniel very calm, though there was something about the hold that didn't entirely feel-

"Daniel?" Jason asked, his eyes bleary, his skin glistening with sweat.

"Yes, it's me! What happened to you? How did you get here?"

"I'm not sure," Jason wheezed as he clasped Daniel's hand.

"What do you remember?"

Jason's other hand grabbed Daniel's wrist. A hot, soothing feeling spread through Daniel's body, melting his worries and concerns. Did he really care how Jason got here or why he was in pain? Daniel had fixed everything, and now that Jason was better, they could go home. Daniel felt giddy with the possibilities of his newfound power, and his mind bubbled with hope as he dreamed of making things better in Ashton as well.

The grip on his wrist tightened.

"Can you help me up, I still feel weak."

"Of course!" Daniel reached his other hand to Jason, who clung fervently, balancing carefully as he lifted himself up. With both their arms clasped, Daniel felt soothing currents flowing through him, as if he and Jason had completed a circuit.

"What should we do now?"

Daniel's jaw collapsed with surprise.

"Jason, I can hear your thoughts!"

"Of course you can, you made it possible."

Daniel frowned.

"I... I did? I don't remember doing that?"

"You don't remember? That's okay; the only thing that matters now is getting home. You have a lot of work to do."

Deep in Jason's glinting eyes, Daniel saw a reflection of himself.

"Your mom is scared all the time, scared of losing you. You can help her not be so afraid, can't you?"

"Yes! I want to, but how can we get home without the ship?"

Jason's eyes were wide and bright; Daniel's reflection smiled back at him.

"You close your eyes, and will it to be."

Jason's grip tightened further and Daniel's eyelids became heavy. They closed like velvet theater curtains blocking the image of himself that shone in Jason's crystal eyes...

$$-\text{☺⋔ဒ}-$$

... EARLY MORNING—DAWN'S FIRST RAYS CREEP UNDER MY BLINDS AND SKATE ACROSS THE FLOOR TO REST ON MY CHEEK. I HEAR HER COMING TO WAKE ME, BUT I'VE BEEN UP FOR HOURS. I WATCH THE DOORKNOB TWIST SLOWLY, LIKE THE CREAKING GEAR OF A TIRED MACHINE. THE DOOR GROANS OPEN AND SHE STANDS, DAPPLED IN SHADOW, UNDER THE THRESHOLD. I PRETEND TO SLEEP, BUT PEEK AT HER

THROUGH TINY SLITS IN MY EYELIDS. SHE SURVEYS THE ROOM TO MAKE SURE EVERYTHING IS IN THE PROPER PLACE, AND THEN WALKS TO ME WITH ROBOTIC MOVEMENT. I WAIT FOR HER SOFT KISS, BUT FEEL ONLY A ROUGH HAND ON MY SHOULDER, SHAKING ME GENTLY. I PRETEND TO WAKE, OPENING MY EYES GROGGILY AND RUBBING THE SLEEP FROM THEIR CORNERS. SHE SEEMS WORRIED…

"DANIEL," MY MOTHER WHISPERS IN MY EAR, "IT'S NOT SAFE FOR YOU HERE ANYMORE."

I SIT UP AND CAST THE HEAVY BLANKET OFF MY LEGS. I TELL HER IT'S VERY SAFE WHERE WE LIVE, THAT SHE DOESN'T NEED TO WORRY. I WON'T DISAPPEAR LIKE MY FRIEND.

SHE DOESN'T BELIEVE ME. "DANIEL, I HAVE TO KEEP YOU SAFE, YOU'RE MY ONLY SON."

I TELL HER I KNOW THAT. I TELL HER SHE DOESN'T NEED TO BE SO AFRAID. I LOVE HER AND I'M NOT GOING TO RUN AWAY. MY MOTHER CURLS HER LIP AND FROWNS, HOW DARE I SAY SHE'S AFRAID! I JUST DON'T UNDERSTAND, SHE SAYS. I'M TOO YOUNG… I'M FAR TOO YOUNG TO UNDERSTAND. ONE DAY I WILL, ONE DAY I'LL UNDERSTAND WHY I CAN'T STAY HERE ANY LONGER: "IT ISN'T SAFE."

I ASK HER WHERE I'M SUPPOSED TO GO.

"THERE'S A DOOR BENEATH YOUR BED. I MADE IT WHILE YOU SLEPT."

I TELL HER I WANT TO STAY, WANT TO TRY AND HELP. SHE SMILES; IT'S NICE TO SEE HER SMILE. SHE PUTS HER SOFT HAND AGAINST MY CHEEK AND TELLS ME I'M VERY SILLY AND MUCH TOO SMALL TO HELP. ONE DAY I'LL UNDERSTAND, SHE SAYS. I TRY TO SPEAK, TO TELL HER SHE'S WRONG, BUT SHE PUTS A THIN FINGER TO MY LIP. WITHOUT A WORD SHE COMMANDS ME TO GET OUT OF BED. SHE KNEELS AND PEERS INTO MY EYES. I SEE MY REFLECTION WADING IN THE WATERS OF HER IRIS.

I FEEL WEAK AND TRY TO SIT BACK DOWN. SHE
CATCHES ME BEFORE I FALL. MY BED IS GONE. ONLY
DUSTY PILES ON THE FLOORBOARDS REVEAL A BED
WAS ONCE THERE. I STARE AT A TRAPDOOR MADE OF
HEAVY OAK AND STEEL. THERE'S A LATCH SET
BETWEEN STEEL RIVETS. SHE TELLS ME TO OPEN THE
DOOR... I TRY, BUT IT'S TOO HEAVY. SHE LAUGHS, "I
TOLD YOU; YOU'RE WEAK."

SHE WAVES HER HAND. THE LATCH UNFURLS AND
THE TRAPDOOR CREEPS UPWARDS AS THOUGH PULLED
BY AN INVISIBLE CORD. MEAGER POOLS OF LIGHT
CREEP ALONG THE EDGES, AND I SEE THERE'S A SPIRAL
STAIRCASE LEADING DOWN. SHE RESTS HER HANDS ON
MY SHOULDERS. WE DESCEND INTO THE DARKNESS
TOGETHER.

SHE WAVES HER HAND, AND TORCHES LIGHT THE
WAY WITH RUSTY-ORANGE FLAME. WE WALK DOWN
AND FURTHER DOWN, STEP-BY-STEP, FOR HOURS. SHE
SINGS ME LULLABIES AND TRACES THE SPIRITS OF THE
SONGS IN THE AIR BEFORE US. I CAN SEE THEM, THE
SONG-SPIRITS; THEY LOOK LIKE TURQUOISE MISTS
FEEDING THE ORANGE FLAMES.

THE STAIRCASE SEEMS TO HAVE NO END, BUT
EVENTUALLY THE SMOOTH STEPS GIVE WAY TO
JAGGED ONES. THE TORCH LIGHT STOPS ABRUPTLY,
LEAVING CONSUMING SHADOWS BEYOND. SHE SEES
THAT I'M FRIGHTENED, AND SHE STROKES MY HAIR.
"YOU DON'T NEED TO FEAR THE DARK." SHE BRUSHES
THE SMALL OF MY BACK AND A PLEASANT WARMTH
COURSES THROUGH MY BODY. THE PASSAGEWAY IS
SUDDENLY FILLED WITH A MELLOW LIGHT. I HOLD UP
MY HAND AND REALIZE THAT THE LIGHT IS COMING
FROM ME.

WE REACH THE BOTTOM AND PASS THROUGH A
NARROW CORRIDOR COARSELY HEWN IN THE GRANITE.
HER HAND NUDGES ME FORWARD. THE PASSAGEWAY
SOON ENDS, AND I AGAIN SEE THE SPIRITS OF HER

LULLABIES SWIRLING ON THE ROUGH STONE. THEY LOOK AT ME--I DON'T KNOW HOW--BUT THEY SEE ME, AND TRANSFORM INTO A PERFECT CIRCLE OF TURQUOISE LIGHT.

I TURN TO HER. SHE'S SMILING BRIGHTLY. I ASK HER WHERE WE ARE.

"SOME PLACE SAFE."

I RETURN TO THE TRANQUIL LIGHT. I'M NOT SO SURE.

SHE FEELS MY FEAR. "WOULD I LIE TO YOU?"

I'M ASHAMED. "OF COURSE NOT," I TELL HER, BUT WONDER WHERE THE PATH LEADS.

"SOME PLACE SAFE."

I ASK WHAT THAT MEANS.

"A DIFFERENT WORLD, A DIFFERENT EARTH... THE WAY I WANT IT TO BE."

"WHAT DO YOU WANT?" I WONDER.

SHE PUSHES ME TO THE END OF THE CORRIDOR AND MAKES ME TOUCH THE MILKY GLOW. THE TIPS OF MY FINGERS BRUSH THE SURFACE AND... AND...

$$-\text{ⓞ}\text{↑}\text{ȝ}-$$

A crushing jolt rushed through Daniel and shattered the jagged walls of the corridor. The light emanating from him was extinguished.

"Stop!" The word shattered his vision into atomic dust. He recognized the voice immediately.

Daniel opened his eyes, though he couldn't remember closing them. To his dismay, he found himself kneeling, and surrounded by the stark white walls of a massive room he knew too well.

"No!" Daniel screamed until his blood curdled. "It was real this time! It was real! Why did you take me away?" he wailed.

His inner voice, speaking through the suit, held no pity.

"You were going to kill us... again."

"I did what you told me to do! I found Jason, at least I-"

"That was not him, just an illusion."

"I know that!" Daniel snapped. He gazed at the giant white walls and recalled a ghost story he'd once read on Halloween. A lonely spirit couldn't remember how it had died. The spirit was destined to wander the endless halls of a strange castle until the memory returned. He'd been too scared to hear how the story ended, and he berated himself now for his weakness. He wished he knew if the ghost ever escaped from the prison.

The enormous room was as silent as his first encounter. If the walls knew the secrets of this place, they weren't telling.

"This is insane."

"It is a reflection of you, nothing more."

"What are you saying, I'm crazy?"

"No, you are not crazy, just…not prepared. You should not have chosen this path."

"I didn't choose this! Jason jumped through the portal and Nierion followed him. What was I supposed to do, stay on the surface and wait to die?! Besides, the portal was supposed to take me to a city, wasn't it?"

"But it did not. It took us here."

Daniel threw up his arms in disgust. "I can see that!"

"And you do not want to leave."

"I know tha—Wait, what do you mean I don't want to leave? What the hell do you think I've been trying to do?!"

"Transform."

Daniel dropped his arms and surveyed the silent, mocking walls. "What does *that* mean?! I've been doing what you told me to do! Make a path to Jason, so that's what I did!"

"I know, but that did not work. It is not what you wanted."

"I want… to get out of here!" Daniel was again losing patience with this annoyingly cryptic, inner monologue. He vowed to make a harsh examination of his subconscious if he ever got home.

"I think we can leave whenever you want… but only if that is what you really want."

"That *is* what I want!" Daniel sniped through clenched teeth.

"Clearly this is not the case. It is fortunate the Archivist gave you the suit; we would have died many times in this place, otherwise."

On the verge of a sarcastic retort, Daniel was struck by something his inner voice said, or rather not said.

"You told me... you... we... whatever. You said, deep down we could feel Jason, I mean the real Jason, not some imaginary one."

"I felt him for a moment, a star burning bright, but very far away. I cannot feel him anymore."

Daniel nodded and wiggled his fingers about as he formulated a hypothesis.

"What about Nierion, do we sense the Archivist?"

"No, we do not sense anything resembling the Archivist."

Daniel stood up and put his arms akimbo. He saw the white walls as if for the first time. Then, he tried to empty his mind of hopes, judgments and fears. He focused solely on his desire to occupy a point in space beside the Archivist.

The wall at the far side of the chamber began to shimmer. The material liquefied and white became black; leaving a perfect circle.

Firmly keeping in mind the one thing he wanted, and nothing else, Daniel raced to the circle. He struggled to stay focused, as each step brought intoxicating possibilities that threatened to displace his one firm desire. He ferociously fought the tide of wondrous potentials for his life... he could make them real... he could make them happen like magic... he only had to will them into being... The portal began to look hazy, as if fading away.

He hardened his mind into diamond.

"No!" He wheezed a few breaths as he sprinted towards the black circle. He tightened his solitary desire in a vice and refused to let go as he leapt into the portal. His body felt ripped apart at the seams in an all-too-familiar fashion: the Travel Sequence. This time, he happily endured the pain.

Chapter 29: Eye of the Storm

Jason pulled his finger out of the turquoise pool. He noticed small ripples on the surface and assumed he'd made them. The liquid was cool, yet slightly sticky. He held his index finger to his nose but there was no discernible scent. Meanwhile the shadows of the serpentine creatures on the far side of the cave continued their whirling dance of agony. The fact they made no sound reminded Jason of some bizarre silent film. He began to circumnavigate the pool's edge, searching for the physical source of the shifting shadows, but he was alone.

The shadows were a vision of some other time, when their miserable souls were captured and held on display in the strange cave. With each step, the peculiar feeling that this world was not quite as real as it should be tiptoed beside him matching his cadence. The other side of the cave was farther away than he anticipated, an illusion created by the shadows. He'd assumed they were about his size, but as he approached the wall, he saw that they towered above him.

He gazed at the puckered mouths set at the edge of the bullet-shaped heads and swore the aliens were calling for help. They were prisoners here, with nothing waiting for them but insanity and death. Jason was furious at whomever, or whatever, had shackled them. He wanted to help them escape, but the notion seemed silly. How could he help shadows on a wall? He twisted to see how he'd possibly missed the source of the shadows, and was suddenly sure he was being watched. He spun to face the wall again, but knew that the eyes he felt upon him didn't belong to any of the hulking shades.

Jason slunk into the writhing, alien shadows.

"Who's there?" his voice cracked. There was no echo of his words but the surface of the pool rippled in response. The jagged stone against his back reminded him that he was also a prisoner.

"Please… I didn't mean to disturb you. I'll leave… just tell me how."

The wall behind him let out a croak, like the grunt of a starving man, and began to move towards the pool. Jason pushed back with all his might, but his feeble effort was no match. The spiked rock tore into his hands and became freezing. He pulled his hands away. They swelled with pain as if stung by hornets.

He darted his eyes to see that the entire cave was converging upon the turquoise pool. To his dismay, the silently thrashing shadows had stilled. Their hidden gazes bore into him without pity.

"I've been looking for you," a voice rasped from behind him.

Jason shot around to see a massive body emerge from the pool. Milky liquid fell from broad, sloping shoulders that met at a taut neck chorded with muscle. Above that, he recognized the alien shadows' head, like a bullet tipped by a pinched mouth lined with small, blunt teeth. Unlike the shadows, however, atop this bullet-head was a mound like a tank turret, and set within a thick brow was a single, glowing yellow eye. Jason averted his eyes from its penetrating gaze to view the being's four muscled arms. They ended in blunt hands with powerful fingers that dragged the remainder of the smooth, serpentine body from the murk.

"Are… are you a Ranis Aun?" Jason whispered.

The being raised its bulk to rest on its coiled tail. The alien didn't answer, but waved a heavy hand. Suddenly, the shadows' hands emerged from the wall to grab Jason. He gritted his teeth and fought the spectral bonds to no effect; he was cruelly trapped.

Jason watched in terror, struggling against the shadow's grip, as the being dragged itself towards him. Despite his fear, he could tell the creature was hurt, and that the dragging was not a normal movement. The monstrous body stopped perhaps three feet away and plunged its huge arms onto the sharp rocks on either side of him. The alien's broad chest and enormous head covered Jason's view of the cave beyond. The solitary eye widened and shone like yellow flames dancing in a cook-fire.

A burly hand clasped Jason's head like a nutcracker. His jaw was pinned shut and his temples squeezed so he had no choice but stare directly into the raging fire of the being's eye. At first this felt pleasant, a calming trance, but after a moment became a searing hook driving into his brain. He wailed into the cave's darkness. He screamed until his lungs could bear no more, but razor claws he couldn't see still tore through him.

"Stop, please!" Jason cried. "What do you want from me?!"

The creature answered question with question.

"Where did you come from?" It screeched in an unknown language, but somehow Jason understood every word.

"Earth," he sputtered, but he knew the word was meaningless to the abomination that held his head in a vice-like grip.

"Where are you hiding It?"

"I'm not hiding anything!"

The serpentine being didn't believe him.

"No sense of It now… but before, felt It burning through me. I know It came from you… Jirnkaa Bira'anan!"

"Please!" Jason croaked. "I don't know what that means, I'm not hiding anything!" A wave of pain blistered through his body like the pounding of a hammer.

The biting rasp grated at the skin on Jason's face.

"Which one gave you its strength?!"

"I don't know what that means," Jason sobbed. The pain was too great, and he felt himself drifting away like he was separate from his himself... watching his body being tortured from above.

"You're lying!" roared the alien.

Jason's body was pressed against the rock like a ragdoll. His mind was being gutted. Just when he was about to surrender, an intense fury billowed within him, fighting total enervation. He managed to syphon strength from the belief that he'd done nothing to deserve this abuse. He deserved better than a lonely death at the hands of a monster light-years from home. And he refused to die. At all costs, he had to let his mom know he didn't run away from her.

This determined heat stoked within him, growing until he felt like an expanding star.

"Yes!" the being cried, and its puckered mouth pulled back into a rictus of stained teeth. "I knew you were hiding It from me!"

Jason couldn't hear the alien's words. He heard nothing but the throbbing heart of anger that coursed through him. He was lightning, he was thunder...

A hazy blue-and-white sheen swirled from his limp body. He peered into the malevolent yellow eye and felt no regret for what he was about to do. He heard the strange words "Jirnkaa Bira'anan" repeated in a fog of spit and dread, but they weren't going to distract him. He closed his eyes and unleashed his storm.

The creature, the shadows, the murky pool, the cave in its entirety was obliterated in a blinding fire, consumed by a hungry stellar maw, and Jason was its mighty core. In an instant, the tempest ceased, and everything was dark.

A massive stark-white room surrounded Jason when his vision returned. The creature's body lay before him, scourged and revolting. The face was a smoking crater, the skin of its burly arms and serpent tail were melted to the ground. An iridescent, turquoise fluid oozed from the alien's open wounds.

Jason gazed into its now vacant eye. A gurgling noise trickled from its throat. He felt sick, not just because of the be-

ing's horrid appearance, but because he knew he was responsible.

Sorrow rushed up his throat like acid. Something about
the terrible sight made Jason forget that not moments before
this alien had held no value for his life... but maybe it was
scared too. Maybe it hated being trapped against its will as
much as he did. Maybe it also suffered a great loss and didn't
understand why... The compassion that now enveloped Jason felt hollow, too little and too late.

He knelt beside the dying body.

"What are you?"

The gurgling increased; the creature was trying to speak.
"Nothing... anymore."

Jason felt pinned by the anguish in his throat.

"What... were you?"

Turquoise ooze trickled from the corner of the creature's
mouth. "Cohev...Senar..." it whispered.

"Cohev Senar!" Jason exclaimed. "You are a Ranis Aun!"

The wounded being strained to turn its neck. Its dull eye
met Jason's. A faint smile lifted the edges of its mouth--a
smile of fondness, of remembering.

"Once... once. Before..."

Jason crouched until he was inches from the Ranis Aun's
mangled face. The alien's breath was putrid, but he didn't
care.

"Before what?"

"Darka... Aravan."

Jason's eyes opened wide and his jaw dropped; he knew
those words.

"Is that where we are? Is this the Night Path?"

The Ranis Aun's brow twitched and a hidden, heavy lid
closed over the fading glow of its eye.

"Never should have come... Followed another who had
been given the Gift... Left, left me behind..."

"That's what you were trying to take from me--a gift? You
mean the Touch?"

The dying Ranis Aun didn't understand. "... You know,

the Touch, Esan's Touch... from the Shantar Anar."

The lid retracted suddenly, and a pulsing flare of fear and hatred blazed from the eye.

"Their world... This is *their* world." The lid descended again, this time consuming the eye entirely. The Ranis Aun's head loped to the side, exposing the charred remains of its broken skull.

"Wait!" Jason bawled. "How do I get out of here?!"

"Follow me," it wheezed, and then died.

The serene relaxation that washed over the alien corpse chilled Jason to the bone. He could only imagine what agony the Ranis Aun had endured in this place, and for how long, to seek death as a welcome escape.

He stepped from the limp body to survey the massive room, which was eerily quiet. He shivered. *Why would the Shantar Anar make this place?* One glance at the dead Ranis Aun convinced him that he needed to find a way out. He was desperate to avoid the same fate.

From the Ranis Aun's cryptic response, Jason reasoned that the other--the one with the gift--had managed to escape somehow. And if that gift really was the Touch, then he had a chance, too. But how could he use the Touch to escape? He'd used it to create illusions of his father and mother and his old room, and he'd used It to destroy the Ranis Aun. Both of those times, he had no rational, thought-out plan; he'd simply reacted instinctively to strong desires. Maybe all he had to do was wish really hard to leave.

Could it be that easy?

Jason inhaled deeply and closed his eyes. He focused inwards and found the Spark eagerly waiting for him. Touching It this way felt like being reunited with a lost friend. He let the Spark blossom and felt Its immense power, again firmly in his grasp. But before he could articulate his wish, his mind was bombarded by images of possible futures and changed pasts. They were all so wonderful, and so real, and he knew he had the power to make them happen. If he just waved his finger, if he just willed them to be he could...

"No!" his shout filled the vast room.

He tried to steel himself from the accosting visions that slid through his mind like sickly sweet syrup… His parents smiling and holding hands, watching an older version of himself… A quiet kiss shared with a dream girl somewhere outside of time… A star-filled sky above the planet Earth, now at peace and free of all incurable disease… All of mankind thankful, grateful to him, their savior, their protector, their…

"Lava Mind," he got out in tapered breath, and pushed away the intoxicating fantasies. "Lava Mind… Lava Mind," Jason repeated. He held the swirling dreams at bay by imagining a point on the far wall as a tiny blip of empty space. He extended his hand at this fictional point, and the far wall peeled away like a banana until the empty space was the size of his fist. He reached further, and felt a warm tingling, as if he'd placed his hand in a hot bath. He thrust deeper, until he could almost touch the emptiness, and the wall bloomed again. The void was now the size of his head. Beyond lay impenetrable darkness, as if Jason was staring into the end of everything.

Wispy waves of green light spread over the infinite hole as he clutched his fist to his body. The waves solidified into a translucent disk that glowed green. As he approached, the center of the disk protruded. Crevices and shadows, hills and valleys emerged like a topographic map. By the time he'd crossed the room, he recognized a generic human face. More features appeared, and he realized the face was his own.

He stared at the green-hued phantom of himself, but there was nothing behind the replica's eyes. The face drew in upon itself, from convex to concave until he was looking at its hollowed-out interior. There was only one thing he could think to do: he leaned his face into the perfect, seamless mold, which disappeared, as did everything around him.

Jason stared ahead, expecting to be consumed, and sure enough, the abyss pulled him in, disassembling him piece-by-piece, fragment-by-fragment, atom-by-atom.

His senses failed and his memories fell away. Stripped of

his identity, he felt like a drop in a vast ocean. But then he was reassembled, and distinguished from the ocean by the unique torrent of his feelings and memories. The sudden burden of his mass was excruciating. The strain of being re-made was agonizing. He felt crushed by the terrible and wonderful vulnerability of having people to hold dear. Yet that awareness eased the pressure weighing him down.

He knew that the Darka Aravan was not a prison, though it seemed that way. The Night Path was like a towering stone wall set with ramparts and guards. But in the center was a feeble wooden door with no lock, and if he wished to leave, he merely had to push the door open and walk through.

Jason opened his eyes to reveal another portal. He cast a pitiful glance at the remains of the Ranis Aun he'd killed--and also set free. He took a deep breath to prepare for the pain he knew was coming. Then he jumped through.

–◎⋔ຣ–

Jason tumbled from the portal and hit solid ground with an involuntary "umph!" He rested on his hands and knees to make sure he'd again survived the horrible effects of the Travel Sequence. Eventually, he rallied the strength to stand. He was in the middle of a box-shaped room, perhaps fifteen feet by fifteen feet. The area was illuminated by a direction-less, dim light, which let him see that every inch of the walls, floor and ceiling were covered in the scrawling script of the Ranis Aun.

It would be really helpful if I could read all this, he thought as he crossed to examine the writing up-close. Of course, proximity didn't improve his comprehension. *Maybe I can use the power of the Touch to understand the words!* He reached within to summon the Spark of energy and awareness, but It remained the tiny bulb hiding in a corner of his mind. He tried again to harness It as he had in the Night Path, but the Spark was unrespon-sive to his efforts. Jason cursed under his breath.

"Why can I only use It sometimes?!" He grumbled as he

scanned for the door, but there was no door. There was no visible exit other than the portal leading back to the dead alien's tomb.

Total exhaustion swept over Jason. He sank to his knees and let gravity pull the rest of his body to the ground where the uneven, embossed script bit into him. After all he'd learned, he was still trapped.

His mom sprang to mind. He wasn't sure how long he'd been gone. Traveling on the ship and navigating the Night Path had distorted his sense of time. *She's got to be frantic by now*, he thought. He was helpless to reassure her, which made him sad, but also angry. Angry at himself for being so hard on her. For not tolerating a little boredom for her sake.

If I could've just been happy…

Jason filled with regret as he lay on the uneven ground. He was about to close his eyes, content to let fatigue carry him away, but a new light filtered across him. He followed its source to a tiny tear in one wall, as if the material was made of fabric, rather than metal or stone.

Suddenly, that wall pushed inwards and he fumbled on his backside away from the intruding light. The tear opened further, and through it he soon saw four familiar visors. His heart pounded with newfound hope as he heard a glorious sound:

"There you are, Jason," the Archivist said.

Chapter 30: Reunited

The pain of the Travel Sequence was too great to bear after Daniel's experience in the Night Path, and he lost consciousness before being spit out the other end. Though his vision was blurry, comforting light illuminated walls that appeared to be covered in trickles of liquid mercury. In his periphery, he noticed the shadows of two figures talking. He shot to his knees in fear, but when his eyes focused he realized he saw Jason and the Archivist. Daniel's heart beamed with hope.

"Are you real?" he dared to ask.

Jason spun at the sound of his voice.

"You're awake!" Jason cried, as if Daniel had been asleep for days. "Am *I* real? I should be asking you the same question!"

That seemed a good response in Daniel's estimation. Apparently, Jason's adventure in the Night Path had been as strange as his own. He wiped the sleep from his eyes.

"How long have I been passed out?"

Jason tilted his head to the side.

"Not long. You tumbled out of the portal shortly after I did and slid right onto the floor, unconscious. Nierion checked on you. There didn't seem to be anything wrong, you just needed to rest."

Daniel turned to gaze at the ominous portal towering above him. He shuddered.

"This isn't just another illusion is it? I'm not still in that place am I?"

"No," the Archivist said, focusing its visors on the portal

as well. "According to the writing around this entrance... or exit, depending on one's viewpoint, this hidden chamber is on the outskirts of Spiria Inan, the great city of the Ranis Aun."

Knowing he was safe for the moment, Daniel heaved a sigh, but then a jolt of anger flushed over his fatigue. He stood up and cast Jason a fierce glare of rebuke.

"You had to go through that portal, didn't you?"

The contrition on Jason's face was surprising.

"I know... I'm really sorry. I should have listened to you."

"Well..." Daniel stumbled. He hadn't expected a quick and genuine apology. "Lesson learned... I guess."

The Archivist glided to Jason's side. Though it conveyed no emotion, there was something about Nierion that comforted Daniel.

"What was your experience, Daniel?"

"You mean, after you both left me?"

The Archivist seemed oblivious to his self-pity.

"Yes, after that, please."

Daniel sighed and scrunched his shoulders.

"Well... at the beginning it felt just like back on the ship, when we traveled to this planet. Then... there was something different, I can't really explain, but it felt like I was being examined from the inside out, every last part of me. I ended up in this giant white room, and I had no idea what to do."

"I was in the white room too!" Jason exclaimed, "But... I didn't see you there."

"Perhaps you were there at different times," the Archivist suggested.

"Or maybe there's more than one white room," Daniel proposed. He furrowed his brow and tried to think of how best to describe his experience.

"Anyway, then I was just trying to find a way out, but all I ended up doing was sending myself into these strange hallucinations. They were so real, I think I could've actually hurt myself, only I didn't because the suit interfered."

He put a speculative finger to his lip, "Actually... it *told* me to stop."

A muted grey light appeared in the Archivist's visors.

"The suit communicated with you at a conscious level?"

"Not the whole time," Daniel replied and sat down to stretch his aching neck and back. "I heard my voice, but it was more like I was speaking in a binary code, something super basic, and a piece of my brain was also translating. That's the best I can explain."

"So how did you escape?" Jason pressed.

"That's the weird part," Daniel said, glancing at the portal, "I think everything that happened in there was kind of my own doing. When I tried to leave for real, I just sort of... left"

Nierion turned to Jason. "That does not sound like your experience."

"Why, what happened to you?" Daniel asked, intrigued.

Jason paced as he spoke, "Sort of the same at the beginning. I had a similar feeling, like I was being examined, only then I felt like a lock fitting into a key... or a key fitting into a lock? I don't know which one I was. I had power in there Daniel... Amazing power... But it wasn't real, at least not in the way I wanted. And I wasn't alone."

"Who was with you? Nierion?"

"No. It was not me," the Archivist responded. "And that is another matter, I was transported directly to this room and felt no... examination during the Travel Sequence."

Daniel was mystified. "Then who was with you, Jason?"

"One of the Ranis Aun."

Daniel heard reluctance in his friend's voice.

"You found them! Is that where they all are, in the-"

"No!" Jason interrupted, and then his steady voice returned. "No... just one and I... I don't want to talk about it." Jason spun away, like he was going to walk to the other side of the room, but then turned back abruptly. "Nierion, what does Jirnkaa Bir...An..."

"Bira'anan?" the Archivist suggested.

Jason nodded, "Yes."

Nierion pondered the correct translation for a moment and then said, "Key to Locked Doors."

Daniel watched Jason slowly nod, as if something had fallen into place. He wanted to know more, but the pensive expression on his companion's face kept Daniel silent. Suddenly, Jason stood firm, a bright fury apparent in his eyes.

"Why did the Shantar Anar make the Night Path?"

The emotionless Archivist was nonetheless stunned, "I don't-"

"Don't lie to me!" Jason snarled, "The Ranis Aun called itself Cohev Senar. It knew about the Shantar Anar... It said that place was *their world!*"

Daniel tried to intervene, "Jason relax-"

Jason's gaze was hot as burning coals.

"No! You didn't see it... you didn't see its pain! It wanted my gift, MY GIFT... The Key to Locked Doors. I had to *kill* it, or it would have killed me!"

Jason lunged towards the Archivist.

"And it was happy to die, Nierion... Happy to escape that nightmare! What kind of monsters would make that place?!"

Daniel's attention flitted back and forth from Jason to the Archivist. The scorn scratched into Jason's brow met a searching silence from the Archivist. The tension in the room was suffocating, until eventually Nierion spoke.

"I... I do not have an answer for you."

"Of course not. You say you don't know anything, but I'm not sure I believe that!"

"Jason, calm down." Daniel grabbed his friend's arm, but Jason tore away.

"No, don't you see? *They* made that hell, Daniel." He pointed a sharp finger at the Archivist. "Nierion knew what the Night Path was, of course he did. How could he not have known?! This was his plan all along!"

"I am not a he," the Archivist interrupted.

Jason twisted to confront the four empty visors. "Whatever you are, stop lying to me! Stop pretending not to know anything! You wanted us to be trapped in there forever, didn't you! "

Daniel felt helpless as he watched a dim blue glow emanate from the Archivist's visors while two black tendrils rocketed from compartments in Nierion's chest. They gripped Jason's arms and all Daniel could think was that Jason was right; they'd been horribly fooled and this was the end. But then, the blue light shot from the visors to cover Jason's body like the photons were seeping into the microscopic space between the suit and his body. Jason slumped as if the anger hoisting him up was being been squeezed out the bottom of his feet. His gaze became downcast, almost ashamed. Again, Daniel breathed a sigh of relief.

"I have never lied to you." the Archivist said. "I am not human, but neither am I cold and heartless."

"Then why did you let us go in there?" Jason sobbed.

"I am sorry; I truly did not know what was going to happen. There is no mention of 'Darka Aravan' in the Archive."

"But the Ranis Aun... It told me the Shantar Anar made the Night Path."

"I... do not discount the truth of its conviction." Daniel heard sadness in Archivist's words. "I've seen much, including the portals of entrance and exit, that lead me to the same conjecture."

The bindings loosened their grip and retreated into the Archivist's chest. Jason's exhaustion took him to his knees. Nierion sounded weary as well. "Right now... I feel as lost as you Jason, like my perspective has been shattered. But we must press on; we must discover what happened here!"

Daniel was puzzled, "Here? You mean in the Night Path."

"That as well," Nierion replied, "But I was referring to the city. I have attempted to use Esan's Eyes and still cannot locate any of the Ranis Aun."

"What do we do now?" Jason asked as he regained his footing.

"There is a small probability that the problem lies in the equipment, and I will not be satisfied until that can be completely eliminated. Therefore, we will explore the city to dis-

cover what happened to its inhabitants. And of course...
there is also the other issue."

Jason gave the Archivist a look of surprise.

"What's that?"

But Daniel already knew.

"We can't get back to the ship, except, maybe, by the way
we came." Daniel eyed the portal darkly.

Jason didn't understand.

"What do you mean? You can use Esan's Eyes to find the
ship... right?"

"I should be able to," the Archivist replied, "except that
that connection is lost as well."

"Then it *is* the equipment," Jason confirmed.

"No, something is messing with us," Daniel whispered.

The Archivist surveyed the room carefully.

"Perhaps, Daniel, or perhaps whatever is breaking the
connection is unaware that it is doing so. All the more reason
to continue exploring. I promise you both; we will find the
answers, together."

The Archivist seemed to want to give an innocent conclusion the benefit of the doubt, but Daniel peered suspiciously
at the script-covered walls of the room. The city of Spiria
Inan waited, just beyond.

Chapter 31: The Golden Fleece

Anne hasn't spoken to him in two days. He knows why. She catches a glance at his discerning eyes fixated on the road ahead. Both his hands grasp the wheel as he sings under his breath along with the radio. She hopes to spot a sign of remorse for what he'd done, but he just keeps humming. Driving through the flat fields under a giant sky matted here-and-there with fat, lazy clouds, it almost feels like the car isn't moving. Everything is still and waiting, expecting an apology. But the clouds pass and don't care. The fields bristle and sway in a churlish wind that whistles through the car, and he sings...

"Got cut off on the road today
Missed the light, missed the train, didn't mind too much
I was fine, just fine, but saw the frown greeting your face..."

...She barely remembers what they'd been arguing about; something stupid, she's sure. All that remains is the anger festering like some disease, keeping her from seeing how silly they were both behaving. She creeps another look at him, suffering a quiet smile as she watches his eyes bug in-and-out when he tries to hit notes too high and too low for his voice...

"... And a thousand other things on other days
Without a single change of the expression on my face
You say I'm indifferent to the world
Lack your passion, lack your flair..."

Is this how life's going to be? Moments of clarity and joy lost in a bog of trivial frustrations? Each day waking to find the light of the sun older, and she older as well? Losing opportunities to the vault of days past, until she slips into a wrinkled husk of her youthful body, riddled with regrets? "I don't want that if you don't Michael," she whispers to him. He is lost in the song:

"…I know you think the days will never end
But I've only got so many times to touch your hair
To kiss your cheek, cause forever is just a word it seems
I'd like it to be more, well, only in my dreams…"

–◦⋔ꙅ–

Dean Kipson's final words to her repeated in Anne's head as she drove back to his house: "Only in my dreams." Despite Captain Willis' insistence, she couldn't forget him. When he'd shared his strange and frightening vision, there was something in his eyes and in his tone, a quality of age that she recognized as the recollection of a painful memory, an old memory. It was all that kept her from kicking down the door and pushing him aside to search for her son inside his house. She knew he hadn't been talking about Jason, and a feeling within her, stoked by the memory of a long-lost car ride, told her to take mercy on his grief. But there was something there, something she couldn't put to rest. She had to speak to him again.

Before she turned onto Cedar Lane, Anne spied a figure darting in and out of her rear-view mirror. Maybe fifty feet back, huffing and puffing to keep pace with the car, was Ashlyn. Anne pulled to the side of the road, but when the girl saw brake lights she darted up a driveway and hid behind a tree. Anne sighed, and got out of her car. With a couple cricks of a tired back, she strolled to the tree.

"Ashlyn?"

A small voice carried around the trunk of the sagging elm, "Oh my god, there are so many ants climbing up this tree! How do they walk straight up and down like that?"

Anne pursed her lips. "Ashlyn."

The girl peeked from behind the tree, her hair strewn about her face. Her cheeks were dappled in red from the bite of the wind.

"Oh… hi, Mrs. Swann!" Ashlyn labored. "Oh wait, you said it was all right if I called you Anne, remember?"

"That's fine, but what are-"

The girl beamed with delight. "Great!"

Anne smiled inwardly; she should've guessed Ashlyn wasn't going to admit to anything without a little prodding. "Would you like to tell me why you're following me?"

The girl feigned surprise and hurt. *She could use a few acting classes,* Anne thought as she crossed her arms, waiting for an explanation of pure invention.

"Following you? I was just riding to… this tree! It's my favorite tree in Ashton. I try to visit it at least once a week."

Anne was expecting better.

"Your favorite… tree."

"Right…" Ashlyn said under a grimace.

"Why are you following me?"

The girl sighed, her downcast eyes hidden beneath her eyelids like waning crescent moons.

"Because I was worried!" Ashlyn suddenly cried.

The fierce change in the girl's demeanor shocked Anne.

"Worried about what?"

"You!"

Anne blinked.

"Why are you worried about me?"

"Not about you. I was worried you didn't believe Captain Willis, that you thought what Mrs. Elliot…" Ashlyn glanced from side to side, making sure they were alone, "… What Sharon said about Dean was true."

Anne was struck by the girl's use of his first name.

"Do you know Dean, Ashlyn?"

"Maybe," the girl said sheepishly.

Ashlyn's clear chagrin didn't quell Anne's anger.

"You told me he was just some strange man your parents didn't want you to be around. Why did you lie to me?"

"I should have never said anything at all!" Ashlyn blurted. "I just... I wanted to be useful."

"Lying is not useful!"

"I didn't lie!" Ashlyn defended. "I... glied."

Anne frowned.

"You glied... what's a 'glie'?"

"A GOOD lie."

Anne could see the girl was invested in the difference.

"I couldn't tell you that I knew him," Ashlyn continued.

"Why not?"

Exasperated, Ashlyn sighed again.

"You're a parent! You have Parent Code."

Anne leaned on her right hip; the girl's jargon was making her weary.

"What does that mean?"

"Ugh," Ashlyn grunted. "It means you would've told my parents what I told you, because you'd think it would help you find Jason."

"I would never have-" Anne stopped herself as she peered into Ashlyn's discerning eyes. "Well, maybe you have a point."

Ashlyn crossed her arms.

"Yeah, believe me; I've been totally burned by Parent Code before."

The girl's hesitation was understandable, but Anne felt deserving of her trust. "I didn't tell Sharon or Coregon who told me about Dean."

Ashlyn nodded, dropping her arms to her sides.

"I only sort of know him," she confessed. "I mean, I've met him a few times, but I know... I knew his son. We were friends."

Anne narrowed her eyes. "Were friends? What happened?"

Ashlyn seemed to be fighting the urge to run. "Are you sure you don't want to talk about ants instead?"

"Who was his son, Ashlyn?"

The girl glanced right and left, still suspicious they were

being watched.

"If I tell you something, can you make me a promise?"

"Of course-"

"And I don't mean a parent promise," Ashlyn countered. "I'm not supposed to know this."

"Whatever you tell me here is between us," Anne said, but Ashlyn appeared unconvinced.

"Tell you what," Anne continued. "I'll do you one better than a promise; I give you my solemn oath that I will never tell your parents, or anyone else."

"Are you sure an oath ranks above a promise? I think they're just synonyms."

Anne sighed. "What about a vow, will you take a vow?"

"I think that's another synonym too."

Anne met the girl's eyes and gave her a smile full of trust and understanding. The girl's defensive posture weakened, she was convinced.

"Mr. Kipson's son was my best friend. His name is… was Leo."

The vision of Dean Kipson's eyes changing when he saw Jason's picture shot into Anne's head… A longing for something lost.

"His real name was Leonard, but we both thought that was kind of lame. He loved mythology and liked to pretend Leo was short for Leodocus, instead," Ashlyn continued. When Anne showed no sign of recognition, "He was one of the Argonauts. Not one of the famous ones but… I guess that fit him."

Anne shook her head in ignorance, which led to a twisted expression from Ashlyn. "You know, the ancient Greek story about the guys who found the Golden Fleece?"

Anne shrugged. "I was more of a math and science person in school." Ashlyn glared at her quizzically. "But, isn't that why you named your son Jason? He's the hero of the story."

"Oh," Anne said, finally understanding. "No, I just always liked the name." She smiled, but found a hint of disdain twitching in Ashlyn's face.

"Anyway… I met him at school my first day of fifth grade. Nobody else wanted to be friends with him because they thought he was strange. Well… that's not true. I think Daniel, Daniel Elliot, was his friend." A strange expression overtook Ashlyn, like she'd just put together two pieces of a forgotten puzzle. "They couldn't have been that great of friends, 'cause Leo kind of stopped hanging out with Daniel when we became close.

"He loved to explore and so do I, so we went exploring all over Ashton. Some nights we'd sneak out and ride our bikes into the woods where it was really dark, so we could see all the stars in the sky. This was only like, three years ago. Then one night, Leo came to my window and woke me up. He told me he was really sorry, but he had to go. I asked him where, but he wouldn't tell me. I wanted to go with him, but he wouldn't let me."

Ashlyn looked into the distance, as if still searching for her friend.

"He made me promise I wouldn't follow him. That was the last time anybody saw him. Not even Captain Willis could find him, and the police had to give up their search eventually. I'd ride my bike by the Kipson's house some nights to see if maybe Leo had come back. I could hear his parents screaming at each other, even from outside. I wish I hadn't kept that promise. I should have followed him!"

Ashlyn's eyes burned resolutely and Anne knew her pain.

"I'm really sorry, Ashlyn. Losing a friend is the worst thing in the world… but what does that have to do with Sharon and Dean?"

"*This* is the part I'm not supposed to know," the girl continued, her eyes wide and clear. "After Leo ran away, Mr. Kipson started acting really weird, like he was losing his mind kind of. Leo's mom couldn't take it anymore, losing her son, and I guess feeling like she lost her husband too. She… she killed herself. Even Captain Willis said it was definitely suicide, but some people blamed Dean like he'd killed her himself. They weren't sad for him at all; it wasn't fair." Anne had a dreadful feeling she knew where the story was headed.

"Sharon Elliot was Mrs. Kipson's best friend," Ashlyn continued. "They'd known each other forever. She wouldn't let there be an end to it. She sent nasty letters about Dean to the college—where he worked-- and got him fired. I don't know if he even tried to stand up for himself. I think he was tired of having to defend himself all the time, of having people look at him like he was the worst thing in the world. Nobody'd even talk to him. I tried, but he'd just tell me these weird things he'd seen... places that didn't make any sense, and I didn't know what to do. He kept saying he had to find the right path, that the ones he picked were always wrong and he could never find his son. I had no idea what he was talking about. I didn't want to be scared of him. I thought I should have been better than that, had more courage... but I didn't.

"Sometimes I see him sitting in the park when I'm riding by, but I don't stop. I don't think he'd even recognize me anymore if I did. Sharon is wrong about him. He's not a bad man; he's just sad and misses his son. I think you should leave him alone."

It was impossible to miss Ashlyn's fury and remorse. Anne was unsure what to say. She recalled Dean's vacant eyes... lost a wife... lost a son. The girl's eyes, in contrast, were hard and firm.

"I... I will. I promise," Anne said. Ashlyn sighed with relief, but Anne felt nothing of the sort. A gnawing ache bit at her gut and a fog lifted from her eyes. What was she doing? Why had she sought him out again? Something in his words, the expression on his face? All it had done was distract her from finding Jason! But what could she do?

"Now, about *your* son," Ashlyn remarked, as if on cue.

Anne was shaken from her winding thoughts. "Jason, what about him?"

"I'm going to help you find him," Ashlyn replied, her words brimming with confidence.

"That's very sweet but-"

"You said you wanted my help!" Ashlyn reminded, and

rested her fists on her hips. "I'm the one who found the footprints in the woods, *not* Captain Willis! I mean, he probably would have eventually but I-"

"And I'm grateful you found that clue, Ashlyn-"

"Ugh, let me finish!" the girl pouted, and then remembered herself. "Sorry, I'm sorry."

"It's all right. *I'm* sorry. I did ask for your help," Anne said, hoping to mollify the girl. Each second that passed was another she wasn't trying to find Jason.

"Right, only you didn't realize whose help you were getting," Ashlyn continued, oblivious to Anne's mounting anxiety. "I don't often share this with people, especially adults, but I possess excellent detective skills. Captain Willis is my teacher... He says I'm not supposed to call him that, teacher I mean, not Captain; I'm always supposed to call him that. He...says a lot of things I try not to pay too much attention to."

"I don't understand, you found another clue?"

"Not yet," Ashlyn replied, as a blush spread across her cheeks in acknowledgment of her failure. "But I didn't really have the opportunity. I would've done a more thorough job, but Captain Willis kept threatening to tell my parents where I was. I bet if we went back I could find something else, something not even the Captain could find!"

Anne crooked her eyebrow. "We?"

"I know, and normally I wouldn't involve a civilian," Ashlyn responded, glancing at Anne coolly. "But it was really tiring following you here, so I kind of need a ride back to the woods."

"This isn't a game. You need to leave this to the police. I'll take you home-"

"Please! The police won't go back to the woods; they think there's nothing else there. But they're wrong, I know it! You think I don't understand what's going on, but I'm thirteen... not dumb. Let me help you!"

What if Coregon really did miss something, Anne worried. She might regret indulging the girl, but desperation held a firm grip on her. As foolish as she rationally found Ashlyn's request, the thought of not following all the leads and leaving her son's fate totally in the hands of the police, however capable, seemed more ridiculous by far. The twinkling green of Ashlyn's irises couldn't have agreed more.

Chapter 32: Eureka

Ashlyn stared out the passenger window of Anne's car while her bike rested in the back on a thin trail of dirt from its tires. Ashlyn had tried to apologize, but Anne didn't care. The mess was just another of life's trivial imperfections.

Jason's mother didn't speak as she drove, and between her silence and the houses speeding by, Ashlyn felt very small. She worried she'd bitten off more than she could chew, and now a desperate parent was depending on her to fix everything. Her bravado melted like ice in a cup of hot tea, and all that remained was the fear that she'd fail to find Jason, like she'd failed to find Leo. Ashlyn peeped at Anne's mouth, a thin line of determination; she felt like a fool. *Why do I think it'll be different this time?* she wondered.

Nobody knew, not even Coregon, how hard she'd tried to find Leo. Many nights, she'd snuck out of her room and scoured Ashton's streets-- and the surrounding suburbs--on her bike. Sometimes she didn't get back home until dawn and had to fight exhaustion to get through the next school day. She never found his trace. True she was older now, and had more experience. But passion had driven her then, and the fear that if she didn't find him, she'd never have another friend like him again. The drone of the car on mostly empty streets made Ashlyn feel like she was halfway between consciousness and sleep, and she was trying hard not to fall into a bad dream. She was far more worried about failing Anne than facing her parents' disapproval of where she was and what she was doing. There'd always be plenty of excuses for them.

The car pulled into the Swann's driveway and Ashlyn was

anxious to get out and shake the doubt from her normally stout resolve. As soon as the car's engine turned off, she leapt out, opened the latch on the driveway gate and raced into the backyard, which butted against the woods. She moved like a bloodhound, retracing the path she'd taken to the clearing where Coregon had found her. She glanced back to make sure Anne was keeping up with her rigorous pace. The woman was breathing hard but didn't complain; she seemed eager.

Ashlyn stopped to examine a familiar fork, then was off down the right path. She eased to a quick walk, and kept track of Anne by watching the woman's shadow in her periphery. They soon found themselves in the clearing with the boys' footprints.

Anne needed all of her endurance to stay close to the darting girl. The cold morning jogs were finally paying off. She happily rested her hands on her knees for a moment when she reached the meadow.

"Is this where you found the footprints?" she called to Ashlyn. Before the girl could answer, Anne was overtaken by a queer anxiety as she felt the invisible current of Jason's presence sticking to the trees, rocks and grass. She pictured him standing in this spot, safe, close to home, and then … gone.

Ashlyn's harried voice brought her back to focus. "Over here!"

She ran to where the girl was pointing and saw a long, curving, shallow scar in the earth, just as Coregon had described. Ashlyn stood nearby with her fists resting on her hips. The girl looked contemplative, trying to unravel the mystery.

"The footprints are about ten feet that way," she said.

Anne watched her survey the surrounding area until Ashlyn's gaze rested on an outcropping of small boulders. Then the girl shot off towards the heavy stones and fumbled her way up, apparently to get a better vantage point of the meadow. She wiped scatterings of debris from her pants, then motioned for Anne to join her. Anne silently cursed, then shrugged, and hurried to the rocky outcropping. After one failed attempt, she found a natural ramp of dirt and exposed roots leading to the top. Finally, she joined the girl and gazed across the meadow, trying to match Ashlyn's line of sight. She saw both curved indentations in the trampled meadowgrass, but they gave her no better idea of what had happened here. If anything, she was more confused. The markings clearly weren't natural and yet, she couldn't imagine what had made them.

In an authoritative voice Anne was learning not to take as a sign of disrespect, Ashlyn told her to "keep looking." The girl then jumped off the boulders, landing gracefully on the uneven ground at their base. She raced back to the first indentation, sank to her knees, and brought her head down almost to the grass line.

Anne cupped her hands on each side of her mouth: "What are you looking for?"

"Anything out of the ordinary," the girl called back.

Anne wondered what was ordinary about any of this, but kept the discouraging thought to herself. She was struck in the next moment by the fact that she was a grown woman staring at a child pretending to be a detective. The girl's plan sounded so promising, but as she stood on the boulders staring at Ashlyn foraging through the crumpled grass, Anne felt ridiculous.

She navigated her way carefully off the rocks, down the natural ramp and approached Ashlyn, who lay pressed against the ground--tasting the dirt, feeling the grass--doing everything a thirteen-year- old imagined a good detective should do. Anne felt a pang of sadness watching this girl try so hard to find something that wasn't there.

Adrenaline seeped into the deep cavities of Anne's body, making her heart race. After a few breaths, despair returned.

"Ashlyn," she said, but the girl ignored her, or was too lost in thought to hear. Anne knelt down. "Ashlyn," she repeated. "Let me take you home, there's nothing to-"

The girl leapt to her feet, almost knocking Anne over. "I

think I know what this is!"

Anne was stunned. "What? What is it?"

Ashlyn's exuberance died suddenly, replaced by suspicion. "I'm not sure I can tell you."

"What do you mean? Why?" Anne demanded, ready to shake the answer out of the girl's head.

Ashlyn grimaced with dread. "Because… You aren't going to believe me."

Anne was not to be denied. "Nobody else has any idea what these are, so if you think you do, even a guess, then tell me!" She followed with a softer tone, "You don't have to be afraid."

Ashlyn stared back boldly, and Anne knew the girl wasn't afraid of her. "I've… I've seen something similar before," she said. "Not personally, but I saw it on TV. Episode twelve of… 'Dead Nebula,' the show on the Science Channel, with Dr. Isaac Hampton."

"Who?"

Again perplexed by Anne's ignorance, Ashlyn frowned. "Dr. Isaac Hampton… You've never seen 'Dead Nebula?!'"

Anne still didn't appreciate her tone. "No, I… wait, you're saying some guy on TV was talking about marks like these?"

"Not 'some guy,'" Ashlyn retorted. "Dr. Isaac Hampton, the smartest man in the world… at least I think. The show's on Friday nights. He explores unsolved mysteries of science and bizarre claims sent in by viewers."

Anne was incredulous. "I don't understand, is the show real or fake?"

"Real! I mean…"

"What?"

"Real. It's real."

"And the host was talking about marks like these?" she asked, pointing at the enigmatic indentations.

"Yes, precisely."

Anne couldn't guess what the lines in the ground had to do with a science program, and she wasn't sure she wanted the answer, but she bade Ashlyn to continue with a brisk flip of her hand, and the girl obliged.

"They were made by some kind of surveyor."

Ashlyn clearly expected she'd be understood. Anne sighed, and again hurried the girl's explanation along with another circular hand motion.

"It means…" Ashlyn continued, building suspense, "that Jason and Daniel… have been abducted by aliens!"

Anne gave her a disapproving glare. "If you aren't going to be serious then-"

The girl's lips pursed. "I am being serious!"

Even worse…

"This isn't a game!" she chided.

"I told you, you wouldn't believe me!" Ashlyn wailed, her eyes welling with tears.

Anne realized she'd betrayed her promise, and immediately felt ashamed of her outburst. But that didn't change the fact that the girl was obviously delusional.

Anne closed her eyes to clear her head. When she opened them, Ashlyn was still before her, real, standing where her son should have been. She was too tired to indulge Ashlyn's fantasies any further.

"It's the truth," the girl croaked.

Anne brushed Ashlyn's hair from her damp eyes, and gently wrapped her in a maternal hug. "Come on, Ashlyn, it's time for you to go home."

Chapter 33: Ghosts of Spiria Inan

The city, if it could be called that, was massive. Jason expected to find a system of interconnected caves when they left the secret room, but instead they emerged into a metropolis-sized cavity in the subterranean depths of Ranis Anjiran. Cut into the stone floor were countless bubbles that looked like frosted glass, which were set in clearly delineated rows. Each bubble emanated a pasty light. Tracing the light upwards, Jason saw that the upper limit of Spiria Inan was a dark sea, hundreds--if not thousands--of feet above his head.

There were no buildings, or their alien equivalents, but a cluster of spheres of all different sizes; some smaller than he, others as large as a house. They were arranged at a multitude of heights, from not more than ten feet off the surface up towards the ceiling, disappearing into the vastness beyond his sight. The spheres he could see were connected by an immense network of things that looked like pipes, which crisscrossed and twisted throughout the cavern. The spheres and the piping were all made of a meteor-grey metal that dimly sparkled with a prismatic gloss. Though Jason was no engineer, he was sure he knew where they must be.

"Nierion, I think we're beneath the city, like in a sewer system or... something."

Daniel nodded in agreement as he strolled beneath some nearby spheres. "I didn't think this place would look like Ashton, but... what kind of city is this?"

Nierion glided between the bubbles of light in the floor, casting its visors curiously at the web of interlinked globes. "Our coordinates are correct Jason; this is not a sub-system of the city… However, the configuration does not match the description of Spiria Inan in the Archive."

Jason visually backtracked one large pipe to its origin in the stone wall, which lay in the direction of the hidden room. Grooved lines running along the exterior of the pipe resembled the inside-out rifling of a gun. "Then what are these things?"

"I… do not know," the Archivist replied. Jason caught the hesitation in its voice. He followed the pipe with his eyes back to a sphere a little ways off, about thirty feet above his head. The light from the bubbled floor was strong enough to see that the sphere bore intricately etched swirls and twisting lines, like someone… or something, had gone to a great deal of trouble to decorate the surface. As Jason approached the sphere, he swore the object was calling him, though not with any words. Instead, it was Daniel who spoke, and though his friend was close by, Jason could barely hear him.

"What are we supposed to do now?"

Good question, Jason thought as he stood beneath the sphere, but he was too distracted to care about making a plan. Something between his feet was glowing.

He realized he was standing on a rectangular stone raised perhaps two inches off the surface. In the middle of this platform, a single word of the Ranis Aun language emitted a soothing, violet radiance. Jason was now enveloped in a cylinder of violet light that beamed from the perimeter of the stone beneath his feet to the sphere above his head.

In an instant, he was transported inside the sphere, which was filled with a viscous substance, and he was stuck at the center. He tried wiggling his arms and legs, but he felt like he was moving through honey. He thrashed his limbs furiously in an effort to escape, and gasped helplessly before realizing that his breathing was normal. He tried calling out, but his voice couldn't escape. The sphere was a perfect barrier to the city outside.

Great, Jason thought and tried to shimmy his way towards the sphere's bottom. His skin prickled with goose bumps at the ticklish coldness of the jelly-like goo. The itchy chill penetrated his body, sending shivers through his veins and viscera, until he felt numb.

The tiny Spark hiding in the depths of his mind suddenly blossomed again, countering the ice with a blazing heat. This battle raged inside him as the sphere shimmered with blue and white. Jason's fear returned, though it felt somehow magnified. A small part of him was aware enough to wonder why a sphere in a city of the Ranis Aun could awaken the Shantar Anar's Touch. The question was eerie and puzzling, but the answer was beyond him.

Images appeared on the globe's interior surface, like projections on a movie screen: A Ranis Aun's serpentine body gliding through empty space, its muscular arms extended and its hands splayed out, as if riding invisible wind. The being's glowing blue eye stared at Jason, entreating him to join. The gelatinous material pulsated, replacing the icy chill and anxiety with soothing warmth. The Spark's inferno was calmed and he felt a sense of wonderment, of discovery, of being awakened into an existence he only now began to understand. The Ranis Aun joyously circumnavigated the sphere, and other Ranis Aun materialized into view beside it, as if they'd been called from the ether to join in a celebration of life.

The jelly pulsed in gentle, undulating waves, injecting Jason with feelings of friendship, love, and hope, as if they were his nourishment in this tranquil, alien womb. Then, all the Ranis Aun turned brittle, and cracked. Their skin dissolved, revealing muscles and tendons that were being consumed by thousands of eel-like parasites. Some ripped apart flesh, others ground up bone and feasted on the remains, but the largest congregations formed into devouring hordes at the center of their hosts. The jelly churned around Jason, grating against his skin like sharp flakes of stone. He was filled with despair.

The parasites gorged mercilessly, fighting each other between voracious bites, also killing each other as they fed. Jason felt gnashing teeth drive through his own flesh, and he screamed as if his body too was being eaten, piece-by-piece.

But when the Ranis Aun were nothing more than husks, the eel-like parasites turned fully on each other. Soon, only one remained, and it ravaged its own body, leaving a pool of toxic, purple blood. That quickly vanished as well, revealing still-beating hearts in the ghostly skeleton-cages of the dead Ranis Aun.

The gelatinous goo constricted around Jason. He felt like a piece of grain crushed by a millstone. A draining sadness poured through him as he witnessed the glowing eye of the first Ranis Aun expire. Then, violet light shimmered around him, and in an instant he was back on the ground, huddled beside the rectangular stone, gasping for breath. He peered up and swore he could still see the glowing eye riveted on him. Jason wasn't surprised when the shuddering brightness of the Spark diminished into obscurity, but he still felt an indescribable ocean of sorrow. Though he couldn't see anything, the waves of grief came from a distinct direction: the center of the vast cavern.

Jason fumbled away from the trigger stone, hobbling backwards until he bumped into an oblivious Daniel, who'd been gawking aimlessly at the galaxy of spheres above them. Daniel stumbled forward as Jason spun in terror to see that his classmate was falling towards another trigger stone. He lunged for his friend, ramming his shoulder into Daniel's gut and tackling him to the ground.

Daniel pushed Jason off of him, and gingerly stood up. "What the hell's your problem?!" Jason rose quickly to meet his companion's indignant gaze. "You don't want to step on that stone," he said, pointing to the raised rectangle.

Daniel examined the trigger with a frown. "Why, what does it do?"

"Didn't you see what just happened to me?!"

"No... I was examining the floor lights with Nierion," Daniel said, pointing in the direction of the Archivist, but Nierion was no longer there. He turned back to Jason, his frown transformed into a narrow-eyed mask of confusion. "Where did Nierion-"

Jason firmly grabbed Daniel's shoulders. "Listen to me. That stone… I stepped on another one and was transported into one of the spheres." Daniel's reaction was not as sympathetic as Jason anticipated.

"That's awesome! Why did you stop me?"

Jason bit his tongue. "No, not awesome! It was full of weird goo that-"

"What kind of goo?"

"That doesn't matter! Please, just… the goo triggered the Touch. I don't know how! Then these terrible images of the Ranis Aun appeared in the sphere and… I felt their pain."

Jason stared intently into Daniel's eyes, waiting for a moment of clarity that was all too slow to arrive. Then Daniel stepped away from the trigger nervously. "How is that possible? How could the Ranis Aun have… Where is Nierion?"

The boys swung their heads back and forth like awkward birds, seeing only as far as the floor lights carried through the cavern. Only then Jason realized not all the glass bubbles glowed, just those in a large, circular perimeter around them. Suddenly, the Archivist materialized, like a stalking ghost, behind them.

"I am here, Daniel," but Nierion's voice rung hollow and unsure.

Daniel's response, "What is this place," was cut off by Jason, "What are these things?!"

"Where did you go?" Daniel added.

The Archivist's visors, empty of light, now seemed full of dread. "I… I have been trying to locate any of the Ranis Aun with Esan's Eyes, but this city… if it can even be called that, is devoid of all life save ours."

With that creepy sentiment hanging in the air, Jason wondered why, if the city was deserted, he was so sure he was being watched. The feeling wasn't ominous, like in the Night Path; he felt more like the ongoing waves of sadness from the cavern's core belonged to someone who knew he was there.

"Nierion, did you hear what happened to Jason?" Daniel posed to the Archivist. Nierion answered, but Jason barely listened to the Archivist commiserate with Daniel:

"... Yes, it should not be... No, I have no idea how..."

Jason no longer cared about Nierion. *What good is the Archivist if it knows nothing? What good are Esan's Eyes if they can't sense the being calling me?*

"You're wrong!" he spat at the Archivist, "Someone else is here."

"Who?" Daniel asked quietly. Jason spun on him in wonderment and disgust. "Can't you feel it?" Jason then accused the Archivist, "Nierion, you *have* to feel it!"

Daniel meekly shook his head. But Nierion calmly replied that it sensed no one else.

"Why am I the only one who feels it?!" Jason growled.

"Must be the Touch," Daniel reasoned, but the obvious remark infuriated Jason. He roared at the Archivist, "What did you do to me?!"

Nierion glided effortlessly towards him, but Jason shied away.

"What did you put inside me?!" he cried.

The relentless waves of hurt and sorrow were wearing him down. Now they engulfed him like the raging rapids of a river. He sank to his knees and gasped, then pounded the Archivist with a glower of hate. *Is there any mercy in those empty visors?* he wondered. *How could I tell?*

Daniel rushed to his side and Jason felt his friend strain to lift his bulk. He threw one arm around Daniel's neck and his agony diminished enough to arch himself onto his feet.

The small boy's face was pale, his eyes wide as a frightened rabbit's. He swiveled to the Archivist, maneuvering Jason's weight from one side of his body to the other.

"We have to figure out who's doing this!"

The Archivist's visors shone a startling cobalt blue in response to Daniel's plea.

"The city of Spiria Inan was built into the deep crust of Ranis Anjiran," Nierion said, as if reading from a book. "Solid rock was hollowed into a half-sphere four miles in diameter. At the center, a massive spire was built to let the rulers of

Spiria Inan claim absolute dominion across their city. Not a single shadow could hide from their sight…"

The visors blinked out, and Nierion said, "Come, it is clear where we must go."

Jason was now so weak he had to lean further onto Daniel. Rancid guilt shamed Jason as his friend grit his teeth. Daniel would have to expend reserves of strength that he may need for himself, but Jason couldn't walk on his own.

A good friend, Jason thought warmly and wondered for a moment if he should just give up. *Yeah, that'd be much easier.* He could fall on the ground and close his mind to the penetrating wail of misery felt solely by him. *That would be nice, to leave everything behind.* He was so tempted to let go of his grief for his father and be at peace; to leave behind his excruciating worry for his mother and allow her to forge a new life and find happiness… even though that meant he'd never see her again. But he doubted he had the strength to surrender his own hopes and abandon himself to oblivion.

Chapter 34: Secrets in the Spire

The two-mile walk to the center of Spiria Inan felt like twenty. Every step Jason took required more effort than the last, as if he was confronting the headwind of a hurricane. But instead of rain or sleet, he was battered by howling gusts of gloom that felt as real as any squall. And yet, every arduous step was made possible by Daniel.

Jason leaned on his friend's quivering shoulder like a boulder hedged against a sapling. Nierion glided beside them unable to help as its exterior proved too slick--and too awkwardly shaped--to support Jason's weight. Daniel took up the charge, with no complaint ... *And after everything I've gotten him into,* Jason thought, while struggling to fight the storm of sorrow raging at him.

Reaching the city's center, they were awed by an immense meteor-grey spire, illuminated by several arrays of the bubble lights ringing the tower's circumference. The structure was at least a couple hundred feet wide, but Jason couldn't tell how tall, as the top of the spire disappeared into the darkness of the cavern above.

The bottom seemed to be supported, around forty feet off the ground, by the massive network of pipes, which penetrated the tower at hundreds of points. Overlapping spirals, ranging from the size of his fist to several feet in diameter, were etched into the exterior in a tapestry of rich detail. Notched into the spirals were hundreds, if not thousands, of circles of varying sizes as well. Together, the spirals and circles resembled overlapping solar systems fanning across a galaxy. Curiosity filled Daniel's face, but Jason felt only crippling fear;

either the spire itself, or someone within, was undeniably the source of his misery.

"Can you feel it now, Nierion?"

"I still sense nothing Jason, I-"

Jason shifted his weight against Daniel's body and stood up straight.

"How can that be?! Don't Esan's Eyes... see anything?"

"They do not," the Archivist answered, uneasy.

He had to get inside! Jason was sure answers were there. He stumbled away from Daniel to position himself under the spire. From there he saw that the core was a hollow tube, perhaps fifty feet across, extending into infinity. Jason searched for anything resembling a hatch or a ladder to lead up into the spire. He nearly tripped over a raised object on the ground beneath the very center of the tube. He looked down, and gasped...

"Those are just like the symbols on the ship! What are they doing here?"

Jason spun to find Daniel right behind him. He wasn't surprised he hadn't heard Daniel sidle up; he could barely perceive anything beyond the never ceasing torrent of pain that assaulted him.

The Archivist glided beside them, focusing its visors at the unexpected symbols. They appeared to be made of the same metal as the spire. The visors swirled through shades of electric blues and greens, then ceased.

"They *are* Arcon Drei," the Archivist said grimly.

The confirmation seemed obvious to Jason.

"You said other archivists visited in the past. Maybe one of them put the symbols here."

Nierion shifted its inspection to the hollow interior of the spire. Jason wondered if the Archivists' sight could penetrate the distant abyss.

"You do not understand. The Arcon Drei are not lifeless controls like the levers of a machine. They require a profound level of knowledge to create and to use. None of the archivists are capable of doing this."

Bewildered, Daniel furrowed his brow.

"So how did they get here?"

"There is only one possible answer... One of the Shantar Anar was here." Nierion's unfailing calm was dispelled and Jason sensed true anger and fear in its next words: "Why was this kept a secret from me? Why was I not told? If they knew... if they knew... then what am I doing here?! This should not be!"

"Maybe they think you wouldn't understand," Jason muttered, recalling his last conversation with his mom.

The Archivist stared at Jason fiercely.

"What would I not understand?!"

He ignored the inhuman glare of Nierion's visors and felt only sympathy.

"Maybe there are answers here for you, too."

Nierion said nothing and returned its attention to the circle of Arcon Drei. Jason stood still for a moment; the sorrowful wind of the spire matched his own regret. He noticed Daniel flash him a nervous glance and realized he was shivering. At the same time, he felt beads of sweat feverishly mat his forehead.

Jason sighed and shuffled back towards Daniel for support. The Archivist's body burst to life in the sheen of blue and white that he recognized clearly now as an activity of the Touch. But if that was the case, why couldn't Nierion also feel the hopeless crush of ruined dreams filling the city of Spiria Inan?

The Arcon Drei glowed red, like a brand ready to be worked in a blacksmith's fire. The glow brightened until the symbols appeared as scalding cinders of white with veins of blue. The alien symbols levitated, rotating faster and faster until Jason couldn't discern their individual shapes. A spinning halo of white light was all he could see.

"Jason, Daniel, come to me!" the Archivist commanded.

The Arcon Drei rose, only to stop several feet above the Archivist's head. It then glided beneath the center of the orbiting circle.

Daniel helped Jason hobble to the Archivist, its visors bursting into life, and now radiating heat. Soon they shone with the same blinding light as the ring whirling above them.

"Prepare yourselves," Nierion said.

The circle of light slowly descended, stopping at the height of the Archivist's midsection. Jason heard a faint click, like two pieces of a machine fitting together. Then the cavern burst into light. He threw his hands over his eyes to protect them as the thousands of bubble lights in the floor turned on at once. An unseen force pulled his hands from his face and locked his arms at his sides. Jason felt as if a constricting snake was squeezing the breath from his lungs.

For a terrifying moment he thought his bones would be crushed, but the pressure quickly eased, leaving only a snug restraint. From his companion's lack of movement he knew they were held securely in place as well. The boys exchanged glances of trepidation as the revolving circle of Arcon Drei rose into the hollow middle of the giant tower, taking them along for the ride.

At first, they were lifted at a leisurely pace. Jason observed that the interior walls of the spire appeared to be made of the same gelatinous material he'd been encased in earlier. The walls pulsated as they passed, and shifted colors from electric blue, to blood red, to rusty orange. As they floated higher, Jason concentrated on not looking down. He noticed that at certain intervals, cylindrical sections of the spire were translucent, and he could briefly view the cavern outside.

From his new vantage, the spheres and the network of spiraling pipes resembled shining clusters of planets and stars. Suddenly, his stomach lurched and his vision blurred. He thought something was seriously wrong with him, then realized that their pace of ascension had quickened to a horrifying speed. His teeth chattered as his jaw shook. The visible cavern became a haze of amorphous shape and color. The sensation didn't last long before the lift came to a halting stop. If he'd been mobile, he was sure that momentum would have carried him through the cavern's roof.

When Jason recovered vision and balance, he realized they'd stopped at one of the spire's translucent sections. The spheres and pipes appeared much smaller than just a minute before. The expanse of Spiria Inan rested below him--several thousand feet-- and he wasn't too disoriented to notice there was still no solid ground beneath his feet.

The invisible grip loosened slightly, and for a moment Jason wondered if he'd come all this way to be dropped to his death. Though his bonds didn't feel as tight, they kept him aloft while a bridge of metal slats converged from both sides of the spire to connect in the center and lock under his feet.

The whirling Arcon Drei slowed until Jason could make out individual runes in casual orbit. Their color dimmed from blazing white through shades of orange and red until they settled again into cool metallic grey. Then the alien symbols descended, presumably to rest again at the spire's base. Although relieved to be standing on a solid surface again, Jason was anxious to move on because the bridge was quite narrow.

However, at either end, hugging the gelatinous walls, were ten-foot portals of swirling black. He shot Daniel a grimace of despair, but they'd have to choose one way or the other.

Nierion barely hesitated, headed towards the portal at their right. Daniel sighed and Jason shrugged; what else could they do? With Jason still relying on Daniel for support, together they followed the Archivist through the ominous liquid.

Gasps of relief left Jason and Daniel at the same time. After only a second of unnaturally cool dark, they had emerged through the portal, and were clearly just on the other side of the translucent wall. The anticipated pain of the Travel Sequence was thankfully avoided.

Jason's reprieve was short lived as he was struck by a fresh blizzard of sorrow, stronger than anything he'd felt before. He crumpled to his knees and felt like a hobbled, old man.

"Daniel," he wheezed.

His friend sank to ground beside him.

"What's wrong?"

He retched like his lungs were full of dirty water. Between

heaving coughs he murmured, "It's close."

Daniel was so frightened he could barely think. Jason's agony reminded him too much of their illusory encounter in the Night Path. This time his companion's suffering was real, and being in the spire clearly intensified Jason's anguish. He could think of only one solution.

"Nierion!" he yelled, though the Archivist was beside him. Its visors were fixed on Jason as if on the verge of a great discovery. "We have to go back!"

"No!" Jason garbled. "We're close. I can keep going!"

"No, you can't. I have to get you out of here!"

Nierion assessed Daniel's request.

"The only way out of the city is how we came in… through the Darka Aravan. There is no guarantee, based on what you told me, that either of you would be able to find your way to the planet's surface again."

"I know that, but…"

Jason's hand gripped Daniel's wrist; determination glistened in his eyes.

"We… keep going, Daniel," Jason's words came in ragged breaths. "You know… we can't go back there."

In his heart, Daniel agreed, but he couldn't bear to see his friend in so much pain.

"Nierion, isn't there something you can do to help him? Can't the suit do anything?!"

The Archivist's visors pulsed with bursts of red light.

"The suit is functioning properly. What is happening must be beyond the suit's abilities to control. But Jason is right, there is no turning back. We must discover what is causing him this pain, and stop whatever is blocking Esan's Eyes."

Daniel sucked in his breath, hoisting Jason to his feet. He dragged Jason behind him, stopping often to make sure he could feel his friend's breath. He followed the Archivist up a gently sloping incline. The familiar globular lights were set into the far wall of the passage. After a few minutes, it was clear they were on a spiral ramp leading even higher into the spire.

After a grueling period of time, the floor leveled out. Daniel found himself peeking from behind Nierion into a straight and dimly lit hallway. He maneuvered Jason to one side of his body and leaned in the opposite direction to support his friend. Jason peered ahead and Daniel watched his face switch from dread to intense surprise.

"It's... a Ranis Aun," Jason whispered in a hoarse voice.

Daniel was confused. "Where's a Ranis Aun?"

"... so sad... It found me when I was in the sphere..."

"What are you talking about?!" Daniel demanded. He peered into the dim passage, but saw nothing. "What found you? The Ranis Aun?"

Nothing Jason said made any sense and Daniel wanted to shake him until he stopped speaking in riddles. Instead, the Archivist gently nudged Daniel out of the way and stood before Jason with new life shining in its visors.

"You can sense the Ranis Aun's emotions?" Nierion asked.

"It's not a sense!" Jason cried. "I *feel* its loneliness... like a fire burning my own life away!"

Jason's legs shuddered and gave way. He sank to his knees, covered his face in his hands and wailed into the gloomy corridor.

Daniel fell beside him and pulled Jason's hands from his face. For a moment, time seemed to stand still. He thought he could see, as Jason described, the brightness of his friend's life being extinguished. *What does courageous Daniel do...?*

He imagined his friend's pain as black spheres he could willfully pull away. With his hands on Jason's heaving chest, Daniel concentrated on his friend's suffering changing into peace and calm. This time nothing happened, he was powerless. The horrible lie of the Night Path made him feel like the worst of fools. His hands clutched Jason's shirt and he pulled his companion's limp weight to him.

"Listen to me Jason, you have to fight through this!"

"No!" Nierion boomed. "That is not the way!"

Daniel twisted to the Archivist in despair.

"What do you mean? Do you know the way?!"

"There is only one possible answer. The Ranis Aun was Touched as well, and the bond was not broken."

"But I thought-"

"As did I, Daniel," Nierion said. "But I have been mistaken about a great many things... far too many things. I fear Jason is not prepared."

The Archivist's words terrified Daniel. *Is Jason dying? Will I be left alone on this crazy alien world?!* Worse still, Daniel had promised to help Jason, and he had utterly failed.

"Pick up Jason!" Nierion commanded. "We must find the Ranis Aun; it is our only chance." These words of hope rejuvenated Daniel. He mustered his strength, and lifted his friend to his feet. He flung Jason's arm around his neck, and followed Nierion down the dimly lit hallway.

"Cruelty is not the reason the bond is intentionally broken," Nierion said, though Daniel hadn't asked the question. "The Touch opens a powerful sense of awareness, especially of other beings who have been Touched. The Shantar Anar discovered long ago that their archival contact could have disastrous effects on life forms thus accessed."

"And that's why the Touch is dangerous?" Daniel found himself asking, mostly out of habitual politeness. All his effort and concentration was focused on helping Jason walk.

"The Touch is not dangerous," the Archivist said. "*You* are dangerous."

"Me?"

"The Cohev Senar."

Daniel immediately dismissed that idea. Dangerous was the last way he'd ever think of himself.

"What is the Touch, anyway?"

Nierion paused.

"A complex question... with a complex answer best suited for a less stressful time. Now we must hurry."

Daniel shot the Archivist a venomous glare. I'd be able to go a lot faster if you could actually help!

Jason let out a weak groan as if in agreement with Daniel's

unspoken thought, but any fury was short-lived.

Fifty feet ahead, the passage came to an end and Daniel found himself staring, not at another portal, but at an enormous door.

Chapter 35: Violet Sky

Jason clung to Daniel's shoulder as an escalating torrent of despair penetrated the massive door, which seemed out of place so far from Earth. The giant block of solid steel would have better fit a medieval fortress. Four long, rectangular bars, which appeared to be made of the same material as the door, ran like ladder rungs from top to bottom. Surrounding the threshold were perhaps forty or fifty Arcon Drei, which cast shadows on the metal directly behind them. Jason realized, just as on the ship, that the runes of the Shantar Anar were not attached to the wall.

The symbols began to glow in bluish-white light and Jason saw that Nierion's visors held the same light. The Arcon Drei moved away from the door, shifting from the rectangular outline into a circle, which performed a half revolution in midair. Once complete, the symbols regained their rectangular orientation and silently snuck closer to the door. In this new pattern, their glow turned a deep violet. The four bars emitted the same violet sheen.

The light intensified and Jason felt piercing heat radiating from the bars. These soon appeared as white-hot bands of molten ore, which were absorbed into the door and quickly cooled, leaving no trace. The violet glow in the Arcon Drei faded until they were again cold and lifeless. There was an audible click and a muted droning as the door slid into the wall. The exposed rectangular cavity was as dark as a starless night. Then the blackness swallowed Jason…

… He thought he heard his body strike the ground, but wasn't sure. He tried to open his eyes, but couldn't find them. The corridor was gone, replaced by pitch-black. Jason wondered if he'd stay in the shadows forever, but light emerged in his periphery, dotting the edges of the impenetrable dark.

The illumination expanded, and he hoped to see Daniel kneeling at his side, but when his vision refocused, he was staring into an endless violet sky. He knew he'd seen this sky before, but he couldn't recall where. He rolled onto his side and tried to scream, but no sound came from his throat. A skeleton of bleached bone rested nearby. Inside the rib cage, a beating heart suggested it might still be alive somehow. Jason recognized the remains as the Ranis Aun in the sphere. Somewhere far away, he heard a familiar voice pleading for him to wake up, but that was easy to ignore.

The caged heart beat faster, and the skeleton sprung to life, propping itself onto long arms and broad hands. A serpentine tail dragged against the ground as the skeleton shambled towards him. The empty eye socket in the long, flat skull stared into his soul. The alien jaw unhinged like a snake, revealing a gaping hole into absolute darkness. A fog of hot, putrid breath kissed his face before the living skeleton lunged forward to swallow him whole...

"No!" Jason screamed.

The force of his denial shattered the deathly illusion like a pane of glass. He found himself back in the spire, collapsed under his burden of despair. He was freezing, as if ice-cold metal coursed through his veins where warm blood was supposed to flow. A hand gripped his own and he saw Daniel's ashen face looming above him.

Then he saw that his skin was covered in crystalline, blue-and-white lesions. His protruding veins weren't greenish-blue beneath the surface, but rather a repulsive mix of silver and grey. A repressed memory arose, and its truth was more than Jason could bear.

Somewhere beside him the Archivist pleaded, "You must not fight!"

He wanted to tear off his skin, to rend his body and throw it away like a worthless husk, until he was just another skeleton beneath the endless violet sky. Then he could leave his nightmare behind and be at peace.

But Nierion wouldn't let him fade away; the fierceness in the Archivist's voice forced Jason to listen.

"You must not fight, or you *will* die!"

Wasn't death the release he wanted? But he recalled the melted face of the Ranis Aun he'd killed and knew he was terrified of dying. Instead, maybe he could simply cease to be; maybe he could tear the fabric of time and space and completely erase his own existence. Then the distant moments of joy in his life wouldn't seem like such a joke. He wouldn't have to dream away his grief or spend the energy to keep alive the possibility that he'd ever have a normal life again.

But even more than this, he was terrified to open his eyes; afraid the sight of lesions and silver veins would be waiting to drive him towards an inescapable madness that was worse than death, worse than never even having been born.

He now felt a part of him--separate from this frightened ghost—that still clung to life, and more than ever he wanted answers to this new fiendish discovery. He let himself drift away, not towards death, but back into the vision of the violet sky…

…The horrid skeleton of the Ranis Aun waited for him, the creature's giant maw ready to consume him. But, instead of recoiling, Jason let himself be devoured, and was carried into the still-beating heart. There he found the source of the creature's agony; an unbearable sense of loss he understood immediately.

He showed the beating heart a mirror glimpse of his own grief; let his sorrow flow from him like blood through ventricles until he couldn't tell where he ended, and the Ranis Aun began.

A sense of overwhelming peace flooded through him, and he knew to the core of his being that the alien had not been trying to hurt him, but instead set him free from his despair. Jason let his anguish fall away, piece by piece like chiseled flakes falling from a marble block. Within the block, a form awaited to be brought to life.

When the final flakes had fallen away the now familiar Spark ignited in a consuming flash. He was bathed in the power of the Touch in a way he had not felt either through the Arcon Drei on Earth, or by the mysteries of the Night Path.

Blissful weightlessness lifted him from the mire as spiraling chords of blue and white energy consumed his body. He could no longer separate himself from the sky.

Flowing through the vast complexity of the universe, he sensed a river of elegant simplicity more wonderful than any fantasy. The river held answers he couldn't understand, to questions he didn't know to ask. Hidden in the current were keys to the locked doors inaccessible to normal human perception. If he could locate the right key, it would somehow help him get back home.

But he was distracted by a vision of Daniel, standing in the shadows beside the river. Daniel was sweating drops of fear, not for his own life, but for Jason's. The beads of fear fell into the river and disappeared.

Jason held his hand out to Daniel. Tendrils of blue-and-white light flooded from Jason in an arching dance and penetrated his friend. In the center of the diminutive boy, Jason found Daniel's spark, or at least that was Jason's description. He wasn't sure what he was sensing though he knew it was a physical part of Daniel, not an ethereal hope given some feeble name.

The spark was as real as anything else, but dormant, waiting to be ignited. Jason tried to awaken it, but using the power of the Touch was exhausting. He had to pull back the tendrils of light before he collapsed. The river, which had been so clear, faded away as Jason reabsorbed the nimbus of energy crackling around him. His body shuddered like he'd been dipped into a cloud of freezing rain. His heart fluttered and the breath shook from his lungs. Only then did he realize he was still shrouded in the darkness merely by his closed eyelids.

Jason opened his eyes, thrust his arm up to Daniel and

squeezed his friend's hand. He was spent, but a smile spread across Jason's face. A mountainous sigh of relief exploded from Daniel. Jason saw that the lesions on his skin had disappeared and his veins returned to their normal color.

"Jason... I don't know what... What just happened?"

Jason shook his head, there were no worthy words. And this time, unlike the others, he knew the power hadn't left him. The Spark was there to be called upon, a supernova of alien potential simmering in his body.

The Archivist leaned over him at his feet.

"You see, the Touch is nothing to fight."

Nierion spun back to the immense doorway and glided through, disappearing into the obscuring darkness.

Daniel tried to help him up, but Jason pulled his hand away. His strength had returned. He propped up on his elbows, then pushed himself to his feet. He felt famished, like he hadn't eaten in days, but a deep rejuvenating breath straightened his spine. His shivering limbs were already a distant memory. Daniel's face held a mixture of awe and fear, but Jason gently took his friend's arm.

"Don't worry, there's nothing to be afraid of here."

Together, they strode through the threshold and into the chamber beyond.

Chapter 36: Myths and Lessons

Light filtered in from the hallway. When Jason's eyes adjusted to the grainy dark, he found himself in a circular room about forty feet wide. His feelings of hunger had begun to abate.

Rising from the smooth floor was a sarcophagus, elaborately carved with the same designs as the spire: circles orbiting spiral lines. Nierion pressed against the wall to Jason's left. The Archivist's visors focused on the decorated coffin. They were in a tomb.

Three words growled from the shadows: "Leave this place."

Daniel slid behind Jason as if for shelter from the words, but Jason was unafraid. He stood firmly and swiveled his head to the far right. There, huddled like a pile of rubble, was a Ranis Aun, eight or nine feet long. Its giant burly hands nervously twitched. Its bullet-shaped head slowly rotated back and forth. The Ranis Aun's dimly glowing yellow eye, pivoted between him, the Archivist, and Daniel near the entrance.

The Spark within Jason pulsed. He saw misery oozing from the Ranis Aun's body, spreading out in waves to fill the chamber. The newness of the perception was uncomfortable, and he was disconcerted that it happened without any conscious effort on his part. Jason still felt the alien's pain, but it was no longer a furious storm. He now discerned a mist of complex emotions seeking understanding. How had he ever mistaken these desperate feelings for malice?

"I was Touched long ago, Archivist. There is nothing for you to do here. Leave me in peace," the Ranis Aun said, its deep voice sodden with sadness.

Daniel crept beside Jason and whispered, "You understood what that thing just said, right?" Jason was surprised by Daniel's question, but didn't answer his friend.

"The suits have to be translating… Jason, the Ranis Aun knows what Nierion is!"

Jason narrowed his eyes sharply and fixed them on the Archivist; Daniel was right.

Silence hung in the chamber until the Archivist spoke in a measured, but alarming, tone. "What is in the sarcophagus?"

"What do you think?" the Ranis Aun questioned with a baiting sarcasm.

Fear clouded Nierion's response, "That is not possible!"

"What's not possible?" Daniel asked.

Jason stepped forward to examine the sarcophagus. "There's another circle of symbols on the lid!"

"Stand back!" Nierion ordered, but Jason held his ground. The Ranis Aun glared at him. Jason was momentarily washed in the being's dread. But when its gaze shifted again to the Archivist, the gloom lifted. "You know not what you fear Archivist," the Ranis Aun said. "You have believed many lies. But you know this… yes; I can see the betrayal behind your blank face."

Nierion didn't speak, but the Ranis Aun continued as if reading the Archivist's thoughts. "I will explain … then you will leave me in peace." Sadly, Jason knew the being had no hope of peace.

"We can't leave; there's no safe way back to the ship!" Daniel cut in, but he was ignored.

"It cannot understand you, Daniel," the Archivist said. Then to the Ranis Aun: "Explain."

The alien slightly uncoiled to place its four heavy hands on the ground. "You may be very old, Archivist. Eons more ancient than I am, but I know far more than you." A crack of pain struck Jason, as if speaking to the Archivist opened the suture of a fresh wound in the Ranis Aun's gut.

"Your kind had been coming here for millions of years,

but we were unaware of them. We progressed naturally, building our civilization in our own way, and that might have continued under your hidden observation for many millennia. However, three hundred years ago, the last spying archivist was discovered, and captured. I do not know how, these events were long before my birth… but I was told the archivist was imprisoned while its fate was debated. Some were of the opinion that the prisoner should be freed. Tampering with the unknown was terrifying to them. Others of my kind were unafraid, and demanded the archivist reveal its purpose here.

"The archivist insisted that the Protocol of the Shantar Anar forbade disclosure. But the Ranis Aun are not easily dissuaded, and my ancestors knew nothing of the Shantar Anar or their power.

"I do not know if your kind scream Archivist, but I imagine this one did. The torment must have been great as it was dissected alive, one piece at a time."

Jason glanced at Nierion, but its empty visors were an impenetrable mask. Jason realized that even with the Touch, he sensed nothing from the Archivist.

"We leveraged the technologies gleaned from torturing the archivist. Of course, the Shantar Anar were aware of our cruelty, but for two hundred years they did nothing in retaliation.

A haze of melancholy shuddered from the Ranis Aun. Jason absorbed the feeling as a vacuum does dust. The Spark pulsed, refining the sensation to bitter loneliness. Jason peered at the Ranis Aun with sympathy.

"I still remember the day that changed our destiny. I was very young. There was no ship like yours. This time the visitor was no archivist but one of the Shantar Anar. I do not know how it got here without a ship, but it appeared at the outskirts of the city, as if emerging from the stone. When it spoke, all of the Ranis Aun heard the penetrating power of the Shantar Anar's voice, which scraped against our minds. There was no fury, no malice. It had not come to annihilate, but to help."

"Which one was it?" the Archivist asked.

"Malchion," the Ranis Aun answered. Jason watched Nierion intently and thought he caught a momentary twitch; perhaps the recognition of a name that proved the Ranis Aun wasn't spewing lies.

"When I first heard the Shantar Anar's voice, I envisioned an awesome being, big as the city itself. But when I first saw Malchion, I laughed. It was no larger than I was, even in its protective suit... much like the one you wear, Archivist." Jason spotted Nierion's almost imperceptible twitch, this time of surprise.

"Oh yes, I know that is not your face. You are within... A tiny piece of one of them."

What does that mean? Jason wondered. On Daniel's face, he found an equally perplexed expression in response to the Ranis Aun's cryptic remark.

"We were Touched directly by the Shantar Anar, Archivist. At first I felt as if crushed by the weight of the planet above me. I cried out and Malchion swept away my fear. I learned not to resist the increased perception I had been granted. Then I felt lighter than air! The Touch was a gift to all of us.

"Malchion warned that the technology we had stolen was not to be misused. We needed time to be ready to use it wisely, or we might destroy all the Shantar Anar loved.

"'Then change us!' my people demanded, 'Make us ready now!' But allowing us to evolve at our own pace was their gift, and we did not understand.

A gift. Wasn't that what the Ranis Aun in the Night Path had called the Touch? Jason tried to remember, but this Ranis Aun's voice was hypnotizing.

"The Shantar Anar were right to be afraid of us, Archivist. For the nine million years of our history, the main way we evolved was through our expressions of hatred and distrust. Even with Malchion among us, even with the Touch, we didn't let go of our hate... we remained children, demanding a power we couldn't comprehend."

The Ranis Aun's head lowered in obvious shame.

"But *I* changed!" it rasped.

A burst of defiance blasted Jason, who almost toppled over. He trenched his feet on the floor and turned to see if Daniel was okay, but of course his friend was unfazed. In that moment, he became determined to find a way to control the alien power.

"Of all the Ranis Aun, only I was set free by Malchion's Touch. For the rest of my kind, the gift remained a crushing weight that was clearly punishment for our cruel acts… or so they believed."

"Why were you the only one able to accept the Touch?" Nierion asked.

The Ranis Aun shook its head. "I do not know…"

"For one hundred years Malchion stayed with us… A blink in time for the Shantar Anar, but for the Ranis Aun… A generation rose and fell, and the young grew old. Eventually, my kind decided that the Shantar Anar was a vengeful god who spoke in riddles and would never release us from the painful confusion of its Touch."

"At the end of that century, Malchion was ready to abandon us. I begged for more time. I told it I could make them understand, that *I* could succeed where the Shantar Anar had failed. But I needed Malchion to stay because its presence supported my precarious self-control. Malchion seemed willing to indulge me a while longer. Then, a tribal war erupted… Nothing special, my species had a tragic habit of violent conflict."

The brutal images flowing into Jason from the Ranis Aun were maddening, but the Spark attracted these memories like a powerful magnet. He knew if he didn't do something, he'd be dragged back into the storm he'd barely escaped with his life. But what could he do?

"Malchion did not try to stop us. It watched dispassionately as we tore our civilization asunder. I would give you the reasons, but I cannot pretend they make any sense. The Shantar Anar decided we were beyond help, and hope.

Malchion led me here, to the top of this spire, to survey the destruction reaped in this one city alone. The Shantar Anar knew it was only a matter of time until we used their technology to spread this carnage beyond Ranis Anjiran.

Jason's body felt frigid, despite the swirling emotional fire dancing within him.

"Malchion's body was soon discovered at the outskirts of the city, in the same place the Shantar Anar first appeared one hundred years earlier. I was dragged from my home and brought to see the remains. My people knew I was… different. They accused me of killing Malchion out of spite… Spite!" the Ranis Aun roared. "My greatest teacher, my only friend… They thought I murdered their god!" The voice grated bitterly, "As if killing a Shantar Anar was even possible."

The Ranis Aun's puckered mouth twisted into a terrible smile. "What they found was just the suit. I tried to tell them Malchion had departed, not died, but they would not listen and I was to be executed."

Jason's heart lurched as he watched the Ranis Aun draw several shallow breaths. Memories of loss dripped from the being's imposing body and scuttled across the floor, but only Jason could see them. In this pause, the Ranis Aun reminded him of how his better sense was overwhelmed by the confusing sensory input of the Touch.

The Ranis Aun regained its composure and continued, "You must suspect what happened next Archivist: With Malchion's presence no longer controlling the Shantar Anar's gift to us, the sickness began, and I was forgotten."

Nierion moved towards the sarcophagus with a defiant glide. "The Shantar Anar would not do that, no matter what your kind had done!"

The Ranis Aun's eye narrowed. "You are wrong." Contempt chilled every word. "You do not understand them any more than I do… You have no idea what the Shantar Anar are willing to do to protect what is precious to them.

"Not even our wars killed us as quickly as the sickness.

Soon millions lay dead, then billions. In the end, I was the only one left. I thought I survived because I had acquiesced to Malchion's Touch, but… I am no longer sure that is what spared me."

Why was he different? Jason wondered. Suddenly, Jason was curious what the Ranis Aun's spark might look like, and he knew he had the power to see for himself. Jason began to focus his mind…

Nierion arrived at the sarcophagus and examined the circle of Arcon Drei.

"If you alone survived, why are you here? The door to this chamber was sealed. Only one of my kind can grant access."

The Ranis Aun glowered suspiciously at the Archivist. "You truly do not know?" Nierion met the alien's piercing eye with blank visors, but didn't speak.

"They came back… Not the Shantar Anar, but the Ebenin, their creations. Not archivists, but others. They razed our cities to the ground, and in their stead built our graves.

An image of the trigger stone Jason stepped on flashed in his mind. He realized the single word must be the name of a Ranis Aun. He pictured his father's name on a stone lost somewhere in the graveyard of floating spheres.

"I was allowed to live, but was imprisoned here with all I would need to sustain me for the rest of my life. And with that…" The Ranis Aun said, lifting a hand towards the sarcophagus.

The Ranis Aun uncoiled its body and dragged itself to the Archivist's side.

"They left me a tomb befitting a god. Laid inside is Malchion's empty suit, a cruel reminder of my arrogance. I wish they had killed me instead."

"Show me," Nierion demanded.

But the Archivist's fury was unmatched by the Ranis Aun, who lowered its massive head in defeat.

"Look for yourself."

Nierion's visors glowed in a hazy blue light and the circle of Arcon Drei alit in matching hue. The halo rotated and broke apart, sliding down the sides of the sarcophagus as four straight lines, two on each side. The heavy lid split into two sections at the middle. With a tired groan, each section pulled into compartments in the rim.

Revealed there, unmoving and lifeless was a pitch-black, metal exo-skeleton shaped with a serpentine body, thick muscular limbs and massive blunt fingers. The head looked like a Ranis Aun as well, except for one defining feature. Instead of a single penetrating eye, four empty visors faced the Archivist. Nierion's visors shifted to a cloudy grey, as it focused on the exo-suit. After a moment, the dusky lights faded and the Archivist slid away. The lid rematerialized, solid and still, as if unmoved since the beginning of time.

The Ranis Aun turned to focus on Jason, as if pleading with him, rather than with the Archivist.

"I did not lie to you."

"I understand," Nierion whispered.

"Then leave me, and take this Cohev Senar with you," the Ranis Aun barked, pointing a blunt finger at Jason. "I cannot bear to feel another's Touch."

"We cannot leave yet-"

The Ranis Aun lifted itself to a towering height.

"Leave!"

Daniel shrank from the rage in the alien being's voice, but Jason let the fury of the Ranis Aun's command break against his body like delicate clay.

The pulsing Spark within him expanded, and Jason felt his new power billowing to the surface. Serene weightlessness surrounded him again, as did the nimbus of blue and white. In his periphery he saw horror overtake Daniel's face but with a gentle hand he quieted his friend's fear. Then he reached out to the Ranis Aun with tendrils of blue-and-white light.

He felt the alien's resistance as a thick aura of sadness that the Ranis Aun wielded as a shield. Jason gave more of his energy reserves to the Spark, and his power surged. He pushed the tendrils forward until the shield broke. The Ranis Aun's glowing eye narrowed in hate, but Jason approached the being without fear. When he was covered in its shadow, he placed his palm upon the alien's, bark-like skin. The tendrils split to enwrap the Ranis Aun's body.

"Please, I do not want this! Just leave me."

Instead, Jason plunged his tendrils inside.

The Rani Aun's eye flared open. Fissures of blue and white light rose to the surface of its skin. Cracks spread out, covering its entire body before fading away.

Jason now found the being's spark, which wasn't dormant like Daniel's, or a scorching star like his own. Rather this spark was withered, almost burnt out. Yet, he knew the spark's presence haunted the Ranis Aun. Jason nurtured the charred remains and worked to restore the broken thing. Expending precious energy, he stretched himself until he had nothing left to give.

The rebuilt spark seemed like a mirror image of his own, and he tried to fathom what that meant, but he was forced to disengage after catching that glimpse.

The blue and white aura dissipated into mist as he fell to the floor in an exhausted heap. Daniel ran to help him, and Jason gladly gave his hand. He leaned against Daniel and gazed proudly at the Ranis Aun.

"I...I don't understand," the alien said in a voice full of wonder. "I sensed you from the moment you entered the sphere. I thought you were like the others. But... you... are different. How did you..."

The Ranis Aun's wide eye peered at Jason. After a moment, the being let out a suppressed sigh that held the weight of a lifetime.

"No matter. Thank you. My name is Laushtee, and I am in your debt. "

"Laushtee?!" Daniel shouted in surprise. "Nierion, isn't this the Ranis Aun you were supposed to find?"

The Archivist remained still and didn't speak. Jason knew what it was thinking: *This was no coincidence...*

Jason decided to deal with that puzzle later.

"You understand me now, don't you?" he asked Laushtee. The Ranis Aun nodded.

"We are bonded."

Of course, Jason thought, *I gave it a piece of me.* But what was that piece? He knew what he'd given of himself was physically real--yet he had no name for it--and he didn't feel any less complete.

"If you're in my debt, will you help us get back to our ship? This all started because Esan's Eyes... the Archivist's tools for finding you, weren't working."

"I know why that is," Laushtee replied. "Now that I am free, I can help."

Relieved, Jason sighed. Then he remembered the terrible journey between Nierion's ship and the city of Spiria Inan... "Wait, Laushtee, what is the Darka Aravan?"

Laushtee narrowed its eye.

"That is an odd thing to ask."

"Why?" the Archivist interjected.

Laushtee warily regarded Nierion, there was still no trust in the Ranis Aun's gaze.

"When I was a child, I learned a story about the early days of the Ranis Aun, millions of years before my birth. Back then, we lived on the surface of this world.

"One day, a child named Nisah was lost in the wilderness while searching for food. It came upon a dark cave cut into the rock, but the shelter was a deception. Inside, Nisah was transported to another place in the universe, where one could mold and shape reality. The story was not clear on how Nisah escaped, but the child returned and told fantastic tales of exotic environments. My kind realized for the first time how hard life was on the surface and were willing to search for a better home.

"Nisah led my ancestors back into the cave of dreams, and they emerged in the depths of Ranis Anjiran. That is when the city of Spiria Inan was supposedly built here, in this cavern. Anyway... that's the myth of Nisah and the Darka Aravan as taught to every young Ranis Aun."

"The Night Path's not a myth! It's real!" Jason exclaimed.

"The human speaks the truth," Nierion said. "As Jason told you, I was unable to use Esan's Eyes. I now understand why. Studies of the captured archivist enabled your kind to develop a means to deaden the energetic connection for which Esan's Eyes search. The boys and I were forced to locate another path: a portal on the surface built into a great wall. Posted around the portal was writing that declared it to be the entrance to Spiria Inan, the great city of Ijiran Ranis Jarna Aun successor of many others... but the first name was Nisah."

Laushtee cast a skeptical gaze at the Archivist, and then at Jason.

"It's true!" Jason exclaimed. "And there was a Ranis Aun in the Night Path with me, but... it never escaped and died in there."

"How did you escape?" Laushtee asked, once again full of despair.

"The Ranis Aun... knew the Touch could help me," Jason said, "and called the Darka Aravan 'their world'... meaning the Shantar Anar."

The serpentine Laushtee literally recoiled at the name of the mysterious alien beings. Resting its head and abdomen on its lower body was a posture Jason took for deep contemplation.

Eventually the Ranis Aun spoke, "Why would they do all of this?"

"We do not know," Nierion answered. "But the Night Path led us here, to a hidden room on the outskirts of this city."

Laushtee stared blankly at the Archivist and said nothing. Nevertheless, Jason perceived a new determination within the Ranis Aun. He didn't doubt it would use its reclaimed freedom to search for the Night Path and discover if it truly was the last of its kind.

Chapter 37: Under Cover of Night

Ashlyn lay on her bed and stared at the luminous stickers of planets and stars she'd arranged on her ceiling with no particular rhyme or reason. She liked seeing the cluster emerge in the night, especially when she was angry. All she'd tried to do was help Anne find Jason, but she'd been reminded--by the annoyance and disbelief on Anne's face--that she was just a child and of course, knew nothing important. As she watched the neon glow of the miniature galaxy, her mind drifted to fonder memories: people she'd loved, and already lost, in her short life.

She envisioned her grandmother's arthritic hands, crusted and worn, and divided by rivulets of bulging veins. These hands were the most comforting things Ashlyn had ever known. In their touch, she felt not just unquestioned affection, but an understanding that only came with time: of what that love really means. When her mother told her she needed to be this, or that, or anything else a girl should be, Ashlyn ran to be caressed by hands that accepted her just as she was.

She recalled Leo Kipson's daring smile as they rode their bikes through Ashton's quiet, night streets. His discarded cells--dead pieces of his body--remained in these streets, trees and rocks. His DNA spoke to her from their peaceful graves as she gazed at the ceiling of stars. Their presence flooded her mind with a torrent of regrets that converged into a glimmer of hope hidden in the night "sky" between the starry stickers. An inner voice she strained to hear told her to be patient, to keep breath flowing in her lungs. Somehow she would find Leo... Jason and Daniel, too. She wouldn't give up.

She had time, all the time in the world... Time enough to

see her own hands become brittle cups of flaking skin.

–◖⋔ꙅ–

Coregon was distracted from the book of poems he was reading. In his cozy study, he was hard-pressed to remember there was anything other than the fantasies contained in his favorite books. He loved disappearing into stories that were so unlike his life.

His younger brother, his best friend from birth, died at seventeen from Non-Hodgkin's Lymphoma. Their parents blamed each other, then divorced. His mother found religion; his father, the bottom of a bottle. But he found no relief after cancer stole his brother's future. He hadn't learned anything from this devastating loss except perhaps that there was nothing to learn. Life was most likely a matter of regaining consciousness a certain number of times until one day you simply didn't.

Coregon's occupation had found him. He'd never lacked for courage, and after his brother's death he didn't fear anything, least of all his own. But something unexpected happened--slowly as all true things do--through his years of service. He felt glimpses of compassion for those whose personal tragedies brought him into their lives. Any attempt to restore to them what he couldn't regain himself, if not a purpose, then a reason to get out of bed each day. He found he could occasionally laugh again, and become more than a deteriorating piece of matter afloat in an uncaring universe.

Thus, despite the absence of any solid clues, he was compelled to find the missing boys. But the pattern was tragically familiar. He remembered Dean Kipson's eyes the day the search for Leo was called off. There was no anger, only misery and complacent understanding, which made Coregon sick. If not for Sharon's scorn, he would've left the poor man alone. But the shrill reminder of his earlier failure in the form of Sharon Elliot forced Coregon to speak to Dean Kipson about Daniel... and Jason.

The fruitless conversation only confirmed what he already knew: Kipson had no idea what happened to either boy.

–◎⋒§–

Anne couldn't sleep. Though she desperately wanted to sink into the comfort of unconsciousness, if only for a few hours to fend off grief; she was too exhausted to try. Her misadventure with Ashlyn, especially the girl's delusional theory, cascaded Anne into the depths of depletion.

What she noticed first, upon arriving home, was how strange everything appeared. Familiar chairs, books, and pieces of art felt foreign. Perhaps she'd remember them if she slept. She also didn't recognize her face in the mirror. Her features hadn't changed, but the visage wasn't hers. *Her* face had a child nearby and a husband as well. With them, she built a life she recognized and owned as a consequence of her choices. Even then, she felt like a stranger to herself.

Anne trudged down the hallway towards her bedroom, keeping a hand against the wall for support. With each step, warmth bled from her body and soaked the floor. By the time Anne reached the threshold, even her name--the five-ton chain of identity hung around her neck when she was born--felt light and tired; as if slipping away. Sobbing, she fell to her knees. She didn't recognize her tears and they, like fools departing an uncomfortable silence, leapt to their deaths rather than keep her company.

She crawled to her dresser and opened the bottom drawer. She saw a rainbow of rolled socks whose colors bled into one under her withering gaze. She peered at her soft hands, wondering why they were still here. Why did she have a body in the first place? To give birth and have her only child taken away? This body wasn't hers anyway; it belonged to the stranger in the mirror, like everything that surrounded her. She was lost in a maze and needed a map or a key, some tangible thing she could hold to recognize her and not shrink away.

She opened the dresser's second drawer and the tears ceased. Nestled at the back of the drawer was a sealed letter for Jason that Michael had written very close to the end of his life. She'd made him this death promise: only Jason would read the letter, and not before his eighteenth birthday. But their son had vanished and she'd never see him again. She needed to break her solemn vow. For a second she found it ironic that a piece of paper could carry so much personal value, but this is where life had brought her.

She picked up the envelope, lifted herself from the ground and sat on her bed. She realized she was about to break a second promise today and offered a silent apology. With the greatest of care, Anne lifted the edge of the crease with her pinky and tore the seal. She pulled out the pages. A tiny part of her hoped Michael's words would reveal that her two-fold tragedy was a joke, not at all a funny one, but necessary just the same. Michael would reveal that Jason wasn't missing, but at a friend's house; and that her husband wasn't dead, but downstairs with dinner made, waiting for her to descend into his arms. They'd share a meal, and then share the rest of their lives until, in a long-off moment of utter contentment and old age, holding each other's hands, they'd quietly exit the world, together...

...Anne's hand wouldn't stop trembling long after she'd put down the letter. She read it over and over, each time discovering the same words, the same disbelief, and the same knife through her heart. The air felt thick, like a dense fog, which clogged her nose and throat, and she couldn't breathe. She didn't mind though; she wanted to drown, wanted to end the terrible folly her life had become.

But a silly thought struck her, and she forced air into her lungs. What if Michael wrote the truth?

Stop being ridiculous! her brain ordered.

But... What if the story *was* true? *Absurd!*

... What if... What if... What else could she do?

Anne threw on a pair of torn jeans and an old sweatshirt, and ran from her house into the streets of Ashton.

Above her spread an immense sky full of stars.

–◎↑§–

Esan Shantar Anar sought the guidance of a star. The answers gleaned were difficult to understand, and always came down to a matter of patience. Despite activity bursting on the surface, including giant flailing magnetic flares and massive emission of stellar wind-born particles; deep in their churning fusion cores, the stars were relatively slow. They did not rush about seeking quick solutions to tough questions.

In the measured splendor of stars Esan found all the reasons the Shantar Anar were compiling the Archive, why they devised the Protocol, and why they gave pieces of themselves to their creations so the Ebenin could traverse the cosmos.

But Esan did not know what to make of the transmission from Jiarnu of the Ebenin, and the stars provided no answer.

Even more mysterious was the ship-log of the archivist Nierion, which Esan examined after receiving Jiarnu's unprecedented transmission. The ship's navigational programming had been altered to visit Ranis Anjiran... which should *not* have been.

Then, there was the issue of the human child, a first among his kind. Maybe these perplexing events presented an opportunity to correct prior failures. If the Shantar Anar were not willing to try again, why had we bothered to build gateways to the Night Path on the four planets of the Cohev Senar? We gave the Ranis Aun a second chance, though that attempt ended in disaster.

Perhaps humans were worthy of another opportunity well...

Chapter 38: A New Journey

The ship's interior was the sweetest sight Jason had ever seen. Laushtee had led them to a chamber above Malchion's tomb. There they found a metallic cube suspended from the ceiling by thousands of needle-thin strands. Blazing red Arcon Drei were affixed to each of the cube's six sides. Nierion had only to disarm the box, extinguishing the red glow, and the Archivist could again sense the ship's presence with Esan's Eyes. Laushtee bid them farewell, claiming it felt reborn. The Ranis Aun was deeply grateful, and hoped to live up to their bold example.

Jason lounged beside Daniel on the floor of the ship's central cabin while Nierion checked for any transmissions received while they were gone. The two boys had taken the opportunity to share their stories from Ranis Anjiran.

Daniel was amazed at how much Jason had changed. He'd hoped Jason had a clear explanation, and was disappointed by his friend's limited understanding of what had happened to him. Beyond that though, something still puzzled Daniel.

"Why did the Shantar Anar send Nierion to Ranis Anjiran? They've got to know what happened there!"

Jason nodded.

"I know, nothing adds up…"

Daniel agreed.

"These god-like beings have been around for billions of years, and can do things we can't even dream of… And they just *accidently* screw up, leaving you with this power they seemingly give and take at will… And they *accidently* send Nierion to study some aliens they themselves destroyed?! No way."

Jason knew Daniel was right. Something deeper was going on and Jason had a gut-wrenching feeling he and Daniel weren't going home… at least not yet.

He silently prayed for his mom to be strong, and watched Daniel as his friend thought deeply, index finger pressed beneath his lower lip. Jason hid a grateful smile. Without Daniel, he never would've made it back to the ship alive. Yet, Jason was afraid to share the terrible truth he'd learned in the spire. Somehow, telling his friend would make the horror more real than if he kept the secret inside and pretended it was only a dream.

But Jason knew he had to face the fact that this wasn't the first time he'd seen the blue lesions on his skin, and the silver veins that ran through his arms, while outside Malchion's tomb: In the waning hours of a night he'd tried to forget, they covered his father's body before his death.

Daniel was speaking again, but Jason didn't hear him. He watched the interlocking bands fitted to the cylinder that gripped the Archivist like a prisoner. Nierion's visors dimmed to a soft white glow, and Jason could've sworn he saw compassion in the fading light, before the illumination extinguished completely.

–◎⋔§–

END VOLUME ONE

Acknowledgments

The process of writing my first novel was about as slow and aggravating as I pretty much imagined, and though the experience in and of itself was very rewarding, no doubt it was truly a *labor* of love. That being said, I never would have accomplished this feat without the support and inspiration of the following people and forces:

My assorted hodgepodge of family and friends whose frequent queries into the status of my book and demands to read it only furthered my quest to see it complete if for no other reason than to end the nagging.

My publisher, Valerie Woods, for taking a chance on an unknown voice, and my editor, Shari Goodhartz, for walking me through the process of making what has been put to page the best that it can be and not letting me settle for a story that was less than my finest effort.

My wife Amy; it's one thing to love a person and believe in him in your heart, but quite another to prove this through action. Thank you for pushing me to pursue a dream whatever the result, and being there to support me in every way possible through the twisting road the dream set before me.

The Wimpole Street Writers and Jill Schary Robinson for starting me on the path and enabling me to see that taken one step and one page at a time, a story builds a life of its own and if it truly wishes to exist, the author will see it through.

THE WIMPOLE STREET WRITERS

About the Author

J.M. Kay started writing seriously his sophomore year of college at University of California, Santa Barbara. A few poems here and there led to several collections of poetry, a book of short stories, and many other writing projects. ***Under the Shadow, Children of the First Star: Volume I*** is his first novel. He, his wife and their adorable Shih Tzu all hope that it is just the first of many, as being a writer, for all of its aggravations, is still way more fun and rewarding than what he used to do.